Sex Lounge

Sex Lounge

Rachelle Chase

APHRODISIA

KENSINGTON BOOKS

http://www.kensingtonbooks.com

APHRODISIA Books are published by

Kensington Publishing Corp.
850 Third Avenue
New York, NY 10022

All Kensington Titles, Imprints, and Distributed Lines are available at special quantity discounts for bulk purchases for sales promotions, premiums, fund-raising, and educational or institutional use.

Special book excerpts or customized printings can also be created to fit specific needs. For details, write or phone the office of the Kensington special sales manager: Kensington Publishing Corp., 850 Third Avenue, New York, NY 10022, attn: Special Sales Department, Phone: 1-800-221-2647.

Aphrodisia and the A logo are trademarks of Kensington Publishing Corp.

ISBN-13: 978-0-7582-1650-2
ISBN-10: 0-7582-1650-5

First Kensington Trade Paperback Printing: May 2007

10 9 8 7 6 5 4 3 2 1

Printed in the United States of America

Acknowledgments

To my family, who has always believed in me and supported my every dream. I love you.

Special thanks to: My editor, Hilary Sares, for taking a chance on me—I've framed that napkin you gave me . . . Leigh Michaels, for teaching me and believing in me when I didn't yet know I could write, and then becoming my friend . . . Lori Foster, winning her contest for writers forced me to finish my first manuscript . . . Alicia, for answering yet another last-minute plea for help and providing invaluable feedback on this book . . . Mary B. Morrison, for eating a bowl of orange chicken so slowly that we became friends . . . Dan, for driving to my very first book signing and becoming my personal stalker . . . and, most importantly, to my readers, for without you there would be no books.

1

Fingertips slipped under her skirt, skimming her thighs.

Nichole gasped and stumbled backward, the book slipping through her fingers as she fell off the stepstool.

Strong hands gripped her hips, righting her.

Taking a deep breath, she opened her mouth to scream, and . . .

Stopped.

That scent. A blend of sandalwood, cloves, leather, and . . . man. Only one man.

Her scream became a whimper.

"Shhhhh . . ." Derek whispered against her neck.

A shiver rippled through her.

Thumbs hooked into the waistband of her Nina Ricci thong, sliding it down over her hips.

"What—"

"You know 'what.'"

Hands gripped her hips, pulling her back. Rigid muscle nuzzled her ass.

She moaned.

"Shhhhh . . ."

She was *trying to remain quiet. But after enduring months of teasing, months of taunting . . .*

"Oh, Derek . . . please." Nichole *groaned and reached behind her. Frantic, needing, wanting . . . NOW.*

Here. In the library. In—

At the sound of a throat being cleared, Nichole Simms jumped and slammed her hand over her notebook.

"Good afternoon, Nichole."

Her startled gaze honed in on the perfectly shaped lips, nestled between a neatly trimmed mustache and goatee.

If I nibbled his lips, would it tickle or scratch? If—

She yanked her gaze to his eyes. "M-Mr. Mitchell. Y-your appointment's not until one."

"I know." Emerald eyes ensnared hers, stealing her breath, jolting her heart.

He stared.

She blushed.

"I'll . . . see if Richard can meet with you now." The mesh penholder toppled onto her desk as she reached for the phone.

Fingers pressed down on hers, the touch light, the sensation searing. "No."

No . . . ?

Nichole raised her eyes, staring at the collar of his shirt, afraid to look higher, for fear that he would read her illicit thoughts in her expression. Not that staring at his collar helped, for the crisp whiteness set off his tawny skin while the red silk tie complemented the navy suit. From the corner of her eye, the broad shoulders, accentuated by the tailored drape of his jacket, beckoned her to inspect, to slip her hands under the silk and touch and stroke and—

She returned her gaze to his.

His eyes glittered.

Her knuckles tingled.

Though he stood perfectly still, power seemed to roll off him in waves, mingling with his body heat, concocting a potion impossible to resist.

Okay. She could handle this, maintain the professional façade she always wore like a shield when Derek Mitchell was in the office. He'd just caught her by surprise, that's all.

Uh-huh. Lurid fantasies in which he'd starred had left her feeling more than surprise. Try hot, bothered, wet—

Her face heated. Sliding her hand from under his, Nichole took a deep breath, imagining the air entering her lungs, entering her bloodstream, and dispersing calmness throughout her body. Erasing the feel of fingers caressing her skin. Sweeping away even more sinful acts not yet written . . . but imagined. Restoring order, normalcy, control.

Breathe in . . . Hold it . . . Breathe out . . . One more time . . . That was it. She felt better.

Nichole replaced the pens, careful not to look at him.

"Actually," he said, "I wanted to see you first."

And knocked them over again.

"I see." No, she didn't see. She had no idea what he meant. Oh, she knew what she wished he meant—that he wanted to *see* the real her; the passionate seductress hiding behind the no-nonsense woman who managed Talentz's established and wanna-be models and actors. Of course, there was no chance of that happening. A sexy, wealthy man like Derek Mitchell didn't really *see* a woman like her, a woman lacking the practiced persona of a sex kitten. Which is why he'd been perfect for the lead role in her fantasies. Because there, her understated, girl-next-door prettiness made him wild with need. He craved her. Devoured her.

All within the safe realm of fantasy.

She stared at him, her gaze impersonal—or so she hoped.

He stared back at her, his gaze intense, seeming to peel the layers in her mind, delving into the core, and uncovering the luscious fantasies of her being stripped and caressed. Outdoors, indoors. In a forest, in a library—

Nichole's eyes darted to her forgotten notebook. She snapped it closed and stacked a pile of papers, casually placing them on top of the notebook. Pasting a polite smile on her face, she struggled to keep her voice even. "How can I help you, Mr. Mitchell?"

"Derek."

Oh, Derek . . . please.

Her smile felt like a grimace.

His smile didn't reach his eyes.

"I need some information on Jeremy Smith."

"Oh." Nichole ignored the pang of disappointment at the mention of Talentz's top male model. "I don't know what I can tell you about him, but please have a seat."

He remained standing.

She waited, aware of an undercurrent of tension she'd never before felt coming from him. Or maybe it was just that she'd never before had his full attention on her for more than a few seconds at a time. Or maybe the tension belonged to her, a result of the lingering visions of him, sans the navy Di'Cicco suit and stark white shirt, standing over her, waiting not for information about a model in their database, but rather, waiting for her to inch forward, this time slipping *her* hands under *his* briefs, pulling downward, uncovering—

"Did you send him to the audition for the Jag City car dealership on the twelfth?"

She blinked. *Did I send who to Jag City?*

"Or did Jeremy call and request to be sent?"

Oh right. Jeremy Smith. "I sent him."

"Are you sure?"

"Yes. I called all the models matching your requirements for that job."

"Do you know Jeremy?"

"No. He's only been in our database for a few months, and that was the first job I'd sent him out on." She shook the rest of her haze off, all business now. She took pride in those she offered representation by Talentz, as well as those she sent out on jobs. The high percentage of talent that the agency placed was a result of her selections. "What is this about, Mr. Mitchell? Did Jeremy do something wrong?"

"I don't know." His tone implied that she should know, his eyes once again probing the corners of her mind, seeming to skip the images of him shirtless and her hands rubbing over his chest. Instead, he was looking for . . . something else. He was waiting for information, not her caresses.

"If Jeremy was not to your satisfaction, I'd like to know about it. I want you . . ." *NOW. Here. In the library*. Heat returned to her face. ". . . to be happy with Talentz. We value your business."

"I'd like another copy of his resume," he said, ignoring the inquiry.

"Certainly."

"And since you value my business . . ."

That smile again. The quirk of lips that seduced, despite the fact that it didn't touch his eyes. Or maybe the fact that his eyes remained untouched made it seductive. His secrets remained hidden, the meaning elusive. Nichole could relate. She had her own secrets that, though obviously much different and of no interest to him, she had every desire to keep hidden.

"I'd like talent for an event on Friday."

Relieved by the excuse to look away, she turned her attention to her computer screen, forcing her mind back to his request. A couple of clicks and Jeremy's resume was printing. Okay. The other request . . . an event on Friday. . . . Her mind scrambled to focus, grasping for the occasion that flittered around the edges of her memory. There it was. The one she'd read about in the *San Francisco Chronicle*. "For the grand opening of The Decadent Chaise?"

"Yes."

She smiled and relaxed slightly, pleased by the accuracy of her guess, and turned to him. "What—"

His gaze dipped to her lips.

Her smile slipped.

"How did you know that was the event?"

His gaze was still on her lips.

Her breathing quickened.

"I-I make it a point to keep track of . . ." *everything you do* ". . . all our clients, Mr. Mitchell." That was true. Notices of upcoming events were passed to Richard to convert into business. Other information—like the photos of the Derek-designed chaises in *San Francisco Magazine*—she saved for herself. Decorative fodder for her notebook, around which she wove images of flesh starving for touch, lips dying for a kiss—

"Really?"

She nodded, afraid to speak.

He pulled up a chair in front of her desk and sat. Legs parted, elbows resting on the armrests, index fingers steepled and touching, resting against his mouth.

His lips pursed.

Nichole's lips parted.

"So what else do you know about me, Nichole?"

His tone was light but his gaze resembled that of a hawk's, right before it swooped down for a kill. Or an inquisitor's, seconds before the torture began. Somehow, she didn't think he was asking about tabloid gossip, like whether or not sexy supermodel Melissa Moore was soon to be the first Mrs. Mitchell, or if he was really going to give *Playgirl* an exclusive.

Her breath caught at the vision of Derek Mitchell naked, splayed on one of his own Decadent Chaise creations, smooth, nutmeg-tone skin glistening against the plush, burgundy velour, a muscular leg draped over the side—

Just like she'd penned in her notebook, right under the photo of her favorite chaise lounge.

Nichole turned and placed her hands on the desk, interlacing her fingers. She relaxed her grip. "Mr. Mitchell." She stopped and cleared her throat, attempting to rid her voice of that embarrassing breathiness. "What is it that you really want to know?"

He shrugged, sending her his sexy not-quite-a-smile smile. "You said you track all your clients. I'm just curious as to what you found on me."

Which meant that he obviously wasn't going to tell her the real reason for the question. Maybe this was some sort of test to see how well she knew the talent and the business. But why? And how did this tie in to his earlier question about Jeremy Smith? It made no sense.

"Well?" he asked, his voice mocking.

She bristled. "I know that The Decadent Chaise will feature one-of-a-kind lounges, created using imported fabrics and materials. . . ."

Combining the actual design in her notebook and the imagined ones in her head, she warmed up to the subject.

". . . all sleek lines, with frames covered with smooth curves and embellishments—swirls and curls . . ."

She drew them in the air with her fingertip.

He watched their movement, his eyes bringing the words of her notebook to her mind.

His eyes drifted closed as he leaned back, one arm resting against the mahogany backrest.

". . . made from polished dark woods, like mahogany and cherrywood, topped with plush cushions . . ."

His hip rested against the smooth fabric, its hardness buoyed by the cushion's softness.

"... that give the impression of strength but surround your body, adjusting to individual contours ..."

Crimson velvet cupped his thigh, caressing the skin like she craved to do.

"... like a glove, while the rich, deep colors—crimson, burgundy, chocolate—make it impossible to resist sitting or reclining or ..."

Nichole stopped, forcing the images from her mind, embarrassed by the dreaminess that had snuck into her tone. "... that's just what I ..." *wrote* "read, Mr. Mitchell."

Her face burned.

His eyes seared. "You have very good sources, Nichole."

She ignored the soft silky sound in his voice, the intensity of his stare, and turned back to her computer, desperate to get back to business. "Thank you, Mr. Mitchell."

"Why is it that you won't call me Derek?"

God, more questions. Why'd he care what she called him? And why wouldn't he stick to business? Well, if she looked at this logically, he was sticking to business. Though she had no idea where these questions were coming from or why, nothing he'd said gave her the impression there was anything personal in their exchange. Even his question about his name. She called everyone else by their first name.

Oh, Derek ... please.

She was the one with the problem keeping her mind on business. "You're a client, Mr. Mitchell."

"And that means ... ?"

Nichole forced her breathing to remain even, to treat this abnormal conversation as if it were normal. "'Mr. Mitchell' is more professional."

"I see," he said, repeating the words she'd said to him. But, whereas she hadn't understood why he'd wanted to talk to her when he'd walked in to Talentz, his tapping fingertips, the slight smirk, and narrowed eyes said that he did see—that she was lying. She could only pray he didn't know why.

Ignoring the heat once again rushing to her face, she clicked the keys that launched the search screen. "Now then, w-what type of talent do you need?"

His smile remained.

Her face flamed.

"Lingerie model types."

"Is there a certain look you have in mind?" she asked, pleased to hear the strength back in her voice.

Nichole didn't wait for a reply, happy to be back on familiar ground. She knew what look he wanted. Not only because she was good at her job, but from personal experience when she had been on the other side of this business, in front of a camera lens. Once. A long time ago. A time that she didn't want to remember.

Long hair, big breasts, flat stomach, long legs. She typed a few keywords and hit ENTER. Images of Candy, Brittany, Holly, and Shawna filled the screen, with dozens more a click away.

She turned the monitor toward him.

His gaze flickered briefly to the screen.

"No. I'm thinking short, dark, curly hair . . ."

Nichole resisted the urge to smooth her loose kinky black curls, clicking away at the keyboard instead.

S-u-z-e-t-t-e, M-i-s-s-y, M-e-c-h-e-l-e, ENTER.

She looked at him.

"Less bust and more curves."

She forced the movement of her 36B-cup chest to rise and fall with normal breaths and shifted her 38-inch hips in the seat.

C-h-a-r-l-o-t-t-e, K-e-i-s-h-a, C-l-a-r-i-s-s-a, ENTER.

She didn't wait for the images to load before looking at him.

He wasn't looking at the monitor.

"No. I want . . ."

His steepled fingertips were back at his lips, stroking, tapping, as he thought about what he wanted.

Only his eyes said he already knew what he wanted.

". . . a more innocent look . . ."

His voice deepened.

". . . a woman whose smile says . . ."

His eyes drifted to her lips.

". . . she's oblivious to the fact that men desire her . . ."

His gaze flickered to her breasts before returning to her face. His expression was hooded. "Do you know anyone like that, Nichole?"

Her muscles locked, refusing to expel the air trapped in her lungs. Ten years ago, she'd worn exactly the look he described when she'd posed for that lingerie ad. This couldn't be a coincidence. He knew.

But how on earth had he found out about that photo? And why was he mentioning it now? The interrupted fantasy, his presence, the mysterious questions, and now this. Her heart raced. The room seemed to tilt.

Maybe she was just being paranoid. But maybe she wasn't.

Nichole rose. "I-I'm sure I can find women who meet your requirements, Mr. Mitchell. In the meantime, I'll see if Richard will see you now." Bypassing the intercom, she left Derek in her office, walking slowly enough that he wouldn't think she was running away from him—even though she was. When she reached Richard's office, she knocked briskly on his door and opened it without waiting for his answer.

Richard Dalton, deep in conversation on the phone, looked up in surprise. *Wait*, he mouthed.

Nichole nodded. Seconds turned into minutes.

He finally flicked the mute button. "What is it?"

"Mr. Mitchell is here to see you."

Richard glanced at the clock on his desk. "He's early. He won't mind waiting."

"He does."

"He does what?"

"Mind waiting."

He looked at her, his eyebrows raised in inquiry.

Nichole remained silent.

Richard unmuted the line. "Give me a day or so to work on it, Jim." They exchanged a bit more small talk before he turned to Nichole. "All right. Send him in."

With a nod, Nichole exited the office. After closing the door, she leaned against it and closed her eyes. What was happening? One minute, she was in the midst of an innocent fantasy—okay, a deliciously sinful fantasy—then Derek Mitchell was in front of her, asking her questions that made no sense, revealing information that he shouldn't know about that one regrettable act that had changed her life.

A frisson of fear shuddered through her. What if he was planning to blackmail her?

Right. She almost chuckled at that. And just what would he get by blackmailing her? Her six-year-old Honda Accord? The dead plants decorating the balcony of her two-bedroom condo? The only place she'd find a successful, sexy—let's not forget wealthy—man blackmailing her was between the pages of her notebook.

She shook her head in disgust at the reminder of the notebook. Maybe that was the root of what was happening today. The universe was letting her know that this fantasy life was getting way out of hand. What had started out as an experiment to see if she could write—to supplement the creative writing class she had been taking from San Francisco City College—had turned into an erotic obsession with Derek Mitchell. She'd started writing with the intent to eventually publish, but now it was just to satisfy her own prurient needs.

And just why was she featuring him in her writing, anyway? It wasn't like he'd given her any encouragement. He rarely smiled, using his full, kissable lips and deep baritone voice sparingly, only when necessary. He was polite, but reserved. He didn't flirt, never made small talk. But his eyes, green with cinnamon flecks, accented by thick, naturally arched eyebrows and framed by long lashes, were beautiful. And when he looked at her, his gaze probed, seeming to look inside her, behind the words escaping her lips, and she could barely focus. If his eyes had this effect on her when he was all business, what would it be like to have that gaze, his intensity, aimed at her sexually?

And then there were his long, tapered fingers and broad chest, perfect for resting her head against and trailing kisses across, and those muscular arms that'd bulge as he held himself above her, and—

She snapped her eyes open.

This had gone on long enough. As soon as she left the office today, she was going to shred that notebook. Then she was going to give in and sleep with her sometime-date, David. So what if his conversation was limited to stock trades and mutual fund transactions? Maybe he'd be less boring in bed. Anyway, that's what this fantasy obsession was showing her. That she needed to file away her two-page list—typed in ten-point, Arial Narrow font—of relationship requirements and engage in a quick romp. This was about sex, pure and simple. About the need to get laid.

But before she did that, she was going to deal with Derek Mitchell. Whatever his reason for bringing up her secret, she knew it wasn't with the intent to blackmail her. There was something else. It seemed as if he'd been trying to rattle her since he first walked into the office, and it was past time to find out why.

Feeling better, Nichole ran a hand over her navy skirt and patted her hair, hoping to squash any loose curls into place. She took a deep breath and slowly made her way down the hall.

When she reentered her office, Derek was in the same position as when she'd left. Only now, his arms were relaxed, resting casually against the armrests.

"Richard will see you now."

He rose, leather briefcase in hand, and walked toward her. His stride was slow and purposeful, with a hint of a . . . swagger, which threatened to pull her eyes to his hips with each step.

Nichole pivoted, intending to lead him back to Richard. "I would like to talk to you when you are done," she said over her shoulder.

Fabric rustled, moments before the scent wafted under her nose.

Sandalwood . . . cloves . . . leather . . .

Her stomach flip-flopped.

Fingertips brushed her forearm.

She jerked around, barely avoiding the brush of his body inches in front of her.

"There's another requirement."

"R-requirement?" she asked, staring into his unsmiling eyes, eyes which seemed to have darkened since she'd last looked.

"For the models I need. She must look good in a Nina Ricci thong."

Nichole's mouth dropped open.

Derek winked and walked away.

2

Heart racing, Nichole ran back to her desk. Pushing papers aside, she looked for the powder-blue cover of her notebook. When the search of the desk failed to uncover it, she yanked open drawers, knowing before she even checked what she would find. Or rather, what she *wouldn't* find. After slamming the last drawer shut, she fell into her chair.

Why had he taken her notebook?

She mentally flipped through the pages of the book.

Oh. My. God.

Her breathing quickened as she replayed each vignette she'd penned. Leaning forward, she tucked her head between her knees to get rid of the dizziness.

Okay. She needed to think about this rationally. There were over a hundred pages in that notebook, of which maybe half were filled with erotic fantasies. And of those pages, maybe ninety percent were of Derek. What were the odds that he'd read the whole thing?

She raised her head. Slim, that's what the odds were. So maybe things weren't so bad. Maybe—

Oh. My. God.

She thrust her head down, putting it back between her knees. Even if he hadn't read the whole thing, he'd obviously read what she'd been working on today, the library scene. And there was no way he could have missed the chaise lounge scene, considering she'd taped a picture of it on a page, which caused the book to automatically open to that page. And then there was that let-your-fingers-do-the-walking bit in the movie theater.

Nichole suppressed a groan. What was she going to do? What—

Voices sounded behind her. ". . . it was a work-for-hire situation," Derek said.

She jerked her head up, banging it on the desk. Damn.

"You okay?" asked Richard.

"Yes . . . I just . . . lost an earring."

"You must've lost two earrings," said Derek.

"What?"

He tapped both of his earlobes. Was that a flicker of amusement she saw in his gaze?

"Nichole."

She dragged her gaze back to Richard.

"Derek wants to set up Decadent Chaise as a separate account and—"

"Excuse me." Derek tapped Richard's arm. "I've got to go. I'll let you two talk business."

"No problem. We still on for racquetball at four?"

"Of course. I always like beating you."

Richard grumbled.

Derek laughed, a foreign sound, all deep and rumbly, that sent shockwaves through her numbness and caressed her unwilling eardrums. He nodded to Nichole and walked to the door, one hand reaching for the knob, the other grasping the handle of the briefcase.

The briefcase that most likely contained her notebook. Panic blossomed in her stomach.

"Um, Mr. Mitchell, don't you want that list of models?"

He turned, his expression polite. "I'll log in to the database and search myself. Thanks for your help."

And he was gone.

"Nichole, when you set up Derek's account . . ."

She stared at Richard's moving lips as if she were watching a silent movie, the words wiped out by her overwhelming panic. She fidgeted. Richard droned on. Which meant the meeting must've gone well because Richard only came out and gave lengthy instructions when he'd gotten what he wanted. Otherwise, he stayed in his office and sulked. Or hit the booze, though he didn't realize she knew that. "Excuse me, Richard. I have to . . ." She scurried around the desk to the door. "I'll be right back."

"Wait. Derek wants time with you—"

Nicole didn't wait to hear the rest of his sentence, uninterested in what *Derek* wanted. Tearing down the hall, the heels of her pumps clicking furiously on the marble floor, Nichole rounded the corner and skidded to a halt in front of the bank of elevators. Heaving a sigh of relief at the sight of an open door, she rushed inside.

"Nichole. What a pleasant surprise," said Derek, removing his finger from the "Door Open" button.

The doors swished shut.

Inwardly, Derek smiled as he watched Nichole Simms struggle to catch her breath. Her face was flushed, her curly hair tousled more than usual, and those full, Kewpie-doll lips . . .

His smile faded as he stared at her lips. Until today, he'd admired them with a distant sort of admiration, like he'd admired the James VanDerZee photograph he'd purchased as an investment. Now, after catching a glimpse in the lingerie ad of the talent they hid, he stared at them anew, parted and glistening in some reddish shade of lipstick that made him want to lick and nibble it off. He wanted to see if it tasted like strawberries or raspberries, suckle that bottom lip and see if it was as soft and moist as it looked.

"You . . . you . . . took my book . . ."

His gaze drifted to her chest. Each ragged breath beckoned his hands to the vee of the cotton blouse, to slip inside and cop a feel.

His groin tightened.

He turned away in search of a distraction, and pulled the STOP lever. The elevator jerked. Nichole stumbled. As he reached to steady her, she took a step back, grabbing the railing as if hanging on to a life jacket.

Not that that was going to save her.

Her eyes darted to the digital readout above the door. "What . . . are you doing?"

"I thought we'd have a little chat."

"I don't want to 'chat.' I want my book, Mr. Mitchell. Now." Her voice was steely, though the breathless undertone gave it an entirely different effect.

His cock twitched.

Derek leaned back against the railing, staring into her wide brown eyes. "*Derek*. I know you are capable of saying it. And quite well, I might add."

Her face went crimson. "You had no right to take my notebook."

"You had no right to take my notebook, *Derek*."

Her lips tightened—whether in disgust or anger, he didn't know—making him want to restore their softness by licking away the tension, one lap at a time.

"Derek," she said—this time there was no mistaking the anger—making his name sound like two pieces of sandpaper rubbing together. This aroused him more than if she'd whispered it seductively in his ear.

"I want my book. And I want to know why you brought up my . . . past. Now. Because I need to get back to work—"

"Shhhhh," he said, quoting from her book.

Her gasp injected arousal into his bloodstream, making him want to take the tiny step necessary to touch her. Instead, he said, "I asked Richard for a bit of your time and he said to take all the time I needed."

"Why?"

Why had Richard given him her time? No. Judging by the way her back stiffened and her lips thinned, he'd be willing to bet that wasn't what she was asking. More like, why had he asked Richard for her time or why had he taken her book? Both very good questions, since his current actions had nothing to do with his initial purpose in approaching Nichole. The initial purpose had been to discover if Jeremy Smith and his sister, interior designer Barbara Randolph, were in cahoots on the bogus Jag City lawsuit. And since Jeremy had come from Talentz, Derek wanted to know if either Nichole or Richard knew anything about him. Or if Nichole was in on it with Jeremy. That was a long shot, for Derek couldn't see a motive for Nichole's involvement, despite the fact that there seemed to be a skeleton or two rattling around in her closet.

So why was he locked in an elevator with a hard-on for a woman he'd purposely ignored in the past?

Skeletons. Her skeletons were rattling around in his mind, refusing to get out. First, the X-rated photo he'd uncovered while looking for a connection between her and Jeremy. Then the notebook.

Especially the notebook.

Her hips, his hands, her ass.

His cock stiffened.

He ignored his body, reminding himself that the lawsuit, not the notebook, was the important thing. Derek pretended to misunderstand her question. "Because, as you said, Nichole, Talentz values my business. Now, you give me a few honest answers, and I'll give you . . ." he paused, the juicy lower lip that she kept nibbling making him reluctant to finish the sentence. He suppressed a sigh. ". . . your book back and then we'll forget I found it. Okay?"

Distrust flickered in her eyes.

As well it should. He'd get his answers but there'd be no pretending like this had never happened. And he wasn't sure he'd give the book back, now that he had sampled the erotic thoughts that swirled through her mind. In the past, he'd been able to dismiss the fact that Nichole Simms, with messy hair that she was always touching and smoothing—which only made it messier, sexier—and curvy body, was attractive. And he'd ignored the dark something that sometimes snuck into her big brown eyes—and caused a flicker of heat in his stomach—when she didn't think he was looking.

Because he didn't mix business with sex. Because she wasn't his type. Her innocent, girl-next-door look, combined with the words *committed relationship* etched in the depths of her eyes, worked on him like holy water during an exorcism.

Until today. The decade-old photograph of her in the transparent nightgown seduced, while her words in the notebook teased and aroused, begging to be acted upon. Far be it from him not to oblige. And what better way to find out if she had anything to do with Barbara Randolph and her brother? Here was an instance where mixing business and sex made perfect sense. After he got a few answers, that is.

He raised an eyebrow.

She crossed her arms. "It's not like I have a choice, now, is it?"

"There's always a choice, Nichole." He gaze dipped to her

breasts; they were pushed up by her forearms, the plump mounds peeking at him between the folds of her blouse. Bending to remove her notebook from his briefcase, he held it loosely in front of his crotch, using it to shield her gaze from the action behind his zipper.

Or maybe he should move it aside, letting her see the outline of his hard cock. That'd probably get her jabbing the emergency button. On the other hand, maybe it wouldn't.

Her lips tightened. "Fine. I have a few questions of my own, *Derek*."

He smiled, amused by the emphasis on his name.

Surprise flickered across her face as she glanced at his mouth. Then it was gone and her lips tightened. Which inspired him with all sorts of ways of loosening them. Like tracing their softness with his forefinger before pulling the bottom lip gently down, and opening that sexy mouth up to his—

"Why all the questions about Jeremy Smith?"

He wrenched his attention back to business, keeping his position relaxed and his senses alert. "I wanted to see if you knew he was Barbara Randolph's brother."

She gasped, her wide eyes making her surprise seem heartfelt. "The woman suing you over those designs?"

At least she didn't pretend not to know. "The very same."

"And you think I had something to do with that?"

Either the sense of outrage in her voice was real or she was an excellent actor. "The thought crossed my mind."

She laughed, a light tinkling sound that rolled over his abdomen as if her fingers were caressing it. "Why on earth would I do that?"

Derek tapped the notebook, letting his eyes drift down the front of her blouse to the round hips filling out the blue skirt, hips that he could almost feel under the pads of his fingers. He looked back at her face, much to the dismay of his cock. "Why on earth would you write this?"

The laughter faded, and her expression shuttered.

Silence.

"Why did you bring up my . . . photo?" she asked finally.

"Why did you do it?"

Pain flickered through her eyes.

Annoyance snaked through him. Annoyance at himself for actually wanting to know the answers—why a woman who seemed to go to such lengths to hide all passion had posed nearly naked with an expression of bliss on her face. Why a woman who created such sensual and graphic fantasies featuring him made no effort to make them real with him.

Why the hell did he care what the answers were? The only thing he should care about was her possible involvement in the lawsuit. And whether he could get her to act out any of the fantasies spelled out in such glorious detail. Simply for fun, for both of them.

She made an impatient gesture. "I had nothing to do with Jeremy and Barbara Randolph. As I already told you, I don't know him. And why I did that photo is none of your business." Anger vibrated through her tone. "And as to that—" her gaze flickered to the notebook—"I wrote it because I'm taking a creative writing class, and I wanted to see if I could write something totally outside of the box. To see if I could take something totally unbelievable and make it believable."

Derek smiled. "An exercise in creativity, so to speak."

"Exactly."

"Then why not use Richard?"

Why the fuck do you care? He didn't care. It was a rhetorical question, asked only because he'd found his name in her book.

Her gaze sharpened. "Why would I use Richard?"

Because he has the hots for you. But Richard hadn't mentioned Nichole in months.

Maybe he was over her. Or maybe he'd already had her.

Derek forced his grip on her book to relax. "Women seem to find him attractive."

She shrugged, though her eyes still flashed. "I needed someone who was distant, emotionally remote, on the verge of being cold."

Derek stiffened.

Nichole continued. "Who . . . who wouldn't let anyone into his life. And you came into the office at the right time and fit the role and so I used you."

Even though body language—like the fact that she slid her gaze away from him, suddenly enamored with the paneling to his left, along with the teeth nibbling nervously at her bottom lip and that breathless note to her voice that left him hard—told him she was lying, something about her flippant tone grated his nerves. She said "distant" as if he'd woken up one morning and said "I think I'll be emotionally remote today" the same way he'd say "I'll have the scrambled eggs with linguisa sausage." And she decided to "use him" because he happened to be at the right place at the right time?

He ignored the blood beginning to boil in his veins and forced all emotion from his voice. "Well then, since this was all for the sake of art, satisfy my literary curiosity."

"It wasn't—"

"After I slide the thong over your hips . . . and pull you against my cock . . . what happens next?"

Nichole gasped. Oh God. He hadn't just asked her to tell him what was next. She'd wanted to make him think that the stories were mere words, of no significance, but somehow, her attempt to downplay the words in her journal had backfired. Instead, he'd found some unintentional significance to something she'd said. The flat, emotionless voice gave her the impression he was angry. And the smile—no slight quirk of lips this time—was dangerous. The Big Bad Wolf kind that ate big girls, savoring every bite.

She shivered.

"Do you reach for my hips?" His voice was like steel.

Yes . . .

"Or do you run your palms down the front of my jeans, making me groan, forcing me to grip your hips tighter, making me beg for you . . ."

Yes . . .

"No!"

"Or do you reach for the front of my jeans, unbuttoning, slipping a hand inside, touching, stroking . . ."

Oh, Derek . . . please.

Her gaze slid to his crotch, before she jerked it upward, mortified by the unconscious act his words had invoked. Thank God the notebook was still there, hiding what she . . .

. . . wanted . . .

. . . didn't want . . . to see.

She had to stop this before it went . . . before it went . . . right where she'd devoted pages of ink detailing where she wanted it to go.

He took a step forward.

There were no more steps backward for her to take.

He dropped his hands to his sides.

Her eyes dropped to his crotch, to the bulge no longer hidden.

The dizziness she'd felt when she had discovered her notebook missing returned. She pressed her thighs against the railing, but he was still mere inches away. All she had to do was lean forward and she could rest her head against his chest or stand on tiptoe to press her lips against his or extend her hand and she could reach his pants, unzip them, slip a hand inside and see if he felt smooth and hard at the same time, see if he'd gasp at her touch, if—

She had to get out of here.

She couldn't get out of here.

Oh God, he wants me. If he didn't want her, this wouldn't be happening. Her words would just be words on paper, instead of slipping from his sexy lips. And she wouldn't be here struggling to be strong, fighting to—

Why are you fighting it?

Because . . . because . . . she was supposed to fight it. Because fantasies were supposed to remain fantasies, separate and distinct from reality. Because blurring the two had gotten her into trouble in the past.

He took a final step forward—so close that her breasts would rub up against him if she took a deep breath—forcing her to look up. His eyes were dark pools, delving, probing. He said, "Which one?"

"I can't tell you." It was a whimper. Her last attempt to prevent fantasy from becoming reality.

"Yes. You can."

Her lips parted.

His nostrils flared.

"Tell me," he rasped.

Tell him.

"Y-you already s-said it."

He reached forward and stroked her jaw with his fingers. Feather-light flicks.

Nichole gasped.

"Which answer?"

His thumb traced her lower lip.

Nichole fought the urge to lean in to him, to stand on tiptoe and press her lips against his, press her body against his—

His thumb gently parted her lips.

Oh God.

"Which one?"

"I . . . make you beg."

He inhaled sharply. "What do I beg for?"

She couldn't tell him.

She wanted to tell him.

The pads of his fingers burned her skin while his eyes burned her soul, stirring and mixing longing and want with fear. Longing and wanting to let go. Afraid to take the risk.

Going to take the risk.

"I r-rub my palms down your cock and you b-beg for me to touch you . . ." she whispered.

His fingers tightened under her jaw.

". . . to stroke you . . ."

He exhaled roughly.

". . . to rub my ass against you, letting you feel my skin against yours. So close to the wetness that you crave, but not close enough . . ."

He groaned, his grip almost painful.

She felt lost in the depths of his eyes, seeing her own lust reflected within. Lust she'd never expected to see in a man she barely knew. Gone was the distant, remote look. Instead, she saw fire simmering inside. Because of her words. For her. A fantasy come true.

She leaned forward.

Surprise flickered through his eyes.

Nichole gave up on fighting the urge and stood on tiptoe, finally discovering the feel of his lips. His moustache felt both soft and rough. She moved her lips over his, exploring, tasting.

A groan rumbled deep in his throat, seconds before the hand against her jaw pulled her closer, allowing him to go deeper. Tongues met, tasted, and explored. Gentleness fled, displaced by need.

His tongue probed deeper.

Her hands wound in his hair, dragging his head closer, as her mouth opened wider, wanting all of him, while her body melted against him, wanting more of him, wanting—

Her hands slid under his jacket.

His hand slid up her back, pulling her shirt until it came free of her skirt, then slipped under the cotton, searing her skin, burning, caressing.

Yessssssss. She wanted this. For once, to go with something that felt good, without thinking about right or wrong. Whether her behavior was appropriate. Whether people would disapprove of her. To be wild, excited . . . alive.

She clung to him.

He placed his hand against the wall beside her head, the notebook banging against it, reminding her of how this all started, making her thankful that he had taken it—because if he hadn't she wouldn't be here, living the words instead of writing them; feeling his arms, experiencing his kiss, feeling—

He pressed her hard against the wall. The railing dug into her thighs, while his cock sought her warmth through their clothes.

She groaned.

Derek lifted his head away.

Her eyes flew open. "No . . ."

His smile was pained. "Time to get out of the elevator."

"Oh." She blinked, becoming aware of where she was, what she was doing, who she was with. The *real* version of reality crashed through her mind, smashing the desire to give in to wildness. Tensing, she pulled back.

He pulled her forward. "No."

He was not referring to her physical movement. "What do you want from me?"

"Come on Friday."

Her breath caught in her throat, until the real meaning of his words hit her. He meant the grand opening, not her physical release. Her laugh was shaky, sad because that's what this was about. The photo. "I don't model lingerie." *Anymore.*

"I'm not asking you to model."

"Then what are you asking?"

"I asked you to come with me."

"I see," she said, once again not seeing, as she stared up into his green eyes, still hazy with desire. She pulled away. "I can't."

"You can."

"I'm . . . busy Friday." *Oh really?*

"Then come with me now."

Hands stroked her back, persuading, coercing, bribing.

"Why are you asking me?" She didn't know what kind of reason she wanted. She didn't even know if she wanted a reason. Nor did she know if she would accept his invitation.

Silence hung in the air. One second became five, creeping onward to ten.

"Because you still don't know that men desire you." He backed away from her, breaking contact. "And it's time someone showed you."

3

Nichole sagged back against the elevator wall, thankful for the railing, which seemed to be the only thing holding her up. She had never wanted a man so strongly before, to the point that the physical sensations swirling through her body had overwhelmed her, making her forget where she was, filling her with unquenchable craving. In public. In an elevator.

Nor had she ever felt so desirable.

Because you don't know men desire you.

Derek's words hovered in the air, floating above her, making her want to reach out and pluck them and slip them into her pocket, saving them to replay over and over again later.

She left the words, plucking the book from his fingers instead.

His hand fell to his side, drawing her gaze. Which reminded her just how tensely *all* of him waited for her answer.

Her flesh tingled.

She couldn't do this. Casual sex was not her style, was totally outside of her experience. Giving in to it could only lead to pain at best or blow the lid off of Pandora's box at worst.

Blood thundered through her veins, roaring through her head, deafening the voice of reason.

She slid her gaze from him, took a step forward, and flipped the STOP lever to unlock the elevator. She then pressed the button to return to the sixteenth floor.

"I'll be right back," she said to Derek once the doors opened. She scurried down the hall before she lost her nerve. Back in her office, Richard's nonchalant "sure" confirmed that Derek's request for her time had been granted. After grabbing her purse, she took a moment to make sure the phones were forwarded to the answering service, before heading back.

She couldn't believe she was going to do this.

Derek was where she'd left him in the elevator, though her inability—once again—to look above the collar of his white shirt prevented her from guessing what he was thinking.

She entered and stared straight ahead, memorizing the grooves in the marbleized floor.

The elevator descended.

Silence swirled through the tight space, disturbed only by the muted "ding" of the bell seconds before the elevator stopped. Derek held the door open for her.

As they walked through the lobby, Nichole refrained from asking where they were going or what they were going to do. Thoughts of the work she left behind fought to enter her mind, reminding her of what the responsible Nichole Simms should be doing.

But the newly discovered wild and reckless Nichole Simms followed Derek Mitchell across the pavement of the parking garage, her heels clicking a staccato beat that sounded ominous bouncing off of the concrete walls.

Derek stopped beside a black sports car that gleamed, despite the dim fluorescent lighting. The logo on the hood, a coat of arms featuring antlers, red-and-black stripes, and a prancing horse, let her know it was a Porsche; the perforated metal covers dominating the back, behind the two seats, told her it was a Carrera GT like the one she'd seen in a brochure once. Uncertainty seeped into her heart. What was she doing here? A man who could afford a $440,000 car was so far out of her league she doubted she would register on his radar.

So what was Derek doing here with her? What—

The whoosh of the Porsche door drew her attention to where Derek stood holding it open for her. She still had time to change her mind, to offer a hasty apology and race for the safety of her office . . .

Emerald eyes stared back at her, giving away nothing.

Heart racing, she slid into the seat, the soft click of the door reminiscent of a jail door locking.

Derek slid into his seat and started the car. The engine roared as the car took the circular ramps to the exit, its tires squealing around each turn. Once outside, he slowed the car and, with the press of a button, retracted the convertible top. The glare of the sun had Nichole reaching for her sunglasses, while the breeze had her other hand going to her head in an attempt to hold her curls in place.

And still he said nothing. Why didn't he say anything?

Jeremy Smith. Barbara Randolph. The names had become Derek's mantra, his attempt to focus on the primary reason for Nichole being in his car.

It wasn't working.

Out of the corner of his eye, he caught her fiddling with her hair, trying once again to control it. By the way she continued nibbling her lip, which sent the blood straight to his cock, he guessed she was nervous. Or maybe she was still uncomfortable.

She'd had a problem with his car. He could tell by the way she'd come to an abrupt halt and stiffened as her eyes roved over it. The irony had made him smile. The fifteen-year-old Mercedes coupe that he usually drove to leave the image-conscious models he dated unimpressed—now, that would have put Nichole at ease.

But he hadn't had dating on his mind when he'd gotten behind the wheel today.

Nor was *dating* on his mind now. The notebook had taken his thoughts way beyond dating, zooming into the realm of lips meeting, tongues mating, flesh rubbing.

Derek shifted in his seat and glanced over at her.

Nichole stopped fiddling with her hair, and clasped her hands in her lap—or more like, *gripped* her hands in her lap.

Anticipation coiled in his stomach, surprising him. When was the last time he'd felt that? Hell, when was the last time he'd felt anything but mild interest in a woman or had the urge to seduce? He couldn't remember when. Probably because the women with whom he came in contact were the pursuers, after him because of what he could do for them. Like Melissa. Though, contrary to what people believed, he'd never been in a relationship with her. Thank God.

Not that he'd minded women being with him because of what he could give them. It was easier that way.

But then here was Nichole, creating imaginative sex with him on the pages of her little book, with no intent of ever acting on it. A definite first. Which, of course, made him want her.

Nichole's hand went back to her hair.

He pulled her hand down, enjoying the smooth silkiness of her skin, reveling in its heat, wanting to feel it wrapped around him.

She jumped at his touch.

"You all right?" he asked, breaking the silence.

"Yes."

He laced his fingers through hers, rubbing his thumb against her baby finger, round and round.

She tensed, then relaxed, her thumb stroking his hand. Each rotation injected a jolt of lust into his veins.

"Cold?" he asked, heat snaking through his voice.

"No."

"Would you like to know where we're going?"

"No."

The urgency in her tone made him laugh, dousing a few of the sparks ignited by the friction of their skin. He shot her a glance.

She smiled. A fleeting smile, her attention seemingly riveted on their hands. But it drew his gaze to her lips anyway, taking his thoughts back to the elevator when she'd leaned into him, pressing her body against him, the soft parts (lips and breasts) making his lips ache to explore while the hard ones (her pelvis and thigh) made him burn to crush her beneath him.

"So, if you don't want to know where we're going," he said softly, "what is it you would like to know?"

Nichole couldn't tear her gaze from their caressing fingers, the movement seemingly synchronized, hypnotizing her mind while sending bursts of delicious prickles throughout her body— up her arm and over her shoulder, before spreading through her breasts to her nipples.

He removed his hand to shift gears, breaking her trance.

She turned away and glanced out the window, staring blindly into the office buildings they passed along Montgomery Street. Letting one marble lobby blur into another, she tried to ignore her hardening nipples and the heat pooling in her stomach.

His fingers returned to her hand, resuming their circling.

The heat continued to flow inside her, spilling from her stomach, inching lower.

"What would you like to know?" he repeated.

The husky sound was back in his voice, returning her to her obsessive thoughts of *why me*. Which she pushed aside. What did it matter why he'd chosen her? Even before she'd discovered her notebook missing, she'd decided on the need for a quick romp. A quick romp did not require answers to irrelevant questions. All it required was hot and heavy sex.

And, miracle of miracles, here she sat buckled in the candy-apple-red seat with the wind tangling her curls, zooming off into the sunset for exactly that.

She wanted him. He wanted her. It was time to stop thinking and time to act; to seize this opportunity by the horns—or rather, by the hips. Or by the cock.

That made her smile.

Just as she turned to him, the car slowed. He let go of her hand yet again, to seize the stick shift, backing and turning the car until he'd parallel parked.

Her breathing quickened.

They were here, wherever here was. The plateglass windows gleamed in the sun, while the burgundy drapes hid the interior from view. Then, as she took in the silver cursive letters stenciled into the merlot-colored awning above the shrouded entrance, her breathing stopped altogether.

"Welcome to The Decadent Chaise," Derek said.

4

Derek got out of the car, closing the door almost soundlessly behind him.

Nichole remained in her seat, heart pounding, the dizziness that had attacked her at the office once again flooding her brain. When Derek had said, "Then come with me now," she hadn't thought he'd meant, "Come to The Decadent Chaise now." She'd expected . . . his place, maybe. Or a hotel room, more than likely. Because those choices seemed . . . impersonal. The usual locations for sex.

The Decadent Chaise was not the usual location for sex. For one thing, it was newly completed, and thus could not yet have become Derek's preferred locale of seduction. And it definitely was not impersonal. Its starring role in her notebook made it *intensely* personal. Intensely intimate.

Her door opened.

She sat, staring at the shrouded windows, struggling to stop the glass from dancing before her eyes.

"Nichole?"

Nichole tore her gaze from the scarlet velvet curtains that

hid the showroom from view, to the dark green eyes that hid Derek's thoughts from view.

Get out, Nichole.

She remained glued to the seat.

Get out. Don't blow this. Don't act like a frigid, inexperienced schoolgirl.

But that's what she felt like. There was a very good reason why her fantasies had remained fantasies. Because her mind could imagine anything, and in her stories, her body could do anything.

That was why she was so creative when she wrote. Because, with words, she could put herself in the moment and be someone else. The sheer anonymity of secret words freed her to be what she couldn't be in her real life.

That same inhibition had made her fail at acting. Because she *couldn't* let go and put herself into the moment. She was always aware of people watching, waiting, expecting her to be what their script depicted that she be. And she just couldn't surrender to the moment.

You did one time.

She pushed that aberration from her mind and glanced at Derek. His hip rested against the corner of the car door—ankles crossed, hand dangling by the wrist over the doorframe, his gaze unwavering. Waiting . . .

"You read the chaise scene." An unnecessary inquiry.

He answered anyway. "Yes."

"Which is why you brought me here."

"Yes."

Her fantasy lover stood in front of her fantasy location, placing her, once again, in the role of the actor. Only she wouldn't really be acting because this was her script—which was infinitely worse because, while Derek would be the actor, she would be . . . real. Authentic. Vulnerable. There was no anonymity here.

Derek held out his hand to her.

She could refuse his hand, thereby putting an end to things that had barely started, and returning her to a world of words strung together to form erotic tall tales.

Or she could take his hand, and follow him down a road much more treacherous than the yellow brick one Dorothy had skipped along, infinitely more dangerous than the rabbit hole Alice had tumbled into. Secrets would be bared. Souls would be exposed. *Her* secrets. *Her* soul. Just like before.

Anonymity . . . vulnerability . . . anonymity . . . vulnerability . . . anonymity . . .

Nichole made one last feeble attempt to resist. "But you have a racquetball game at four."

Derek flipped open his cell phone and dialed. She listened to him leave a message for Richard.

"Not any more," he said.

Heart racing, once again, Nichole placed her hand in his.

Derek smiled as he pulled her to her feet.

Before she had a chance to change her mind, they were at the entrance. Derek turned the key in the lock, then ushered her inside, flipping the light switch.

Nichole gasped, her apprehension giving way to awe at the sight in front of her. Chaise lounges of every size, shape, and color were sprinkled throughout the cavernous showroom. The absence of color—charcoal-toned cement floor, smooth as marble with a glossy finish, and matte charcoal walls—along with light beaming from the recessed lights in the high ceiling intensified the colors of the chairs. The eye took in the chairs and nothing else.

Derek gestured at the room. "The showroom will be transformed on Friday. Each chair will have its own room, designed to complement the chaise. The rooms will be small, of course. Mini-rooms."

"Wow," she breathed, taking a step forward and stopping at the nearest chaise. She ran her fingertips over the nutmeg-and-gold damask, tracing the silky flowers, before moving to the chestnut frame. "The swirls and curls . . ." *were just as I'd imagined them.* ". . . they're beautiful."

She turned back to look at Derek.

His gaze was amused, just as it'd been when she'd stared at his car. Which reminded her that she was being gauche. Her face felt warm.

"Did you design all of them?" she asked, struggling for sophistication.

His amusement disappeared. "Depends on who you ask."

"What do you mean?"

He watched her intently, as if searching for something. "Jared Morgan claims that I stole them from him."

Nichole's mouth dropped open. Another lawsuit? "I . . . hadn't heard that."

Derek continued to stare at her.

Nichole closed her mouth.

"It's not public knowledge."

And yet he'd told her. Why? "Oh. Well. That explains it . . ."

He continued to stare, his expression unreadable.

Nichole stared back, her expression confused. Once again, he seemed to be waiting for her reaction. Just like he had in her office. Suddenly, she smiled. "Let me guess. You think I'm behind this one, too."

His silence gave her the answer.

"I don't know Jared Morgan. Nor, to my knowledge, his children, siblings, parents, or anyone else in his family tree." She raised her right hand. "Scout's honor."

"You have to be a Scout to make that pledge."

"Hmmm . . ." Nichole lowered her hand and drew an X across her heart. "Cross my heart."

His gaze followed the invisible X, lingering on her breasts. Slowly, amusement returned to his features.

Pleasure rippled through her when she saw that she'd made him smile.

"Well then, back to what you were saying . . ."

Nichole scanned her mind for the previous topic.

His smile grew. "'Swirls and curls.'"

This time, her amusement vanished, replaced by humiliation. "You find that . . . me . . . funny?"

"I don't find anything about you funny, least of all your words."

When his eyes turned dark and moody, and he seemed to be combing through her thoughts, she couldn't breathe. Or think. Or hold his gaze. She turned her attention back to the chair in front of her.

"In fact . . ." The soft swish of fabric alerted her to his presence seconds before she felt him beside her. "No one has ever made a description of my designs sound like phone sex."

Her mind zoomed back to their conversation at Talentz, when she'd told him what she knew about him. She returned her gaze to his. "My descriptions aroused you?"

"Your words—the passion with which you said them—aroused me." His eyes glittered in the light. And the husky undertone in his voice was not due to laughter.

He took a step forward. "You—"

Nichole took a shaky breath.

His finger touched her cheek, before moving downward and outlining her lips. "*You* arouse me, Nichole."

Her breathiness worsened, and her inability to form a coherent thought or remember her native language came back. Her lips tingled under his touch, her body wanted to sway forward and press against him for another kiss. Like the one in the elevator.

The intensity of his gaze as he stared at her lips, watching his finger circle, told her he wanted to kiss her, and was probably thinking about the last kiss, too. She forced herself to remain still, and not move her lips across his, nipping and nibbling. Last time, she'd kissed him. This time, it'd be his move.

Or so she hoped. *Please hurry.*

He dropped his hand, taking a step back.

No!

"What do you think of this one?"

Nichole blinked. "Huh?"

He gestured to the left. "I don't think you described this one." The amusement was back in his voice. Only Nichole was beginning to suspect that what she'd taken for amusement masked something else, some emotion he wanted to hide.

She had no idea what Derek could have to hide but it restored a bit of her control, for it made him seem more . . . human. A man with fears and concerns, just like she had. Maybe not the same fears, but fears nonetheless.

Nichole forced her lust into a corner and smiled at Derek.

He gave her a half-smile.

As she looked in the direction he indicated, she kept her smile in place and walked forward, heading toward The Chaise—the infamous chaise from her notebook.

She stopped before she reached it, pausing instead at an ultramodern, S-shaped chair. "This one?" She smoothed the palm of her hands over the dark chocolate suede. "With suede that kisses the skin of a man's naked back as he sprawls on it?" Turning her hand over, she stroked the curves with her knuckles. "And caresses his ass like hands as he shimmies against it?"

Though the half-smile lingered on his lips, his eyes were narrowed.

A thrill of power thrummed through her. The power to incite. The power to seduce.

"Or do you mean this one?" Nichole asked, feigning innocence as she drifted over to The Chaise. She fingered the curve of the mahogany back. "Perfect for a man to rest his arm against?"

She moved to the side, doing a perfect Vanna White imitation as she gestured to the crimson velvet. "With cushions made to cup a man's thighs?"

"Made to cup *my* thighs, if I remember correctly."

"You have a very good memory, Derek."

Derek inclined his head in a silent thanks. He shrugged out of his jacket and let it fall to the floor as if it were a $2.00 bargain from ThriftTown, instead of a $4,000, hand-stitched Di'-Cicco. The red silk tie followed. His fingers moved to the buttons of his shirt.

Every drop of saliva in Nichole's mouth evaporated as her eyes followed the movement of his long fingers as they undid each button. He slid the shirt off his shoulders.

It dropped soundlessly to the floor.

Her heart hammered in her chest, sending the blood racing through her veins, making the room suddenly too hot.

Gripping the bottom of the white T-shirt, Derek pulled it up over his head.

Nichole drank in the sight of his toned flesh, following the dark hair dusting his pectoral muscles, before moving down. Trailing the valley between his ribcage. Over flat abs, and lower, until the trail disappeared at the waistband of his slacks. She wanted to let her hands follow her eyes, rubbing their way over the muscular ridges of his chest and stomach, before dipping inside to stroke the muscle she craved most.

He unbuckled his belt.

Nichole's eyes were riveted on the motion of his fingers.

The rasp of his zipper sounded like a jackhammer in the quiet room. His custom-made slacks and bikini briefs dropped to the floor, pooling around his ankles.

Nichole slowly lifted her gaze, skimming perfectly formed calves, lingering on well-defined thighs and slim hips, before zeroing in on his cock.

The breath whooshed out of her.

His very *erect* cock.

As he walked forward, his cock jutted toward her. Calling. Beckoning her to touch. To stroke its hardness, to feel its softness, to finger its wetness.

She reached out.

Derek moved to the right, bypassing her.

Nichole pivoted.

She watched, dry-mouthed, as he sat on The Chaise. He leaned against the arm at the head of the chair and draped his other arm around the back. Light haloed his body, making his skin glisten.

Her mouth was no longer parched. Instead, the sight of him striking the pose straight from her fantasy kicked her salivary glands into overdrive. As if she were a death row inmate, preparing to indulge in her last meal.

Which she was. Preparing to indulge, that is.

"This is as far as I read," he said.

Her gaze drifted to his hips. Her mind drifted back to her notebook.

His hip rested against the smooth fabric, its hardness buoyed by the cushion's softness.

Derek surpassed that description. When she wrote it, she'd had no idea that the red fabric would accent his skin, bringing out the gold undertones. Or that the curves of his body would be in sync with the rolling curves of the frame, his masculinity transforming the chaise from merely elegant to manly elegance.

Her gaze traced the curve of his thigh.

Crimson velvet cupped his thigh, caressing the skin like she craved to do.

The cushion dipped slightly under the weight of the leg lying atop the spongy fabric, just as she'd imagined. What she hadn't imagined was how his other leg, bent at the knee and propped against the chair back, would look. The lattice pattern of the dark wood emphasized the smoothness of his skin—like silk covering steel—making her want to reach out and trace the underside of his thigh. To lightly rake the pads of her fingers to the bottom of his ass cheek, then move inward and follow his groin—

"What happens next, Nichole?" The question was a plea.

I move my fingers across your groin, skimming the curly hair at the base of your cock, circling and—

No. That's what she wanted to do right now, not what she'd written about doing. She forced her mind back to the words she'd penned.

"You touch yourself, making yourself hard for me."

His laugh was strained. "We can skip that part."

"No." She didn't want to skip any part. This was her fantasy, an opportunity that she'd never have again. And, cliché or not, she wanted to create memories that would last forever. That she could check out from the shelves of her mind and re-play over and over again. "You lean your head back and close your eyes, stroking your cock as if I'm not here."

"That's going to be . . . difficult."

It was going to be difficult for her, too. The last thing she wanted him to do was pretend she wasn't here. She pushed that desire aside, instead focusing on the feminine power swirling through her, and forced a shrug she was far from feeling.

Derek tilted his head against the back of the chaise and closed his eyes. His hand circled the base of his cock, moving up, over the head, then back down. The movement was fluid, like that of a master musician playing a favored instrument. His teeth bit into his lower lip, his facial muscles locked in an ex-pression resembling pain instead of pleasure. Erotic pain.

"That's it," Nichole whispered.

"Fuck."

She chuckled, albeit, shakily. Sexual power surged through her, mingling with the lust roaring through her veins. "Not yet."

He didn't return her laugh. Derek slowed. As he slid his

hand down his shaft, he smeared a drop of pre-cum, coating the head of his cock. It glistened as if Nichole's tongue had been on him, licking and swirling, painting abstract liquid art.

Nichole continued. "Then you open your eyes . . ."

Derek's eyes snapped open.

"And you look at me while you pump your cock."

His hand kept moving, though slower. Perspiration dotted his forehead.

"And then you ask me to come to you."

"Come here," he rasped.

"And then I walk toward you . . ." Nichole walked toward him.

"Yes." Derek's hand stilled.

"Don't stop, Derek."

"I *have* to stop, Nichole."

Nichole shook her head. "That's not what happens in my notebook."

"That's because you're clueless."

Hurt pricked the lust circling underneath her skin. "Are you saying I'm a bad writer?"

"No. I'm saying you're not a man. When I do this"—He slid his hands up and down his cock—"what do you think I'm thinking about?"

"How good it feels."

"I'm thinking about how good *you* feel. I'm imagining that blue skirt you're wearing bunched up around your waist."

Derek's hands pumped faster.

Nichole's heart beat faster.

"I'm imagining you under me, your pussy bared, ready, waiting, and craving my cock."

Her pussy *was* ready, waiting, and craving his cock.

"I'm imagining sliding between your lips and thrusting inside you, hearing you gasp . . ."

On the upward pass, the heel of his palm squeezed the head of his cock.

". . . feeling your muscles clench and stroke me, holding me, drawing me deeper inside . . ."

On the downward pass, the skin drew tight against his cock.

". . . begging me with your body for more."

His breathing was ragged.

Nichole's breathing was ragged.

"*That's* why I have to stop."

He had to stop because she made him lose control. Her words. Her actions.

Her.

Derek stopped.

Nichole sat down and crossed her legs, the cold floor doing little to cool the heat inflaming her body. She didn't trust herself to stand, didn't trust her shaking legs to support her. "I . . ." She cleared her throat. "I've never watched before." It still came out a whisper, barely audible.

"Is that in the notebook?"

She nodded.

"Then you watch. And you think about what's not in the notebook—what I'm thinking about."

His left hand cupped his balls and his other hand went back to stroking. Up and down. Down and up. And all the while his eyes stayed on hers.

Nichole's nipples tightened.

Derek's hips bucked, moving in sync with the up-and-down strokes of his hand. His eyes were half-closed, but he held her gaze.

Nichole dragged her eyes from his, letting her gaze drift over his body, watching his leg muscles clench and unclench as his hips rose and fell.

Her own hips rocked.

Derek's head fell to the side. His lips parted. His tongue curved against his upper lip. And still he didn't look away.

If she'd been the one on the chair, she would've looked away. Or she would've closed her eyes. Hiding, so that he couldn't see her secrets—her need, her passion. Her soul.

That was Derek's point, why he wouldn't look away. He wanted her to see him, wanted to let her know that he had nothing to hide.

Think about what's not in the notebook—what I'm thinking about.

With each thrust of his hips, he was thinking of being inside her. With each stroke and squeeze of his hands, he was imagining her surrounding him. Nichole half-rose, wanting to climb on top of him and hover over his lap, then lower herself, slowly, slowly—

Derek gasped and his head lolled against the chaise back.

Nichole's neck arched.

His legs tensed, unmoving.

Nichole's breath froze.

A groan caught in Derek's throat and his lips drew back, seconds before his body jerked, ripping the groan from his throat.

His gaze lost focus but he didn't look away.

Nichole wanted to look away and pretend she hadn't seen the need and desire churning beneath the surface of his gaze. His hands, caressing his flesh, had stoked his desire to come, but it had been need—the need for her to make him come—that had changed his eyes from emerald to forest.

And since she hadn't looked away, he'd seen that need mirrored back at him.

His gaze refocused. His grip on his cock relaxed. Moisture glistened on his abdomen, a silken strand on the head of his penis glittered in a ray of light. "Is that how it happened in your notebook?"

"No . . ."

In her notebook, his eyes had been closed and he'd been in his own world, lost in his own pleasure. She'd been a voyeur, in her own world, letting his pleasure fuel hers. They'd shared the same room, but had been immersed in different worlds while engaging in private fantasies.

Here, their individual worlds had become joined and their private fantasies had been shared. Desires were revealed. Souls were exposed.

"This was . . ." *scary* ". . . better." Nichole stood, her hands going to her blouse. "But I want more."

And she did want more. Despite the fear of what she had revealed or what she was going to reveal. Maybe she'd be embarrassed or ashamed later. Or maybe not. But, that was for later. Now, she wanted to just be, to just do, without thought or judgment.

"What do you want?"

I want to be the woman in my notebook.

That Nichole went after what she wanted, regardless of whether others would approve and disapprove. She didn't care about projecting a responsible, professional image. She fucked whomever she wanted to fuck, whenever and wherever she wanted to fuck him. She was sexy and sensual, and men desired her to the point of obsession. Derek desired her to the point of obsession.

I am going to be that woman. Just this once . . .

"I want . . ." Nichole began unbuttoning her blouse. ". . . you to want me again."

His fingers circled his cock.

"No. Don't touch yourself."

"All right." He returned his left arm to the back of the lounge and let his right fall to the seat, palm down.

Her gaze flickered to his penis. It rested against his pelvis.

"Don't talk."

She slipped the blouse off her shoulders.

"Don't move."

She unzipped her skirt and slid it down over her hips, stepping out of it.

His gaze slid up. Ankles, calves, thighs . . .

Her skin tingled.

. . . and stopped at the small triangle of her thong underwear.

Her gaze latched onto his cock. "Except that. I want you to move that."

His cock wasn't quite so soft anymore.

Nichole unhooked her bra and let it fall to the floor. "I want to *see* how much you want me." Splaying her fingers on her neck, she trailed them down, tracing her collarbone, then following the curve of her breast. "I want you to like my breasts."

She circled each areola.

Derek swallowed hard.

She grasped her nipples, rolling each between her thumb and forefinger. "And my nipples. I want you to like my nipples."

Derek's eyes caressed her breasts. His eyes darkened. His cock lengthened.

"I want you to crave me." All facets of her: Notebook Nichole and the girl-next-door Nichole, the seductress as well as her no-nonsense counterpart. But, of course, she didn't tell him that. Instead, she kept to the fantasy. She took a breast in each hand and squeezed. "I want you to crave my breasts in your mouth, for tasting and sucking."

Derek's tongue traced his lower lip.

The action made Nichole think of other places she'd like him to lick. She ran her tongue across lips that suddenly felt dry as she slid her hands down over her ribcage, fingers spread apart, fingertips lightly caressing.

Derek seemed hypnotized by the downward path of her hands.

Nichole was hypnotized by the intensity of his stare, spellbound by the craving that shone in his eyes. The craving that she'd requested.

A trail of need prickled her skin in the wake of his gaze. Her skin burned where her fingers touched.

Hooking her fingers under the elastic waistband of her underwear, she removed her thong and threw it behind her. She let her hands linger on her thighs, thumbs pointing inwards, toward her lips.

"I bet you want this."

His cock twitched, lifting away from his abdomen.

She walked toward him.

His eyes roved her body—breasts, stomach, pussy, legs, thighs, pussy, stomach, breasts—and returned to her eyes. His eyes were darker than she'd ever seen them. No longer green, but not quite brown. And they blazed, confirming the desire evidenced by his body.

She stopped in front of him, her pussy level with his head. "You want to kiss me." She slanted her hips. "You want to stop licking your lips and lap here . . ." She pulled her lips apart, giving him a peek. "So close. If only you could lean forward one . . . tiny . . . inch . . ."

His nostrils flared. He was breathing out of his mouth, his chest rising and falling rapidly.

Nichole's breath was jerky. She was struggling to breathe and talk at the same time. The room spun slightly and her legs trembled, as if she had just downed a couple of apple martinis. Which wasn't too far from the truth, as she was drunk. Drunk from the desire pouring off of Derek in waves that assaulted her senses.

She dipped a finger between her folds.

Derek groaned.

"*I'd* like you to kiss me here . . ." She flicked a finger upward. "And lick me like this." She rubbed, back and forth, then around and around.

Fire sparked from her finger and tumbled outward. Nichole gasped.

Derek gripped the arm of the lounge, his nails nearly gouging the soft wood.

She withdrew her finger and raised it to her lips.

Derek's chest was unmoving, the air trapped inside. His gaze clung to her finger as she puckered her mouth and slid her finger inside. She sucked, sampling the musky taste of lust.

A grunt rumbled within his chest.

His cock jerked away from his abdomen.

Nichole inhaled sharply and paused. She was supposed to be the mistress of seduction, dishing out desire, while remaining in control. Instead, she was a lackey to desire, struggling to resist climbing onto his lap and sliding him inside her.

"Tell me this is where I get to show you I want you," he rasped.

A droplet of moisture trickled over the head of his penis.

Her heart jangled against her ribcage. Every nerve ending seemed to snake through the air, heading to him, seeking the sensation that only his body could give. Nichole yanked her gaze from his cock and, avoiding his eyes, looked for a neutral spot to concentrate on while she summoned back the mistress of seduction.

"No. Not yet."

Derek cursed.

Nichole wanted to smile but the pain of her own desire kept her lips locked in place. She knelt in front of Derek. His breath caressed her cheek. The faint scent of peppermint wafted under her nose.

That made her think of the article she'd read on the sensuality of peppermint and oral sex. Had Derek read the same thing? Had he come prepared?

Excitement and disappointment slithered through her, tangling inside. Not yet, not yet, not yet.

"This is the part where I touch you like this . . ." She trailed her hands over his biceps, feeling the muscles move beneath her fingertips as his hands clutched the chair. She moved over his shoulders, to his chest, weaving her fingers through his chest hair, marveling that it felt wiry and silky at the same time. She stopped at a nipple, circled and pinched, until it became hard.

He inhaled sharply.

"It's hard like mine."

"Baby, it's nothing like yours," he said. The flames of hunger, alight in his eyes, stoked her skin.

Electricity jolted her pussy.

"Stop," she said. Whether she was talking to him or her pussy, she didn't know.

Nichole replaced her fingers with her tongue, licking one pebbled nipple, then the other.

He gasped.

"Now, I tell you how good you taste." She massaged his chest with her hands. "And how good you feel."

She lifted her head, and skipped her fingers down his stomach, circling his belly button. The skin quivered under her touch. "You feel good." She liked the hard muscle and soft skin, the contrast between strong and smooth.

She glanced at his face. She loved the way he looked at her, like she was the last slice of German chocolate cake in the world and he'd do anything to eat it. She loved the way he let her do whatever she wanted, without trying to take over or rush her along, even if that was what his body wanted him to do.

Nichole moved her hand lower, avoiding the cock straining to reach her fingers, brushing the curly pubic hair instead.

"And then I tell you how much I want you." And she did want him. On top of her, under her, in her, his body sliding against hers, slamming into hers, his skin slick with sweat as he let go of the rigid control he'd been fighting to keep in place.

Let go of control because of her—because she drove him beyond all thought, making him feel only her, and want only her.

Like she wanted only him.

"Tell me you want me," he said.

At the rawness in his voice, her gaze jerked to his. The plea burned in the depths of his eyes, igniting the thought that he was asking for something beyond sex. The thought hovered, on the verge of becoming tangible . . . and then it was gone, leaving only the lust.

It left Nichole stunned. Stunned because she'd allowed herself to believe that the urgency in Derek's request had a deeper meaning. Not because it actually did, but because she'd wanted it to have a deeper meaning. God, how had that happened? This fantasy was skittering out of control, veering into dangerous territory, leaving the safety of the physical world for the danger of the emotional world.

Making her imagine emotional needs that were not there.

Nichole wrapped her hand around the base of his cock, yanking the chains of the fantasy back where it belonged—in the physical world. Not silly emotional imaginings. "I want you to fuck me."

She swiveled her hand upward.

Derek's hips jerked downward.

"Do you have a condom?" she asked.

"Yeah. It's—"

A loud crash sounded from an upper level.

Nichole sprang to her feet.

"What the—" Derek jumped off the lounge, grabbed Nichole and forced her back down. "Get under the chaise and don't move until I get back." He yanked his slacks from the floor and ran toward the staircase in the center of the showroom, sliding a leg into each pant leg as he climbed the stairs.

Heart pounding, Nichole inched from under the chair and grabbed the pile of garments. After seconds of fumbling, she found her clothes. And less than a minute later, she'd managed to get her bra, blouse, and skirt on. She rushed toward the stairs just as Derek came down them.

"I thought I told you to stay put." Anger laced his voice.

I didn't want you to get hurt. "I'd rather die with my clothes on."

A smile flickered across his face, diminishing the anger.

"What happened?"

"Someone broke in."

"You mean someone was in here when we . . . uh . . . while . . ."

"Yeah. But my guess is they weren't hanging around to watch us."

He must've seen the doubt on her face. "The office is a mess. Files everywhere, furniture tossed around the room. Whatever he or she came for, they must've found it. The crash was from an overturned vase as they exited the fire escape."

"But how could we not have heard all that?"

"It was probably done before we got here. We interrupted them."

Which meant whoever it was had been up there for a while. Probably waiting for them to leave. Watching. Maybe not intentionally, but what else was there to do?

Nichole turned, suddenly not wanting to look at Derek. She headed back to where they'd been, back to The Chaise, which she avoided looking at as well. She scoured the floor with her eyes, looking for her panties.

"I've got to call the police," Derek said from behind her, his voice apologetic.

"I understand. I'll call a cab."

He came up behind her, turning her around to face him. He placed a finger under her chin. "We're not finished," he said softly.

His gaze on her lips told her he was going to kiss her.

She wanted the kiss.

She wanted to get away, to sort the feelings roiling inside her. Disappointment at the interruption, definitely. Her body still hummed, ready for the fulfillment his body had promised. The morning-after discomfort at her wanton behavior, certainly. But it was the fear that had her rattled—fear that had everything to do with emotional danger and public exposure. And when Nichole was afraid, she ran.

She backed away. "I can't find my underwear."

"I'll find them for you."

"Okay."

"We're not finished," he repeated, as if sensing her panic.

She didn't answer as she hurried to the door. In her panicked state of mind, his words sounded like a threat.

5

"Talentz. This is Nichole." Nichole wedged the phone between her ear and shoulder as she fiddled with the penholder on her desk—the same penholder that she'd knocked over yesterday when the impeccably dressed man came into her office and flustered her.

Twenty-four hours later, she was still flustered. Only more so now. The crash from yesterday in Derek's office reverberated in her mind, begging the question "who had broken in and how much had he or she seen?" and spreading the fear of ruination. She couldn't handle another fiasco like the lingerie ad, not now when she'd gotten her life together.

The man on the other end of the phone brought her attention back to the present.

"What is the date of the shoot?" she asked.

June fifteenth, the man said, then launched into an unnecessary accounting of the production schedule. Nichole's thoughts returned to their previous topic. She had to get a grip on this fear of ruination. True, the public exposure of the lingerie ad had ruined her quiet life in Yuletide, California. But that had nothing to do with yesterday's burglary. What'd she think— that someone was following her, waiting for the opportunity to blow the cover of no-nonsense Nichole? Just as Derek's original intent was to use her notebook to blackmail her?

She'd been writing fantasies and dealing with scripts for too long. Next, she'd be imagining that Derek wanted her to want him—the man behind the cock. Oh, right—she'd already imagined that. Because she wanted him to want her—the woman behind the pussy.

How crazy was that?

She didn't want to think about how crazy that was. Instead, she focused on the words flowing into her ears.

"Who is the client?" she asked.

Didi's Donuts was the client. The man went on to supply extraneous information about the set, while Nichole went back to thoughts of Derek—the man that she'd been about to straddle on the chaise, and rub against, reveling in the friction of his skin against hers, and the roughness of the hair on his chest as it abraded her nipples. The same man she still yearned to straddle and rub against.

Her chest tightened.

The silence on the phone caught her attention.

"What type of talent are you casting?" she asked.

Lingerie model types. Had Derek really been looking for models when he had visited the office or had that just been an excuse? He had yet to make his selection and Friday was only two days away. Of course, in this business, that still left a lot of time. Everything was always rush-rush, as if it had totally slipped the client's mind that he needed a doctor look-alike for the antidepressant drug commercial that had been on the production schedule for weeks.

Just like the harried production director on the phone. Nichole held back a sigh.

But, in Derek's defense, a break-in was a valid excuse to postpone a talent search—and a valid excuse not to call her.

We're not finished, he'd said.

And she wanted them to finish. Despite the fear of discovery that still lingered in her mind. Despite the fear that her desire for sex might blossom into desire for . . . more. Derek's touch was an aphrodisiac. And the look in Derek's eyes—a look that promised to satisfy her every craving, to quench the flame sparked by every nerve ending—and the hardness of his cock, because he was thinking of her, were like drugs. And she was already addicted.

The man on the other end of the line once again interrupted her thoughts.

"I'm sorry. Could you repeat that?"

He gave her an address. She jotted it down and hung up.

Okay. Enough was enough. She'd never let personal issues distract her from business before. But then again, she'd never had anything worth distracting her from business. This was a chance to move beyond a world built of words to one of action. For the first time, she'd felt free to be herself with a man. To enact fantasies some might consider silly. But Derek had not considered them silly. In fact, he'd been just as aroused as she had. She—

She had to get back to work. She would not let fantasy derail her goal of being part owner of Talentz. Even if the fantasy came wrapped in a 6'1" package, with a body that—

Scooping the penholder off of the table, Nichole dropped it into the garbage can. That made her feel microscopically better, more in control. She turned her attention to her computer, determined to find the perfect doughnut look-alikes for Didi's Donuts.

An hour and ten phone calls later, Nichole's eyes were beginning to glaze over—pun intended—from the doughnut search.

She welcomed the sound of the office door opening. Until she saw who it was.

Nichole pasted a professional smile on her face as the woman in the fringed suede jacket and stiletto cowboy boots sashayed through the doors. Silver-blue eyes, collagen-enhanced lips, flawless bronze skin, and blond hair that a hairdresser must've dyed strand by strand, were topped by implant-perfected boobs, and a size 0 body. Melissa Moore flounced to a stop in front of Nichole's desk amid a plume of spicy citrus perfume.

"Good afternoon. May I help you?"

An arctic smile curved the woman's lips. "I'm sure you know who I am."

Derek's ex-girlfriend. "Yes, Ms. Moore. How may I help you?"

"I'm here to see Richard."

"Do you have an appointment?" Nichole pretended to consult Richard's calendar, already knowing the answer.

"No. I don't need one."

"I'm sorry. Mr. Dalton doesn't see new clients without an appointment."

Melissa no longer pretended to smile. "He'll see me."

Nichole dug deep inside for another smile. "One moment, please. Would you like to have a seat?"

"No."

Nichole prided herself on the fact that Talentz didn't represent a single prima donna like the one glaring back at her. And it wasn't because Nichole, personally, did not like the attitude. It was because attitude didn't make for good business. Madam Queens resulted in irate clients, and irate clients resulted in lost business. Thank God Melissa wasn't represented by Talentz. What had Derek seen in her?

The same thing he might still see in her.

Nichole squashed the unwanted thought and dialed Richard's extension. "Ms. Melissa Moore is here to see you. She doesn't—"

"Send her in," said Richard.

"Certainly."

Nichole hid her surprise as she turned back to Melissa. She stood. "Mr. Dalton will see you."

Melissa's smile was a little less arctic and a lot more smug. "Of course. I know the way."

She "knew the way"? To Nichole's knowledge, Melissa Moore had never been at Talentz before today. And yet, here she was, without an appointment. Richard saw very few people without an appointment, Derek being one of the few exceptions, but that was because their friendship went back to their college days.

Nichole frowned as she watched Melissa swish her way down the hall, her perfectly rounded ass bouncing with just the right jiggle.

I wonder if they've invented Botox injections for asses.

Okay, that was catty. No, it was pure jealousy. But not of Melissa's looks. Talentz represented models more beautiful than her, many who even possessed natural beauty. So, no, it wasn't Melissa's appearance: Nichole was jealous of the fact that Melissa had been Derek's ex-girlfriend and had slept with him on numerous occasions. Could still be sleeping with him, for all she knew.

Which was totally, incomprehensibly . . . pathetic. She had no right to feel jealousy or anything else where Derek was concerned. That damn notebook. Why had she written it? And why had she ever given in to desire?

Because she'd wanted to, and still wanted to.

We're not finished.

Derek's words no longer felt like a threat, but a promise.

The phone rang, once again interrupting her thoughts. Which was a good thing because, once again, she'd forgotten about business.

"Talentz. This is Nichole."

"Hi," said Derek, his deep baritone making the word synonymous with sex.

"Hi," Nichole said, breathlessness almost making the word unintelligible.

"Busy?"

Busy thinking about you. "Yes. No. Uh . . ."

Derek laughed. "Which is it?"

"I have a minute." Nichole's heart raced. "Did you catch the thief?"

"No."

"Oh . . . I'm sorry."

"So am I. But that's not why I called."

Nichole held her breath, praying that the reason was not Talentz business, but rather Derek-and-Nichole, limb-and-sheet-twisting business.

"This is where you ask, 'Oh, why did you call?' "

Nichole smiled.

"Or you ask, 'Did you call to invite me out?' "

Nichole laughed. "Do women really ask you that?"

"On occasion."

"Hmmm. Does it work?"

"It would with you."

Pleasure skittered through her. It'd been a while since a man had flirted with her. Or, maybe it'd just been a while since she'd enjoyed flirting.

"I called to invite you to my grand opening on Friday."

"I . . ." *would love to.*

"You'd enjoy it." His tone dropped an octave lower on the word "enjoy," causing a shiver to ripple along her inner thighs.

Yes, she would. That was the problem. Attending the grand opening felt too much like a . . . "date," which would make her want more of him—the man. She needed to keep things in perspective. She needed to treat this as sex. "I can't."

He acted as if he hadn't heard her refusal. "Plus, I still need to return your notebook."

Now, how could she have forgotten about that? "I—"

"And I still have your underwear."

Oh God. She had definitely forgotten about those.

"Which, by the way, I have in my hand right now." He took a deep breath. "They smell like I imagined you'd smell."

Nichole's face burned.

"Only better. Like desire and passion mixed with woman, and a hint of *Eau de Baise-moi*. Actually . . ." He inhaled again. ". . . more than a hint of *Eau de Baise-moi*."

"You de bezzz mwaaa?"

"Fuck-me fragrance." His tone was no longer teasing. "It's a smell that makes me hungry. Hungry for—"

She heard voices in the hall, alerting Nichole to Richard and Melissa's presence. Nichole shook off her hormone-induced haze. "D-Derek, yesterday, I enjoyed playing—"

"You weren't 'playing' and neither was I."

Nichole opened her mouth to deny the truth of his words, then closed it. The conversation in the hallway grew closer.

Silence crackled through the phone.

"You know, now that I think about it, I was playing," he said, finally.

Rational relief warred with irrational disappointment.

"As I lay on that chaise . . ."

She pictured his thighs surrounded by red velvet.

". . . imagining how it would feel to be moving in you, going in deep and coming out slow . . ."

Nichole imagined squatting over him, raising her hips up until only the tip of his cock kissed her lips, then plunging back down, gasping at the thrill of his reentry.

". . . while you gripped my hips, urging me to go faster, saying my name over and over again . . ."

Oh, Derek . . . please.

". . . I *pretended* to come."

Nichole pressed her legs together, attempting to stop the throbbing that had started between her legs.

"And as you bared those perfectly rounded breasts and that most edible pussy, I *imagined* that my cock grew painfully hard."

Nichole inhaled deeply, causing her nipples to rub against her bra and send tingles over her stomach and downward.

"And most importantly, when I looked into your eyes so that there could be no doubt of what you were doing to me, well, I was *acting*."

Nichole's hand tightened on the receiver and she drew her breath in sharply. She couldn't speak, and that was just as well, because as she stared down at the phone, she heard a cough. She looked up in time to see Richard and Melissa enter her office.

Richard. Her boss.

Melissa. Derek's ex.

At least she didn't have the speakerphone on. Only she could hear Derek's seductive voice.

"Now," Derek continued. "Let's talk about you. When you—"

Nichole looked up again at the intruders and summoned her professional voice. "I'm sorry, Der—Mr. Mitchell, but—"

"Is that Derek?" asked Melissa.

"Yes—"

"He must be calling for me. I told him I'd be here."

Nichole placed her hand over the phone. "Ms. Moore—" Then, realizing she was being unprofessional, she turned back to the phone. "Could you hold, please, Mr. Mitchell?"

"No. I'm not holding or hanging up until you say 'yes.'"

"Mr. Mitchell—"

"Is that a 'yes?'"

"No—"

"Would you like me to stop by with a personal invitation?"

"No!" Nichole lowered her voice. "It's not too late to help you with Friday's event. If you—"

"Then I'll see you Friday. Eight o'clock?"

"Of course n—"

"Great." The line went dead. Nichole drew a shaky breath, returned the phone to the cradle, and turned to face a glaring Melissa. "I'm sorry, Ms. Moore. Mr. Mitchell was calling regarding his event on Friday." She turned with relief to Richard. "Is there something I can help you with?"

Richard frowned. "Is everything okay?"

Nichole forced a smile. "Yes."

Richard's frown remained.

Melissa's glare deepened.

"After much persuading—" began Richard.

Melissa turned to Richard and the glare evaporated. She giggled. A high-pitched girlish sound. "Oh, I didn't need persuading."

Richard smiled. A sappy, puppylike smile. "Now, now."

Now, now?

Richard cleared his throat and turned back to Nichole. Thankfully, his expression was the business one Nichole expected. "Melissa is going to join Talentz as a model. I have a few jobs that I'd like you to work with her on. But I'm sure she won't need to audition."

Nichole's lips felt frozen as she turned to Melissa. "Wonderful. Welcome to Talentz."

Melissa didn't deign to answer. She stuck out her hand to Richard. "I'm looking forward to a profitable relationship with Talentz."

"And so am I," he said, shaking her hand.

With a parting smile for Richard and an unsmiling nod to Nichole, Melissa swished her way out the door.

As Nichole stared at the closed door, she wondered if aliens had taken over the bodies of everyone she'd come in contact with in the last twenty-four hours.

Including herself.

"What was that all about?" she asked, turning to Richard.

Richard stared at her through narrowed eyes. "I was going to ask you the same thing."

"What do you mean? *I* wasn't kissing ass."

Richard's smile had an edge. "You sure about that? Three 'Mr. Mitchells' in less than fifteen seconds. And I've never seen you flustered by a client before."

"Stop trying to change the subject," she said, changing the subject herself. "What's Melissa Moore doing here?"

Richard shrugged. "Melissa's here because we were able to negotiate favorable terms."

"But why? She's a bit 'big' for our agency."

His smile was sly. "It seems like there's a certain appeal to being a big fish in a small pond."

"Meaning the La Roche Agency isn't kissing the ground she walks on?"

"Yep. Which is good timing for us."

Nichole sighed. "Uh-huh. You're not the one who's going to have to walk with your tongue to the ground behind her."

"What? You don't think my little display of ass kissing didn't hurt me?"

Nichole snorted. "It didn't look like you were in pain to me."

Richard smiled before turning serious. "Now. You want to tell me what's behind your dislike of Melissa?"

Nichole saw the scene as if she'd written it: *Blond tresses cas-*

*caded over chocolate-colored brocade, as if artfully arranged by
a set designer. The dark-haired man above her lowered himself,
his muscular arms bulging as if he were doing sit-ups. He nibbled her lips, tracing her chin with his tongue as he moved down
her throat. She arched her neck, careful not to disturb her hair.*

Nichole shrugged, banishing the image. "You know I don't
work with divas."

"Yeah. But you seem to dislike this diva more than others."

"Richard, she has a reputation for being difficult. Difficult
models are a problem for us, and for our clients. You know
this."

"Yes, I do. But the benefits of Melissa's name offset the neg-
atives. And any client who uses her knows what to expect. Her
behavior isn't exactly a secret."

Nichole sighed. "Well, I won't let my dislike get in the way
of business."

"I didn't think you would."

"So. What jobs do 'we' have to work with Melissa on?"

"Oh . . . just a little grand opening, for starters. On Friday."

Nichole groaned and let her head fall back against the chair.
"No."

"You just need to take Melissa around—"

"No."

"Introduce her while you're schmoozing—"

Nichole shook her head, eyes still closed. "Nope."

"And let folks know we're representing her."

Nichole took a deep breath, making her decision, and giving
Richard the direct answer she hadn't been able to give Derek.
"You'll have to do it. I'm . . . uh . . . already going."

"You're already going?"

"Yes."

"I see . . ."

He remained silent.

Finally, he asked, "What's going on with you and Derek?" His voice was casual. Too casual.

"I hardly know Derek," she hedged. *But I know how he feels, satin skin over sinewy muscle. I know how his eyes glaze over right before his body shakes. Because of my words. Because of thoughts of me.*

Nichole coughed.

Richard's smile seemed sad. "Nichole, *I* know Derek. He's not—"

Her skin bristled at the patronizing tone. "Look, Richard, we're just talking about a party." *Liar. We are talking about much more than a party. We are talking about panty-melting sex.*

"Women are never 'just talking' about anything with Derek."

She raised her eyes to his, taking in the bland expression belying the sarcastic tone. "Richard, my personal life is *my* business."

"Getting involved with clients makes your personal life my business." He brushed a hand over his spiky short hair. "For Christ's sake, I just signed Melissa with the agency, Nichole."

She stared at Richard, trying to glimpse beyond the anger flickering in his blue eyes. "Why don't we talk about what this is really about?"

Richard said nothing.

"This is about my refusal to date you."

His jaw tightened.

Nichole's voice softened. "Richard, we've already been over this. I thought we'd put it behind us."

"I know, Nichole. We did. I was just being—"

"Hypocritical?"

He raised a brow.

"Melissa Moore doesn't giggle with me."

"Very funny." His smile gave way to sadness. "I know things have been a bit strained between us since . . . that night. But, I'm hoping you're still interested in the partnership."

That sounded vaguely ominous, causing Nichole to reply sharply, "Of course I am. What does that have to do with anything?"

"It's time for you to be more visible. The Who's Who of San Francisco will be at Derek's party, which makes it a good place to be seen. So, while you're there"—his lips twisted—"*with Derek*, you could make a few contacts, hand out a few business cards."

"I can do that."

Richard nodded. "Good. And I'll entertain Melissa."

The way his voice softened when he said her name brought on another alien-invasion moment. Could Richard be romantically interested in Melissa? But he'd never gone for the shallow, self-centered types. He'd never—

Nichole cut off the thought with an inward laugh. Wasn't that the pot calling the kettle black? Since when had Derek been her type? And yet, here she was, becoming more and more deeply . . . involved.

Richard turned, making her realize she hadn't heard a word he'd said. "I'll be right back," he said walking toward his office.

She was definitely letting her personal life get in the way of her business life. She had to stop. After Friday.

Richard returned with two tumblers and a bottle of bourbon. Nichole's stomach tightened. "Richard, I don't think this is a good idea."

"Just one."

"You promised—"

"We need a toast, Nichole." He poured a splash of liquor into each glass and held one out to her. "To increased profits and new beginnings."

Nichole stared at the tumbler, apprehension snaking through her at the "beginning" signified by the amber liquid within. The beginning of Richard's relapse with alcohol? Or the beginning of her decline into . . . uncontrollable passion?

Against her better judgment, Nichole took the glass from Richard, clinked it against his, and took a sip.

6

Friday evening, Nichole stood inside the entrance of The Decadent Chaise, taking in its sudden transformation from a stark showroom to a contemporary bordello. Chaise lounges dotted the room, each housed in a themed setting—or miniroom. Photos of chaises flashed across ceiling-to-floor screens hanging along the perimeter, in sync with the bass-filled beat of the techno music echoing off the walls. Clusters of guests were scattered throughout, talking and laughing, holding tumblers or champagne flutes.

As Nichole's gaze bounced from model to model, pride flickered through her body. The nakedness of the talent hired as waitstaff—the men shirtless with cravats circling their necks and thighs encased in tight-fitting black breeches and the women in lacy black corsets with plunging necklines and Victorian hoop skirts barely reaching mid-thigh—seduced. Her talent choices had been perfect.

She felt herself relax, unaware that she'd been tense. Maybe the tension had been because she hadn't been sure Derek would abide by the condition of her being here: that she not attend as his conquest—*date*—but rather, he treat her like any other guest.

"Why would I want to do that?" he'd asked on the phone two days ago.

She'd meant to say something witty. Instead, she'd blurted, "Because I don't want the media to treat me like the flavor of the week."

Derek had remained silent for a long time. Finally, he'd said, "I would like you to come. So, if that's what it takes . . ." His voice had sounded odd—almost angry, but tinged with something else. Confusion, maybe. Whatever it was, thankfully, he hadn't asked for details.

Nichole let the music pull her back to the present. Her gaze circled the room, looking for the man she couldn't seem to erase from her mind. She didn't see him but she saw that S-shaped chaise—the one she'd run her hands along and taunted Derek with word pictures of naked skin caressed by suede.

She shouldn't be thinking of Derek naked. Not here. Not now. So she yanked her gaze from the chaise to the rest of the room. At the sight of her dress reflected in the mirrored faux wall, Nichole's mouth dropped open.

Of the five dresses that Derek had sent, the white one had seemed less . . . revealing under the fluorescent lighting of her bathroom. But, in the bordello lighting, the near transparency of the material covering her from head-to-toe gave the appearance of nakedness more than actual nakedness would have. The high-neck collar, edged with ruffled lace and tiny pearl buttons from neck to waist, would've been innocent if not for the sheer gauzy material that hugged the outline of her shoulders and breasts, before becoming opaque at the last minute, a scant inch above her nipples. The opaque white silk clung to her waist and abdomen, before hugging her hips. Here again, the skirt would've been modest had not the opaqueness ended right at her pubic bone and turned sheer, dotted with appliquéd satin roses, also white, to reveal the outline of her thighs, legs, and ankles.

As she stared at a spiky two-inch heel attached to the white Victorian lace-up boot, a ripple of unease skated over her skin. In a matter of days, her most intimate fantasies had been discovered by one stranger, while her attempt to act them out had been witnessed by another; she'd been fantasizing at Talentz when she should've been working; and tonight, she'd agreed to attend the party only if she could remain inconspicuous, and yet she'd chosen a dress that shouted "look at me."

Maybe she'd been too successful in her transformation to Notebook Nichole. She needed to remember that the last time she'd shrugged off the cloak of respectability, giving in to the urge for a Victoria's Secret moment in front of a camera lens, her life had crumbled.

But, she told herself, this was different. She was not discarding respectability; she was taking a break from respectability. Just as her notebook of fantasies had a beginning and an ending, her carriage was going to turn into a pumpkin. Hopefully, not at midnight, before she got a chance to taste the beautiful prince. Maybe strip that perfectly tailored suit off his perfectly muscled body and lay back down on The Chaise, running her hands along him, exploring the areas she hadn't been able to last time, feeling him against her like she hadn't been able to do before.

Nichole let the image of Derek splayed out on the chaise wash away her unease, resolving to enjoy her night as Cinderella and revel in what she was feeling: free, horny, and sexy.

Very sexy.

Turning away from the mirror, she caught sight of Richard next to Melissa, talking to a group of people. The woman taking notes must've been a reporter. Though Richard appeared irritated, he did not appear to be drinking, for which Nichole was thankful. Just as she was thankful that he was keeping Melissa occupied.

Nichole's gaze drifted to their newest client. And quickly darted away. She did not want her evening ruined by thoughts of Melissa.

Her gaze landed on a blond man boldly eyeing her. And quickly darted away. There was only one man's eyes she wanted caressing her body.

Her gaze finally found that one man, and the sight of him made her stand stock-still. Derek's white tux seemed to have been made for his body only, the jacket fitting his broad shoulders perfectly. The cut of the fabric draped his chest without a wrinkle, until it parted around his hands, resting in the pants pockets. The black silk shirt, against the white jacket, brought out the tan of his skin, and made his hair look even darker. He looked made for a photo spread in *GQ*.

Nichole's mouth watered.

Derek reared his head back, laughing at something the guy next to him said. At the tail end of the laugh, his eyes met hers.

Her heartbeat suddenly sped up.

Derek's gaze moved slowly over her body, pausing at her barely covered breasts before moving down, lingering at a spot between her legs. Just as she was about to give in to the urge to look down and make sure that the dress's opacity there hadn't suddenly disappeared, his gaze continued on, caressing her thighs all the way to her ankles, before moving back up.

Slowly. Thoroughly. Possessively.

Her face warmed. Her body flamed, as if his gaze had been a physical touch, stroking where it landed.

His eyes were heavy-lidded when they returned to hers. The curl of his lips sensual. A private look. A sexy smile. Both just for her. He tapped the arm of the man next to him, murmuring words she couldn't hear, his gaze never leaving hers as he moved away and walked toward her.

She smiled through lips that trembled.

He smiled through lips that promised.

"You look virginal," he said, stopping in front of her.

Nichole let out a surprised laugh. "Virginal?"

He nodded.

"White is the only thing virginal about this dress."

"*You* look virginal. Fear and desire flitting through your eyes. The flush of innocence on your face."

Nichole felt her flush deepen—this time, with embarrassment. Sexy and self-confident women fell in and out of Derek's bed. Virginal and innocent women didn't make it to the bedroom door.

She searched for seductive words.

Derek's eyes searched her body. "Your body makes that dress look anything but innocent."

He skipped a finger lightly over her shoulder. "It makes me want to rip this away to feel the smooth skin peeking through."

His gaze traced the row of buttons trailing down, over her breasts to her abdomen. "And part this to see the breasts that you teased me with in this very room, and the waist that my hands had itched to circle."

His gaze moved lower, bringing heat to her groin. "That lovely dress would be a puddle at your feet, your beautiful body covered only by the light glistening off your skin."

"W-what about my boots? Would they be on the floor with my dress?"

"No. You'd leave your boots on."

Her blood hummed at that visual.

He returned his gaze to hers. "In fact, I bet that dress makes every man in this room think those things."

You still don't know that men desire you.

She did tonight. Nichole kept her gaze locked with his. "I only care what one man in this room thinks."

Something flickered through his eyes, warming his expression.

She forced herself not to look away. "Maybe you could share your . . . thoughts . . . with me later."

Derek's eyes darkened. "There's no 'maybe' about that."

Her pulse thrilled to the promise filling his words, while her blood raced at the memory of his words in the elevator.

"You're beautiful," he said.

She felt desirable and beautiful. Every word he spoke, every look he gave her fanned the flames of desirability, making her wish that this was a party just for two.

"Thank you. You're beautiful, too." Her voice was breathy.

This time, a smile touched his lips. "Don't you mean 'ruggedly handsome' or 'studly'?"

"No. Those adjectives can be used to describe many men." She let her gaze travel over him. "A beautiful man is a man that a woman can't stop looking at—whether he's wearing a pair of jeans or a tux or nothing at all—simply because she likes looking at him; he's a man she wants to touch all the time, simply because he feels good to touch—"

Something enigmatic flitted through his gaze, distracting her. This time, he was the one to look away.

Nichole kept her expression neutral, holding back her surprise. Had something she'd said made him uncomfortable?

Well, then, she should say more. "A beautiful man is a man whose mind intrigues a woman as much as his body."

Derek gave a polite smile and nod to whomever had caught his gaze, before looking away. He did not return his gaze to Nichole's.

He'd stroked his cock while looking at her and yet couldn't face her simple words? His discomfort encouraged her to continue. "A beautiful man is a man that a woman can't wait to feel inside her. Again and again. Because he shares his body with her. He shares his mind with her. He—".

"I haven't shared my mind with you."

"You haven't shared your body with me, either." She raised a brow. "And yet, in the elevator and in this room, I was given a taste of both."

People laughed. Music blared. Voices rose to be heard over the music. But it felt as if she and Derek were alone.

Derek nodded and smiled again at someone Nichole could not see. "I am not a beautiful man, Nichole."

"Why do you say that?"

Finally, he looked at her. "Because you were right the first time. I'm 'distant, emotionally remote, on the verge of being cold,' everything that a beautiful man is not." His lips smiled. His eyes did not. And the indefinable something in his tone told her that he wanted her to believe that he was right.

But she didn't believe that.

Outside of Talentz, he'd smiled and laughed with her. Need and desire had burned in his eyes as his gaze latched onto hers as he'd pumped his cock. She'd seen him angry—when she hadn't remained under the chaise the night of the burglary, when she'd said she wanted to be treated like a guest, and when she'd accused him of being those words he'd just quoted.

"I lied," she said.

"Oh? Beautiful men *are* 'distant, emotionally remote, on the verge of being cold'?"

She ignored his flippancy. "I was angry because you'd stolen my notebook and were pressuring me for answers I didn't want to give you." She lowered her voice. "I picked you to write about because I *wanted* you to be beautiful. I'm here with you now because I think you *are* beautiful."

Derek remained silent.

Nichole remained silent.

The indecipherable roar of laughter and conversations and music cocooned them.

A smile touched his lips. "You're an idealist, Nichole."

"Thank you."

Derek laughed—a laugh that engaged his mouth and eyes.

A laugh that brought the physical awareness that their conversation had kept at bay burbling to the surface. Desire rippled over Nichole's skin as if Derek's hands, tucked innocently in his pants pockets, were trailing over her shoulders and down to her breasts. The curve of his lips against his white teeth made her want to lean forward, and steal a kiss. His smile would fade and he'd get that smoky look in his eyes that she liked and—

Nichole blinked.

His smile had faded and his eyes were smoky. "Have you changed your mind?"

"Changed my mind?"

"About being my 'date?' No one but us would have to know." He shrugged. "I could just be showing you around the store."

"Have you shown anyone around tonight?"

"No."

She raised a skeptical eyebrow.

"I could make an announcement and tell everyone that I was only giving you a tour. Just in case they got other ideas."

Nichole shook her head and laughed—a breathy, shaky kind of laugh.

Derek smiled—a sexy, mouth-watering, pussy-throbbing kind of smile. He gave her arm an impersonal pat, like one would give a business associate, and leaned his head closer to her ear, like he was a stockbroker ready to impart a stock tip and wanted to make sure she heard. "I love your laugh. It wraps itself around my cock and squeezes."

Nichole gasped.

"And when you do that little catch-in-your-throat thing, I know you're turned on, and it makes me hot."

His words sent tendrils of heat coiling through her chest and stomach.

"I've never wanted a party to end as quickly as I want this one to." Derek dropped his hand and pulled back. "If you change your mind, I'll be around."

Nichole watched him as he walked away. Abruptly, he returned to her. "You may want to join the media tour of the mini-rooms I'm going to lead now." He winked and turned back around.

That wink concerned her a bit. The last time Derek had winked and walked away had been after he'd stolen her notebook. But he knew all her secrets now, so concern for her privacy was the last thing on her mind as she followed him with her eyes. She watched the play of the material against his body as he moved, admiring the confidence in his stride, noticing others, men and women, stop and send glances tinged with admiration, envy, and need. And he seemed oblivious to it all. No, oblivious was the wrong word. More like unaffected or indifferent. And that contributed to his appeal. Since he didn't want, need, or care about the effect he had on others, of course, that made the effect even greater.

Nichole followed him, staying on the fringe of the crowd that was slowly forming. Despite what she'd said about not wanting to be in the spotlight, a part of her wished that she was next to him as he walked from mini-room to mini-room—The Play Room, The Study, The Venetian Room—explaining each setting, describing each chair. An entourage of guests and media hung on to every word. Eyes stared with interest, though sex-me interest battled with polite interest in those belonging to the women. Pens scribbled on notepads.

Derek's words barely registered with her. Instead, Nichole

imagined herself standing by his side and the occasional stroke of his fingertip along her waist, his deep voice vibrating through her from where his chest brushed against her shoulder as he turned to motion to the ebony leather chaise lounge, his breath caressing her neck as he laughed at the brunette reporter's witty comment about the ornately carved chestnut-framed chaise.

"Pretty impressive, isn't it?" asked a voice to her right.

Nichole blinked, coming out of her fantasy. She turned toward the voice, before realizing the woman wasn't speaking to her. As she turned back around, the blond man who'd been checking her out snared her gaze. He smirked and lifted his glass in a mock toast.

Nichole jerked her gaze away. Had he overheard her conversation with Derek? Did he know what was going on between them? Did—

She stopped that thought in mid-sentence with an inner snort. No, what he had most likely seen was her staring after Derek with that moonstruck look she'd observed on the faces of other women when they stared at Derek.

Nichole turned back to Derek, trading her dopey look for one of polite interest, this time actually listening to him. He listed the origins of the Japanese-influenced design for the chair, pointing out that the stark simplicity of the shoji screen enhanced the simplicity of the room's design.

"And now we come to a special chair," Derek said.

Nichole looked away from the shoji screen and, seeing the chair Derek was motioning to, stumbled.

Someone gripped her elbow, helping her regain her balance. Nichole barely noticed, as her gaze was riveted on The Chaise. Their chaise.

"The Sex Lounge," Derek said, his voice seductive, his gaze glittering as he glanced at her briefly, before letting it drift from person to person. "My favorite of all."

Someone to her right made a comment that Nichole missed, having only eyes and ears for Derek.

"The scene is made for seduction . . ." continued Derek.

Nichole's panicked gaze circled the mini-room, dismissing the simulated fire that roared in the stone fireplace and the beige imitation fur rug spread out underneath the lounge angled toward the grate. Her breath grew ragged as she zoomed in on the chaise. There her gaze stayed. Ensnared. Frozen. Disbelieving.

"The chair is made for . . ." Derek paused as if giving it some thought ". . . intimate moments."

Nichole stared at the garments—a woman's blouse, seemingly flung across the mahogany back, and haphazardly strewn atop the cushion, a pair of black panties. A Nina Ricci thong, to be precise.

Nichole's Nina Ricci thong.

Nichole felt lightheaded. She'd never passed out in her life, but if she was ever going to do it, now felt like the perfect time.

"Are you okay?" came a faint voice to her right.

"Ye . . . Yes."

Derek's deep voice rumbled past her eardrums, drowning out her weak response to the man next to her. Someone laughed. But a scrap of black material had rendered her dumb, capable of only a single jumbled phrase that blotted out all other thought and sound:

Mypantiesmypantiesmypantiesmypantiesmypanties.

My God, how could he do this? Now, the whole world knew what she had done on this lounge, knew that those were her underwear, that—

She had to get a grip. There was no way anyone could know that those were her undies.

I still have your underwear. . . . They smell almost like I imagined you'd smell. . . . Like desire and passion mixed with woman, and a hint of Eau de Baise-moi.

Now everyone could share in her *Eau de Baise-moi*.

Oh God. She wanted the ground to open up right now and suck her right out of the room.

"None of the other rooms come with such interesting props. Who was your inspiration?" asked a reporter from the front of the crowd.

A couple of female twitters floated through the group.

"While I'd love to take credit, I can't. A woman designer came up with the concept for this room," said Derek.

A woman designer. There was nothing tongue in cheek about his tone. Nor was there anything to indicate that the "design" had been a mere flick of a woman's wrist as she'd flung her panties backward, to tease and torment the naked man sprawled in front of her. To make him drunk with craving for her, because of her.

Suddenly, their sex play that evening, their flirtation tonight seemed less playful. It felt like a rash had broken out on Nichole's face. She took a deep breath, then another, forcing air into her lungs to be circulated through her body to replace the dizziness with steadiness. This design was aimed directly at her. Why was Derek taunting her this way? What did it mean?

7

From the corner of his eye, Derek gauged Nichole's reaction to The Sex Lounge. Cheeks flushed, lips parted, eyes glossy, she stared back at him, looking stunned. He suppressed a frown. He'd hoped she'd be erotically stunned, but her expression said she could be in emotional shock.

He gave her a small smile.

Her expression remained unchanged.

Shit.

"Looks like the intimate moments have already happened," came a bald comment from the reporter in front of him.

Inwardly, Derek cursed. Outwardly, he smiled and turned his attention to the reporter. He hated these press events. The reporters spouted questions they probably thought were cute but were more often tacky.

Still, he was in business to make money, and the whole point of this event was to garner press attention. If The Sex Lounge did that, all the better. He glanced over at the still-stunned Nichole, and said, as much to her as the reporter, "But that's the beauty of this scene. The visitor can imagine whatever he or she wants. Has the intimacy really already occurred?"

As he skipped his fingertips lightly over the blouse, his thoughts lingered on the image of Nichole as she'd slid a similar blouse off of her shoulders. "Or has the woman simply teased her lover, baring her skin for him . . ."

Derek hooked a finger under the elastic of the thong, letting the underwear dangle from his index finger, remembering Nichole's bare pussy lips, seeming to swell before his eyes, ". . . making him want her and only her, making his fingers throb with the need to touch her . . ."

He stroked the slinky material between his thumb and forefinger. ". . . leaving no room in his mind for thoughts or desires of any other?"

I want you to crave me, Nichole had said.

And he had craved her—still did—like he'd never craved a woman before. He felt teased beyond endurance. And yet, there was something enjoyable about that. When had he ever had to wait for sex? The concept was kind of . . . quaint.

It wasn't quaint. It was damn exciting.

"I choose to believe the latter—that she has left him wanting . . . needing . . . craving."

I don't want the media to treat me like the flavor of the week.

"A craving *immortalized* by the . . ." Derek directed his smile toward the reporter who'd supplied the word ". . . 'props' in this mini-room."

This time, as he skimmed the group of guests and reporters with his eyes, he let his gaze linger for a second on Nichole. Her cheeks were still flushed, her lips were still parted, and her eyes were still glossy. But now he realized it was the same glossiness she'd had when he'd jerked off for her—then, the intensity of the need glistening in her eyes as she'd watched him stroke his cock had floored him, making him feel that only he could satisfy her. That had made him feel like he was doing more than jerking off.

Which was idiotic. Jerking off was just that: jerking off. Nichole had just made it more interesting.

Still . . . he liked that glossy look. *That* was the stunned look he'd wanted to see.

Derek grinned and let his gaze move on. When he saw a blond guy leering at Nichole, he stopped and his smile tightened. As if sensing Derek's gaze, the blond guy turned to him and raised his glass in a silent toast, his expression amused. Derek forced his jaw to relax. He didn't know the man but the man's expression seemed to say he knew Derek. Derek added him to the top of his mental list of people to talk to later. About the lawsuits, of course, not about why he was staring at Nichole, nearly slobbering down the front of her dress.

"And with that, I leave you all to enjoy the party. Please, eat, drink, and buy chaises."

The crowd gave polite chuckles and Derek moved away, giving a comment here, answering a question there, all the while on automatic pilot. He kept Nichole in sight, enjoying the occasional glimpse of her slim shoulders, small waist, and—when he got lucky—her round ass. He ignored the desire to go to her and focused on playing the concerned host, while asking discreet questions of acquaintances and foes alike, looking for anything the slightest bit suspicious that he could pass on to the investigator helping him with the bogus lawsuits. Nothing appeared out of the norm. He stifled a laugh. Nobody hated him any more than usual.

The blond man was nowhere to be seen.

Ridding himself of the last reporter, Derek turned away, pleased to be close enough to Nichole so his approach would seem coincidental, as if he was checking on her like any other guest. Though the need to make it appear natural annoyed the hell out of him, he acknowledged the irony of the situation: On the left, he had Melissa, whom he'd never slept with, managing to appear in his photos and make it look like they were "an item." And on the right, he had Nichole, a woman he was dying to sleep with, avoiding the slightest possibility of being seen with him.

It was funny. Only, he wasn't laughing. And despite the quaintness of blue balls, he was becoming impatient.

Derek felt a tap on his arm. "Great shindig, Derek," said Richard, though "shindig" came out sounding more like, "shin-nig."

Derek turned. Richard's red face and glazed eyes confirmed what his sloppy pronunciation had implied.

"Where's your drink? We need to toast to your success. Here, I'll get us both one." Richard reached out to grab champagne from a passing server and missed. "Hey," he said.

The server turned, saw Richard's outstretched hand, and reached for a glass. "I'm sorry, sir."

"That's okay," Derek interrupted, stopping him. "We're good."

"No, *we're* not," said Richard.

The waiter looked from Derek to Richard and back. "Uh . . ."

"It's okay. Please go give the woman in white"—he motioned with his hand—"a glass of champagne."

The waiter moved away with relief. Derek followed his progress, watching as he held the longstemmed glass out to Nichole. He watched Nichole—her burgundy lips touching the rim of the glass, the ripple along her throat as she swallowed, the glimpse of her tongue as it peeked out between her lips to catch a stray droplet. Desire hit him—the desire to sip of the champagne she had just tasted, to place his lips at the exact spot hers had been, to nibble the lips that had just kissed the rim of the glass, to taste the sweetness of the champagne lingering in her moist mouth.

"Whad'ya do that for?" asked Richard.

"Because you've had enough."

He could almost hear Richard's feathers ruffling. "And Nichole looks like she could use a drink."

"How do you know what Nichole needs?" Anger peppered Richard's voice.

Derek's gaze drifted to Nichole's chest, and his mind filled with memories of seeing her naked, her full breasts quivering with each breath, hips swaying as she'd walked toward him and the chaise. The raw desire shining in her eyes, the rough huskiness of her voice that had told him exactly what she needed. And from whom.

"Let me call you a cab."

"I know what's going on," slurred Richard. He grabbed Derek's arm.

Derek jerked his gaze from Nichole. His jaw clenched. "Let go, Richard."

"I know what's going on. With you and Nichole." Richard shoved.

Derek stumbled, knocking his elbow against the wall.

"You don't deserve her."

Echoes of another drunken voice rang through Derek's brain. Visions of a raised fist rushing toward him and the smack of his head hitting the wall flickered through his mind.

Anger raged in Derek's stomach. He clenched his fists. "You're way out of line."

Anger swirled through Richard's eyes. "To you, she's just another toy for your toy box. You don't deserve her." Then, just like that, the anger leaked from his voice and he gave a sad laugh. "But neither do I."

Derek forced his mind from the past to the present, reminding himself that this was only Richard in front of him.

"Look at me. Sorry, man. I've had too much to drink."

Derek unclenched his fists. "Wait here for your cab." He turned away and motioned to a waiter, intending for him to call a cab.

"Derek!" purred a woman to his left.

He turned toward the voice he recognized and inclined his head. "Melissa."

"The place looks fabulous. You look fabulous." Her lips curved into the smile that had appeared on hundreds of magazine covers. The tip of her tongue traced her upper lip as her eyes swept him up and down.

"Thank you." Derek kept his eyes on her face, refusing to look at the breasts nearly spilling out of the low-cut neckline or the thighs revealed by the slit of her blood red dress. He forced a polite smile to his lips. "If you'll excuse me . . ."

Fury flickered through her eyes before he turned away.

Fury flickered through his body as he walked away, but not because of Melissa. Melissa was angry because he wanted nothing to do with her, despite the fact that she used every wile in her arsenal to lure him. Her anger left him unaffected. So the reason he was furious was because . . . he was furious because . . .

He was mad at Richard for being drunk.

You're not mad at Richard for being drunk.

He was mad at having to deal with this shit on top of lawsuits.

This has nothing to do with being sued.

He was mad at Nichole for making him wait.

Derek's gaze drifted to her, taking in the movement of her pouty lips, watching them open and close around words he couldn't hear, watching them part to reveal straight white teeth when she smiled. He let his gaze drift lower, following the small shiny buttons stretching from neck to breasts, over the swell of tits he couldn't wait to see naked, could almost feel resting in the palm of his hand before he squeezed and kneaded, licked and—

You're mad because Richard is right. You don't deserve her.

I don't even fucking have her!

This was ridiculous. He was not going to stand around and

think about shit that didn't make sense. This was his party, this was a time for celebration, and that—

His gaze traveled back to Nichole.

That was the woman he wanted to fuck. Plain and simple. End of story.

Nichole turned her head and smiled at him. Her smile glowed; her eyes sparkled. There was no trace of the artifice or manipulation that hovered on the lips of the women he usually dated.

Fuck.

Derek's chest tightened.

How do you know what Nichole needs?

He had no doubt what Nichole needed, what she wanted. He'd read it between the pages of a light-blue notebook. He'd felt it when he'd pressed her ass against the wall in the elevator, when he'd pulled her body against his and felt her tense in awareness. He'd seen it shining back at him from The Sex Lounge.

He saw it now.

Just as he'd seen it since her first day at Talentz. That was why he'd kept his office visits professional, never giving in to the urge to see if Nichole was . . . for real. Until that damn notebook.

She's just another toy for your toy box.

He'd never treated women as toys. Yeah, so the relationships he'd had—maybe liaisons was a better word—were superficial. But, he'd always been up front. He'd never led any woman on, never made her believe there'd be anything more than sex.

Yeah, well, he'd never told Nichole anything up front. Just jumped in and started acting out scenarios.

Damn.

Nichole returned her gaze to the man and woman she'd been speaking with and shook their hands. The telltale sparkle lit her eyes seconds before laughter erupted from her throat. A laugh made because something amused her. Not because it was expected, or because it was considered sexy. A laugh that simply expressed enjoyment.

No, he didn't deserve to be with her. That was the only accusation of Richard's that was right.

Nichole wrote fantasies down in a book, a part of her wanting them to come true.

Derek had realized decades ago fantasies never came true.

Nichole hid feelings because she was afraid of being hurt.

Derek had no feelings, so there was nothing to hide.

Nichole was a relationship kind of woman.

Derek was a fuck friend kind of man.

He should walk away, tell her he was sorry, and he didn't want to hurt her. It was the kind, considerate, gentlemanly thing to do.

But Derek had never been a gentleman.

You'll never be more than a pile of shit, his father had said.

You're beautiful, Nichole had told him.

Both of them were wrong.

Derek continued forward, excusing himself as he walked through the crowd. Nichole's black, glossy mane called him like a beacon in a sea of monochrome bodies. He was going to have her, despite the wrongness of it—the wrongness for Nichole. But he'd make it as right as he could. He'd give her the best damn fantasies-come-true possible. Because that was all he had in him to give.

Nichole said good-bye to the Talentz clients she'd been speaking to, idly watching them walk away. Her gaze swung from them, passing over others in the crowd. She tried to tell herself she was just people-watching or admiring the chaises she glimpsed in between the clusters of guests. But she was lying. She was trying not to return her gaze to one man. The sexiest man in the room, his lean body encased in a white tuxedo that brought out the brown in his skin, the broadness of his shoulders. The man who'd lain on that chaise right there, naked, his stiff cock in his hand, doing exactly what she'd demanded.

The temptation could not be resisted. Nichole glanced back in Derek's direction. Richard was nearby, and he looked grim—well, as grim as he could look while edging closer to inebriation. Melissa looked royally pissed as she pivoted and stalked off in the opposite direction. Derek looked angry and determined and . . .

He was striding straight to her.

The breath was wrung out of her lungs.

She'd never before been the dizzy, breathless type. But when he looked at her like he was looking at her now, like he always seemed to look at her—as if she was the only woman in the room, as if she had 200 percent of his attention—she felt as if he saw things that no other man had.

Well, he actually had. No other man had read her secret fantasies. Or lived up to the promise of her secret fantasies.

"Have I stayed away long enough?" Derek asked, stopping in front of her.

Far too long. "Yes. I was on my way to you. I wanted to talk."

"Talk . . ." His lips quirked. "Okay. Let's go somewhere we can 'talk.' "

Nichole let him lead her, aware of little but his hand in hers, reminding herself of her desire to be out of the spotlight and thus, she should probably remove her hand. But she couldn't. She liked the possessive feel, the I'm-his-he's-mine kind of feeling. Even if it was an illusion.

She reminded herself she was supposed to be angry about her panties.

After a few dozen steps, he stopped and turned to her, taking her in his arms. They were on the dance floor. "Dreaming of You" by Selena blared in the background.

"I thought we were going somewhere where we could talk."

"We are." His voice caressed her ear.

Nichole shivered.

"Now. What do you want to talk about?"

"The Sex Lounge."

"Ahhhh." His chin brushed her temple, light as a kiss. "I've been imagining picking up where we left off on The Sex Lounge all evening." His hands caressed the base of her back, stroking lightly.

Her body urged her to forget about talking, to lean against him and ignore everyone and everything around them. Her mind scrambled to remember what she wanted to say.

"My thong . . ."

"I thought it added a nice touch."

"I can't believe you left it there. It was . . . personal."

"Yes." Derek's hand slipped to her lower back, pressing her closer. "That's why those aren't your panties."

His body moved against hers. His chest brushed her breasts. The scent of cloves and leather swirled around her head and under her nose, intoxicating her olfactory glands with their spiciness. She held her breath and backed away, attempting to use distance to get her mind back on track, to make sense out of what Derek had just said. Those were not her panties?

"They're a pair *like* yours. A new pair."

Had she spoken out loud or had he read her mind?

"Oh." Relief wrapped itself around that one small word.

"I have yours."

His knee dipped between her legs.

"And I'm not sharing them or this . . ." his thigh brushed against her pussy. Once. Twice. Again. . . . "with anyone tonight."

Tonight. His words seduced her mind, sending the fleeting

wish that his desire not to share would last beyond one night. She pushed that desire out of her mind, focusing instead on the physical want. His touch seduced her body, sending a rush of wetness between her legs, making her want to feel him naked and on top of her. She pushed the desire from her body.

And failed on both accounts.

Nichole closed her eyes, struggling to regain control.

Derek closed the distance between them, removing his leg from between hers, pulling her against him, forcing her to acknowledge his cock.

His desire twitched against her groin.

Her desire throbbed within her pussy.

She forgot about wanting to avoid the spotlight. She stopped fighting desire and dwelling on what was or was not possible. This was about now—fantasies already written and not yet written. About turning fantasy into reality for as long as the fantasy lasted. Who cared what, if anything, the media thought? Sure, she'd be uncomfortable for a second. But her world would not crumble like last time. It could withstand a whisper of embarrassment. This was San Francisco, not Yuletide.

It was time to stop fighting it . . . right . . . now.

Nichole looped her hands around Derek's neck and moved her pelvis against him. Slowly to the right. Slowly to the left.

His gasp caressed her ear.

"I'm not sharing this . . ." she tilted her pelvis upward, meeting his hardness with her softness ". . . with anyone, either. Until I get what I want." There. She'd said it. She'd staked her claim.

He stiffened.

She stiffened. Damn. Maybe he'd taken her comment wrong, thinking that she meant she wasn't sharing him beyond the duration of this fantasy. Beyond tonight.

"Nichole, you're about to become the first 'guest' I have sex with on the dance floor."

Oh. He'd taken her comment right. Good. "Mmmmm," she purred into his ear. "I love firsts."

Derek's grip on her waist tightened.

"That's in my notebook."

"Having sex on the dance floor?"

"No. Having sex when people are around. Aware but un-aware. Able to see, but unseeing."

Derek's cock felt longer against her thigh. And harder.

Nichole's pussy felt wetter. And warmer.

"Where are you when you have this sex?"

"In the closet. At Talentz."

"We're in that closet now," he whispered in her ear. "What do you do first?"

"I move away." Nichole took a tiny step backward so that a couple of inches separated them. "Then I do this." She parted his jacket and slid her hand inside. "I unzip your pants." She let her hands brush his belt buckle and trace his zipper.

Derek inhaled jerkily.

"I slip my hand inside and take you out." She moved her hand up and around his waist, staying underneath his jacket, as she moved around to the back. "I push my skirt up and do this." She pressed her pussy against his cock, feeling it nudge against her through his slacks. "Burying you inside me with one . . . smooth . . . move."

"You do this." She gasped in his ear. "And this." She grabbed his ass, her hands hidden by his jacket, and squeezed. "'Oh Nichole,' you gasp."

"God, Nichole," Derek rasped.

His thigh slipped between her legs again, brushing her inner thighs, bringing another rush of moisture. "And what do you want, Nichole?" His question bordered on a groan.

"I want—"

His lips grazed her earlobe.

A gasp slipped from her lips, and she leaned against him,

feeling limp. She was tired of words and games and word games. Arousal had given way to frustration. She removed her hands from under his jacket, clasping them, once again, around his neck. She sighed. "I want you to stop teasing me."

"What?" The vibration of his shocked laughter rumbled through her chest. "You want *me* to stop teasing *you*?"

"Yes."

Derek laughed harder.

Couples nearby looked at them and smiled.

Nichole smiled. After the way Derek had looked when he'd come to her, she would've never believed he was capable of such gut-busting laughter.

Derek's arm brushed her back as he raised it. Nichole leaned back to see what he was doing. By the direction of his gaze, she guessed he was checking his watch. "One more song, one more round of smiles, and handshakes, a thank-you-for-coming announcement . . ." He returned his gaze to hers, the fire within turning his forest-green eyes a cinnamon brown. "Twenty minutes tops, and then there'll be no more teasing."

Anticipation circled her stomach, struggling to break free and roar into action.

Derek held up a finger to the DJ and pulled Nichole back to him. They danced in silence. Limbs brushing, breath mingling, thoughts merging—thoughts of what would happen in less than twenty minutes. Tension crackled in the air between them, like a psychic form of static electricity.

Nichole summoned the nerve to ask the question that had been running through her mind ever since she saw what she'd thought was her underwear. Initially, she'd wanted the answer because she'd thought his actions were a cruel joke. But now . . .

"Derek?"

"Hmmm?"

"Why did you create The Sex Lounge? The mini-room, I mean."

The woman next to them laughed. Luther Vandross crooned on about houses and homes. Derek remained silent. Nichole guessed he wasn't going to answer the question.

"You have your notebook. I have The Sex Lounge." He said the words in the same tone one would report the weather.

Nichole's breath stuttered in her throat.

A simple statement with no special meaning. No hidden meaning either. He just meant that, just as her notebook recorded her fantasies of him, The Sex Lounge recorded his fantasy of her.

Warmth wrapped itself around Nichole's heart.

It doesn't mean anything. It doesn't mean anything.

She tried to convince herself of that but . . . she smiled. A happy, dopey smile that she didn't want him to see. Because it did mean something—that he wanted to preserve his fantasies, too.

Luther Vandross stopped singing. Derek stopped moving. Nichole wiped the dopey smile from her face.

Derek stepped back, his hands lingering on her forearms. "Which fantasy would you like first?"

"W-which fantasy?"

"The Sex Lounge or the library?"

Nichole's mouth felt dry. Her gaze flickered in the direction of The Sex Lounge. Of course, with the throng of people milling about, it wasn't visible. But she knew it was there. Covered with memories of his body and her clothing, his hands on his cock, her hands on her breasts. She wanted to leave him with new memories.

"The library," she said softly. "I'd like to save The Sex Lounge for later."

"Okay." His eyes flared. "I'd love to kiss you right now." He kissed her lips with his eyes. "To nibble your full lower lip." His tongue lightly licked his lower lip. "But this will have to do."

He raised her hand to his mouth, his lips pressing against her skin in a feather-light caress.

"The 'library' is upstairs."

His smile was sly.

Her smile was seductive. "Then I'll wait for you upstairs."

8

Nichole threaded her way through the crowd, smiling politely when she accidentally met someone's gaze. If a gun was held to her head and she was asked to describe everyone she'd just passed or smiled at, they'd have to shoot her. She was an automaton, placing one foot in front of the other, forming words of greeting to strangers and familiar faces alike, without conscious thought. Her body tingled in all the sensitive places—lips and nipples begging to be kissed, thighs and pussy begging to be stroked. Keeping her steps slow and steady, forcing the tremors of anticipation to the background, she walked up the stairs and into Derek's office.

Her pulse raced as she took in the floor-to-ceiling bookshelves. Their makeshift library. Nichole stepped closer, running her hand along the spines of the books. Expensive volumes on interior design, architecture, fabric types, and wood were interspaced with models of chaises worthy of the most elaborate dollhouse. She turned away from the books to admire a large desk placed between bookshelves, facing the door, and a chestnut-framed chaise and footstool in the corner.

Nichole resisted the urge to sink into the chaise, instead forcing her feet to take her to the closed door at the end of the room.

Once inside a bathroom bigger than her master bedroom, she stared at her reflection in the mirror.

Sparkling brown eyes stared back at her, seeming to dominate her face. She splashed water on her face and reached for a towel, patting her skin dry. Next, she repaired her makeup— eye shadow, blush, and lipstick.

She dropped her hands and viewed the results.

Her eyes still looked over-bright. Her face still looked flushed. Her lips still trembled.

Nichole closed her eyes and leaned her head against the side mirror. Notebook Nichole was fully in place. In fact, she had been in place ever since Nichole had donned the white dress. No more waffling. No more feeling as if the carpet had been yanked out from under her, dropping her outside of her comfort zone.

It must be a magic dress.

Derek must be a magician.

Nichole opened her eyes. She frowned at the reflection in the mirror, dimming the sparkle in her eyes. She wiped the blush from her cheeks, which made her look a little less flushed. She pursed her lips, which removed their tremble.

The woman staring back at her looked a little more in control—though looks were deceiving, for sensation raged through her body. She wanted Derek here. She wanted him now.

Nichole started at the sound of the office door being flung open. Her silent plea had been answered.

Her heartbeat tripled.

Angry voices reached her ears.

"I am not going to spend another moment being treated like this," came an angry hiss.

Melissa Moore? Nichole's heartbeat slowed. Disappointment washed through her.

"Treated like what?" asked a male voice, his tone was amused. Nichole didn't recognize the voice.

"Like . . . like . . . dirt!"

"How does politely excusing himself equate to treating you like dirt?"

"You know damn well he wasn't just 'politely excusing' himself."

Nichole flashed back to the image of Melissa stalking away after Derek had left her. Was Derek the "he" they were talking about?

"Well, what'd you expect? He's not interested in you. He's *never* been interested in you."

"He *is* interested in me . . ."

Yep. Definitely Derek. But how could Derek have never been interested in Melissa?

Melissa continued sullenly, "Obstacles just keep getting in our way."

The man chuckled. "I thought the dumb-blonde routine was just an act. But . . ."

Nichole walked to the door, curious to witness Melissa's interaction with yet another man who refused to cater to her. Maybe that was the appeal these men held for Melissa—they couldn't be wrapped around her pinky.

". . . now, I'm beginning to wonder."

Nichole peeked through the inch-wide opening. Melissa stood in profile, most likely staring at the man out of Nichole's line of vision. Her eyes flashed. Her mouth was pressed in a tight line.

"Fuck you," Melissa said.

"I was hoping you'd say that." His voice was a low purr.

Melissa ignored him. "What'd you find out?"

"I think he's seeing a woman named Nichole."

"The Talentz church mouse?"

Nichole stiffened.

"I don't know who—"

"What was she wearing?"

"White dress, white—"

"No way." Melissa snorted. "There's no way Derek could be with her."

Nichole struggled between annoyance and relief that Melissa, at least, suspected nothing.

"I saw them together."

"So did I. It was business."

It was the man's turn to snort. "Does this sound like business: 'It makes me want to rip this away and see the smooth skin peeking through?' He was talking about her dress."

Nichole gasped. He'd overheard her and Derek. How could that be? She hadn't noticed anyone paying attention to them. But, then again, she'd been totally focused on Derek. His eyes, his lips, his body, imagining—

The man stepped into view. Blond hair, sexy brown eyes. Nichole recognized him. He was the man she'd caught staring at her.

"And he said something about wanting to see her breasts. But that was probably 'just business,' too. And—"

"Shut up." Melissa crossed her arms and turned away, facing the bookshelves. Her fingertips tapped against her forearm. "I'm sure there's an explanation."

The blond man laughed. "Yeah. He's fucking her."

Melissa stiffened.

Nichole stiffened.

The blond man moved behind Melissa, running a fingertip down the side of her neck. "You have to admit, she's a sexy church mouse."

Melissa's fingers dug into her arm as she made to turn.

The man stepped forward, blocking Melissa's movement and forcing her to step forward until her thighs pressed against the desk. He bent down and kissed her neck. "Though not as sexy as you, Melly."

Melissa jerked away. "Don't call me that!"

He pulled her back and slid a strap of her dress over her shoulder, tracing its path with his tongue. "You didn't mind last week when you were yipping like a poodle as my cock—"

Melissa shrugged his mouth from his shoulder. "If you were half as good as you claim to be, Derek wouldn't —"

"Who needs who, Melly?" The steely undertone in his voice eclipsed the sarcasm.

Melissa remained silent, though the way her body stiffened gave the impression that it was prudence, not acquiescence, that kept her quiet.

"We do it my way or no way," the man sneered.

"And what way is that?"

His mouth moved back up her neck, over her jaw, and stopped at her ear. "The lawsuits first. Well, actually, this is first." He moved his head to her mouth.

The lawsuits? They were the ones behind Derek's problems?

Melissa tried to turn her head away.

His head moved forward, blocking Nichole's view. But Melissa's muffled moan gave the impression that she liked the kiss. He began pulling up Melissa's dress.

Melissa grabbed his hands, wrenching away from the kiss. "Stop it. Anyone could come up at any moment."

Nichole caught a glimpse of her face. While anger vibrated in Melissa's voice, desire lit her eyes.

The man continued pulling her dress up.

"This is Derek's office," Melissa hissed. The breathy quality made the hiss sound like a tire leaking air.

He disengaged his hands from Melissa's and dropped the skirt of her dress, moving back to her shoulders. He pulled both straps down her arms. Or so Nichole guessed. She only had a partial view from the side, but that revealed the top of Melissa's dress pooled around her waist. "I would think that would increase your desire, Melly."

Melissa's eyes flared and her breathing became ragged, giving the blond man the answer he needed.

"Am I right?"

He slid his hand around Melissa's waist and up the front, squeezing her breast.

She gasped.

"Either you turn completely around or I walk out of here."

"You aren't the only person willing to help me. Richard—"

"True. But I'm the only man who gives you this . . ." He pressed his hips against her ass, rubbing against her, before leaning forward. His movement forced her to lean over the desk. ". . . and lets you imagine it's someone else's cock."

Melissa moaned.

"What's it going to be?"

He laved the back of her neck with his tongue and he hooked his hands in the dress bunched around her waist.

Seconds turned into minutes.

"Oh, very well," she said, still striving for anger, but ending up pleading. She placed her hands on the edge of the desk, tapping her fingers.

Even from where Nichole stood, she could see the tremble in Melissa's fingers.

"Just make it quick," said Melissa.

He tugged the dress down over her hips. "Are you sure you want to make it quick?"

His voice was husky.

Melissa's was breathy, making a lie of her words. "Yes. This place doesn't put me in the mood to make love."

The man chuckled without humor. "That's good. Because

we're not making love." Placing his hands on her shoulders, he pushed, forcing Melissa flat against the desk.

Nichole jerked away from the door and leaned against the wall, squeezing her eyes shut. This time, it was her breathing that was ragged. God, what was she doing? It was one thing to fantasize about being a voyeur but another to actually be one. She couldn't watch this.

Notebook Nichole would watch it.

Didn't she just tell herself that Notebook Nichole was fully in place?

"Are we making love, Melissa?"

Nichole put her hands over her ears. She couldn't listen to this. No, this wasn't about making love. It was . . . raw. The literal interpretation of the word "fucking," which was what the man was trying to get Melissa—Melly—to admit.

What you're doing with Derek isn't about making love, either.

True. But, well, it wasn't about fucking, either. It was something in the middle. Wildly erotic, but somewhat caring. Unlike what Melissa and the blond man were doing, it was extremely exciting—

If what was happening in the other room wasn't exciting, why were her nipples straining against her dress? Why did she feel hot all over? Why was she breathing as hard as Melissa?

"Derek's office . . ." The man's voice seeped through Nichole's cupped hands.

Maybe that was it. Because she was in Derek's office, waiting to be fu—. Waiting to have sex. Yes, that was it. She'd been hot for Derek when she walked through the door, so it was only natural she'd be turned on.

Paper rustled. "Derek's desk . . ." continued the blond man.

Nichole imagined that she was the one spread over the top of the desk, that her breasts lay pressed against its glossy surface and her body quivered as she waited for—

The rasp of a zipper interrupted Nichole's thought.

"Derek's cock," said the blond man.

Melissa moaned.

Nichole whimpered.

Yes. Derek's cock. That's what she waited for—had waited for ever since he discovered her fantasies and she'd agreed to let him make them real.

"Isn't that what you really want, Melly? Derek's cock?"

Yes!

"Yes," Melissa said, her answer riding the tail of a moan.

Nichole gasped.

The man laughed.

Nichole lowered her hands. Fire flamed inside her body, causing wetness to fan outward and forcing her to accept the obvious. She had to watch. She had to listen.

Because she and Melissa wanted the same thing.

Nichole turned around, returning her eye to the crack in the door. Her warm breath ricocheted off the wood, sounding like that of a marathon runner to her sensitive ears. The man, still fully clothed, gripped Melissa's hips, and pulled her until her ass jutted off the edge of the desk. His hand dropped to the front of his pants, reaching, Nichole guessed, for his cock.

Melissa wiggled her ass, trying to press against him.

He kept his hips still.

"But it's not Derek's cock, is it, Melly?"

Yes, it's Derek's cock.

"Yes."

He slapped her ass.

Melissa whimpered.

Nichole fidgeted.

A crimson handprint spread over Melissa's ass cheek.

"Is it, Melly?"

"Oh, yes," she said, her voice pleading.

The slap was louder. Her whimper was more excited. Melissa gyrated her ass against his crotch.

"Is it, Melly?"

Yes, Yes, Yes. Nichole's ass stung. Her pussy throbbed. She replaced the man's black tux with a white one, his blond hair with Derek's jet-black strands, and his average voice with Derek's deep timbre. It was Nichole on the desk and it was Derek behind her. It was Derek's cock.

Melissa's ass cheek jiggled with the next slap.

The blond man slammed into Melissa.

In Nichole's mind, Derek slammed into her. Nichole's scream echoed through her brain. She bit her lip, trapping it inside.

Melissa shrieked.

"Does Derek fill your cunt like this?"

"No," Melissa answered, her voice rough.

"Yes," whispered Nichole, imaging Derek's cock inside her, stretching her, filling her.

"Does Derek fuck you fast and hard, making you beg for more?"

"No," panted Melissa.

"Yes," whispered Nichole, almost feeling Derek's hips moving against hers, slow and deep, fast and hard, making her body clench and tighten as the heat boiled inside, banking and building, screaming to get out.

The man's hips pumped harder.

Melissa's whimpers got louder.

Nichole's heart beat faster, circulating heat and fire to her swollen lips. She rubbed her hands against her breasts, imagining it was the wood of the desk rubbing them. She clenched her thighs together and bucked her hips, as if she were the one being ridden.

While pumping his hips furiously, he grabbed a handful of Melissa's hair, yanking her head back. "Come, Melissa."

Melissa's lips parted.

Nichole's neck arched.

Melissa's breasts bounced.

Nichole's breasts jiggled.

Both Melissa and Nichole moved like synchronized dancers, matching the rhythm of the blond man's thrusts.

He let go of Melissa's hair and placed his hands on either side of her, bracing himself over her, hips ramming into her without a change in pace.

Nichole clenched and unclenched her thighs, tightened and relaxed her vagina, sending waves of sensation with every movement. She braced herself with one hand against the wall.

Her hips pumped the air. Faster and faster.

Melissa slid back down onto the desk, her fingers curled into claws, her perfectly manicured fingernails attempting to gouge the wood.

"Now," he commanded, his voice strained.

"OhOhOhOhOh," said Melissa.

"Oooooooh," whispered Nichole, feeling Derek inside her, around her, on top of her, begging for her release, while straining to hold back his.

Melissa yelled as shudders jerked her body.

The man cursed, his body tensing, his hips suddenly motionless.

Nichole fumbled to get her fingers under her dress. She rubbed her clit and worked her hips, desperate to dispel the heat trapped inside of her. Suddenly, it broke free. Nichole stumbled. Her breath froze, her legs trembled, and her pussy spasmed. Then, just as suddenly, the tremors dissolved into mere ripples.

Nichole stilled.

The man pushed himself off the desk and stepped away from Melissa. Nichole heard the sound of his zipper as he moved out of her sight. "I guess you did want it quick, Melly."

"Bastard," Melissa snapped, lifting herself off the desk and grabbing her dress. She turned, facing the bathroom—and Nichole. Her hair was mussed and one side of her face was red where it'd rubbed up against the glossy surface of the desk.

"Where do you think you're going?" asked the man.

"To clean up," Melissa said over her shoulder as she took a step toward the bathroom.

Nichole's heart stopped. She dropped her dress, letting it fall back into place, while her gaze raced around the bathroom in search of a hiding place. Panic made her run to the sink and yank open the cabinet door underneath. Unless she could fit her 5'7" body in a 3' space, she was busted.

Close to hyperventilating, she dashed back to the door.

The blond man had his hand on Melissa's arm. "We don't have time."

"If you had time to fuck me, you have time to wait for me."

His lips twisted. "Fucking is quick. You, in a bathroom, aren't." He handed her a handkerchief. "The party is almost over, in case you hadn't noticed."

Melissa glared at the handkerchief.

Nichole held her breath.

"If you have to use the bathroom, do it downstairs. Use the *public* one."

Finally, Melissa whipped the white cotton from his hand. No other words were exchanged as she dabbed and wiped, dressed and primped. The man straightened the desk. Nichole didn't breathe again until the office was empty.

She fell back against the bathroom wall, this time waiting for her legs to stop shaking. She had watched a woman she disliked fuck—literally—one man, while pretending it was another. Who just happened to be the same man Nichole wanted.

And had she, Nichole, reacted with disgust?

No.

Disinterest?

No.

Shame?

Yes.

Shame because her body still tingled with unfulfilled desire and her heart still pumped hot arousal after watching sex cruder than anything she could have penned. Granted, the pages in her notebook were hot. But her fantasy Derek luxuriated in making her scream with need, his own excitement increasing because of her mindless desire.

Melissa's lover had been affected by her desire only to the extent that he was able to stoke it against her will. His actions were motivated by the power to humiliate.

Derek's actions were motivated by the power to excite.

Melissa's body responded to her lover's physical demands.

Nichole's body responded to Derek's emotional demands.

And despite these differences, despite the fact that she'd just witnessed sex that went against everything she found arousing, her body thrummed like a guitar string plucked by an ivory pick.

What was happening to her? Just when she thought she was within her comfort zone, the boundary was pushed, and she found herself falling, headfirst, down a rabbit hole deeper than the last. Her notebook had, indeed, blown off the lid to Pandora's box. At the rate she was going, she'd all but surpass Notebook Nichole.

What if she couldn't get back to No-nonsense Nichole? Like her mother. Her mother had always sworn she wasn't going to sleep with every loser who asked her. She'd even joined Sexaholics Anonymous, but it hadn't worked. Nichole's motto had always been to resist the temptation of passion, which is why she'd started the notebook.

She'd thought writing would be safe.

You thought the lingerie ad would be safe, too.

Pushing herself away from the wall, she went to the sink and washed her hands. Yeah, right. As if washing her juices from her fingertips could wipe away the lingering images of what she'd just witnessed, and undo her guilty pleasure.

Well, it didn't matter. She was not like her mother. She could go back to No-nonsense Nichole. And she would—after sex with Derek. All she wanted was one time.

As she exited the bathroom, heavy footsteps made her pause, drawing her attention to the door. This time, it had to be Derek. Or so she hoped. She didn't think she was up for more surprises.

The door opened and Derek did, indeed, appear.

"Hi," he said, walking toward her with a smile.

She smiled back. "Hello."

"Thank God you're not naked."

"You don't want to see me naked?"

"I want nothing better than to see you naked." He stopped in front of her and grabbed her waist, pulling her toward him, running his hands over her hips. He slid them around to her ass, rubbing and squeezing. "Except feeling you naked."

He leaned down and kissed her. A gentle kiss, meant to taste and tease. "But I came to tell you it's going to be another thirty minutes or so before I'll be back up." His smile was rueful. "I'm trying to wrap up the party that refuses to end."

Nichole stared at his lips, trying to curb the desire that was on the verge of bubbling out of her.

"God, you're beautiful," he said, leaning down to kiss her. Another gentle kiss, though slower and deeper.

Nichole did not want gentle. Her body still blazed from the illicit acts she had just watched. She wanted fast and hard. She wanted a kiss that demanded, and then took. And she wanted it now, not thirty minutes from now. Pressing herself as close as she could get to Derek, she angled her head, and moved her lips over his. Fast and hard.

Derek hesitated, as if caught by surprise. Then, his lips matched hers, bite for bite.

A moan rumbled in the back of his throat.

A high-pitched scream sounded from somewhere in the hallway.

Derek jerked away from her. Surprise, lust, and disbelief mingled with the frustration and anger in his gaze. His expression was almost comical, but Nichole didn't feel like laughing. She'd bet her expression matched his.

"Fuck! Now what?" Derek said as he ran out the door.

9

Derek slammed the phone down and stared sightlessly at the stack of videotapes from the security camera sitting on the desk in front of him. Neither his high-profile lawyer nor the private investigation firm he'd hired to look into the Jag City and Jared Morgan claims had made any headway in uncovering the source of the bogus lawsuits. Nor had the police turned up any leads on who had broken into The Decadent Chaise and stolen his files, some of which were work-for-hire agreements.

His gaze flicked to the headline on the front page of the *San Francisco Chronicle*.

"Reporter Pushed Down Staircase at Decadent Chaise Grand Opening."

Now this.

Who the hell would start hurting people just to get even with him? Revenge was the only reason he could come up with for pushing the reporter down the stairs on the night of his launch party—to cast a negative light on his store before it officially opened.

Unless the woman who broke her arm was lying about being pushed.

A publicity seeker? Highly unlikely. In Derek's experience, while reporters would do almost anything for a story, they generally avoided intentional physical injury for the sake of fame and glory. So that left the reporter being pushed. And that brought him full circle to the who and the why.

Neither of which he could answer.

Hell, there were probably a dozen people who hated him over deals he'd outfoxed them on, but that was business. In business, revenge was extracted by besting your opponent on the next deal.

Bribing people to lie and pushing a reporter down the stairs in an attempt to destroy a man's reputation—well, that smelled personal. Not that that made it easier to solve. Derek couldn't think of any personal enemies he'd made who hated him that much. Outside of Melissa, he couldn't even think of any women he'd pissed off.

I want you to stop teasing me.

Unbidden, Nichole's words came back to him, drawing an unexpected smile. There was one woman he'd pissed off recently. He still couldn't believe she'd accused him of teasing her.

Just as he'd been about to finally put an end to the waiting, been minutes away from tasting and touching the breasts and pussy, *this* had happened.

Derek shook his head in disgust. Disgust that his cock was keeping him from focusing on this latest mess or the mess itself, he wasn't sure which. Hoping against hope to discover the cause of the reporter's fall, he popped the last of the security videos recorded last night into the VCR. He hit the PLAY button on the remote. The empty staircase of The Decadent Chaise appeared on the screen. He hit the fast-forward button just as his private line rang. Expecting his attorney, he picked up the phone without checking caller ID. "Tell me you've found something."

"Derek?" asked a confused Nichole.

"Nichole." He couldn't keep the surprise out of his tone, since few people had this number. Definitely no women had the number and not because it was relatively new. Instead, it was because he never gave women his office numbers. Women were fun and work was work, and never the two shall mix.

Never? Tell that to your cock.

"Sorry to bother you. I called your other office but . . . Richard suggested that I call you at this number. Is this a bad time?"

"No. I'm glad you called," he said, surprised to discover he meant it.

"Oh." Nichole sounded surprised, too.

Derek moved his finger to the PAUSE button just as Melissa came into the frame at the bottom of the stairs. He frowned.

"I need to talk to you about last night." Her voice was hesitant.

"I need to talk to you about last night, too." His tone was seductive.

She laughed her breathy laugh. The one that stroked his cock.

He forced his mind to ignore his cock and watch Melissa ascend the stairs—now, there was a surefire way get rid of his woody. "Hmmm. Something tells me you don't want to talk about the part that I do . . ."

He smiled at her silence.

"I . . . I just read the *Chronicle* article about last night's accident."

"Yes, I had the pleasure of reading it, too." Derek watched a blond man enter the frame. Melissa raced up the stairs and the man rushed after her. Still frowning, Derek fast-forwarded.

"Well, while I was waiting for you last night in your office, I saw Melissa . . ."

Still in fast-forward mode, Derek watched Melissa and the tall man enter the office. Derek hit PLAY. Their lips moved silently. Derek cursed. Why hadn't he bought the system with sound? He fast-forwarded again, skipping conversation he had no chance of understanding. She turned around, her back to the camera.

The man kissed her neck and pulled her dress up. She stopped him. He continued. He kissed her neck, slid the straps of her dress over her shoulders, squeezed her breast, slapped her ass . . .

". . . and a man in your office . . . well, what I *saw* doesn't matter—"

On the video, Melissa was naked. Derek's jaw clenched as he watched the guy in the tuxedo reach between their bodies, take his cock out, and jerk his hips forward.

"What matters is what I heard Melissa and the man say. I think they came up to your office . . ."

To fuck. In his office, on his desk, at his business. Anger flooded Derek's gut.

". . . to talk. Melissa was angry. She said, 'If you're halfway as good as you claim to be, Derek wouldn't—' and then the man interrupted her."

The man's hips heaved, moving faster, and pumping harder.

Derek's heart raced, spreading anger, and adrenaline.

"This time, the man was angry," Nichole continued. "He told her they would do it his way or no way. When Melissa asked him what that meant, he said, 'the lawsuits first.' "

That caught his attention. Derek hit the STOP button. "What?"

Nichole repeated her statement.

Slowly, his anger receded and Derek felt a thrill of excitement—excitement, for once, that had nothing to do with his cock. "And then what'd he say?"

"Unfortunately, that was it."

"Did you get his name?"

"No. Melissa never called him by name."

That was all right. Odds were, Melissa would see him again. Action items flashed in Derek's mind. Picking up his pen, he made a few notes. First off, he'd notify the investigator, who could then trail Melissa, waiting for the guy to show up again.

Finally, a tip that might lead somewhere.

"Do you think this means—"

"I don't know what it means."

"Oh. Well. I'm sorry there wasn't more."

"No, this is good." His mind still raced. His gaze darted to the frozen screen. If he was able to get a frontal shot, he could provide a photo to the investigator. He pushed PLAY. He watched the man pull Melissa's head back.

The scene no longer bothered him. Anger had turned to gratitude. "Did you see or hear anything else?"

She paused. "Uh . . . nothing pertaining to this."

Derek caught the hesitation—and the reason behind it. He'd been so busy focusing on the drama unfolding on the tape, he hadn't dwelled on the obvious. Nichole had seen and heard the action he'd been viewing. For the first time since he'd watched Melissa and the man bust into his office, he smiled.

The man let go of Melissa's hair and leaned over her, increasing his pace.

Derek shifted in his seat.

The man fucked furiously.

What had Nichole thought as she'd watched this? The possibilities made Derek's cock hard. He glanced at the clock. "Have you had lunch?"

"No. I—"

"Why don't you come over?" The last remnants of anger dissolved. "I'll order something for us to eat. And we can talk."

She remained silent.

"I'd like to see you."

"Oh . . ." Surprise flickered through her voice. Again.

Surprise flickered through his mind. He hadn't planned to admit it.

"What time works for you?" she asked.

"Now."

Women were fun and work was work, and never the two shall mix, huh?

His words were still true, he mused as he replaced the receiver. It was lunchtime and he wasn't working.

Derek pushed the thought aside and hit the PLAY button, continuing to watch the screen in fast-forward mode. He paused when he caught a glimpse of the man's face, not surprised to discover it was the blond man he'd caught looking at Nichole. He noted the position in the tape and moved on. Melissa and the man finished fucking and left the office and it remained empty. Seconds later, the bathroom door opened, and Nichole exited. She was smoothing the white dress he'd fantasized about ripping off.

Derek stopped the tape and pressed the ZOOM button.

Just as he'd suspected, Nichole's cheeks were flushed. Her lips were parted. Her eyes were glossy.

Derek's cock stirred.

He bent down, grabbed his gym bag, unzipped it, and removed his jeans. Standing, he shrugged out of his suit jacket. He grinned.

As Nichole pushed open the door to The Decadent Chaise, an electronic buzzing echoed in the deserted showroom. Once she entered, the buzzing stopped. So did she. Her gaze skimmed the dozens of chaise lounges sitting like sentinels in their mini-rooms, before pausing at The Sex Lounge. Only the edge of the wood frame was visible from where she stood, but she glimpsed the tail end of the blouse, guessing that the thong, too, was still in place.

Ignoring the urge to double-check, she turned right and walked through the room and up the stairs. With every step, her heart beat faster, carrying waves of anticipation and tension through her limbs—anticipation because of the hint of decadent promise she'd heard in Derek's voice. After she'd shared her information, that controlled tone in his voice that she'd begun to recognize as anger had disappeared. In its place, she'd heard innuendo laced with amusement.

Derek wanted to "see" her.

She'd dreamt of him seeing her ever since he'd first walked into Talentz.

Derek wanted to "talk" to her.

She'd craved that flavor of talking ever since she'd written the first word in her notebook.

Anticipation swirled through her at the idea of seeing and talking to him. Tension fought the anticipation at the realization that she was about to live the dream and satisfy the craving.

Or so she hoped.

"Hi," Derek said, standing as she entered the office. His sexy smile sent ripples of sensation zigzagging over her skin.

"Hi," she said, not trusting her ability to say anything intelligent. By now she should be used to the sight of Derek. But she wasn't. She still felt like she'd been sucker punched in the stomach each time he came into her line of vision. Especially now, seeing him dressed in casual clothes for the first time. In fact, he looked almost exactly like she'd penned in the library scene of her notebook. A navy T-shirt that outlined the muscles in his chest, hugging his waist and flat stomach, before disappearing underneath the waistband of his faded blue jeans.

Button-fly blue jeans that she'd love to unbutton. Slowly. Lovingly. One button at a time. Watching as—

There was a definite bulge growing behind the button-fly.

She jerked her eyes to Derek's.

He smiled, his gaze knowing.

She smiled, her face warm.

Derek motioned to a chair in front of his desk. It was new. "Would you like something to drink? Soda? Bottled water? Wine?"

A whiskey sour—her mother's favorite drink—sounded like the perfect sedative for her jumpy nerves. "Water would be great."

"Help yourself to food."

Nichole glanced at the clear plastic containers littering Derek's once-immaculate desk. Egg rolls and dim sum, sandwiches and salad, pastas and garlic bread. She laughed. "This is a lot more than the 'something' I thought you had in mind."

"I forgot to ask you what you wanted."

I want you. Instead, she grabbed a plate and selected a couple of egg rolls, doubtful that the knot in her stomach would unknot enough for her to manage more than a bite.

"Thank you," she said. As she perched on the edge of the wing-backed chair, she watched him walk to a liquor cabinet she hadn't noticed. She liked the way his long fingers circled the bottle as he carried it to her, wishing that they were circling her body—her hips, breasts, neck, head, and all parts in between.

"How's Richard today?"

She blinked. "Fine. There was no mention of last night. All day, he's acted as if it never happened."

Derek made a sound that could have been agreement or surprise.

"Though, I'm not surprised. He's always like that afterward," she said.

He held the bottle of water toward her.

She took it from his outstretched hand, twisted the top, and took a big sip, hoping to flood the fire that had started burning in her stomach.

"Not that he's been drinking recently. In fact, I thought he'd stopped. It's been months since his last . . . episode. Something must've set him off . . ." Nichole forced herself to stop babbling.

Where had this bout of nervousness come from? When she'd entered the room, Derek had overheated her mind and short-circuited her body. She set both her plate and the water on the desk. The same desk that Melissa had lain atop, naked. The same edge of the desk that the blond man had pumped his hips against.

Her face felt flushed.

She thought she'd gotten over the shame and guilt of last night's arousal. But, for some reason, in the light of day, being in the same room in which she'd watched Melissa have sex was . . . embarrassing. And with Derek so near now, embarrassment warred with lust, resulting in discomfort.

And horniness.

In hindsight, she should've suggested they meet elsewhere. Later.

Nichole shifted in the chair, trying to get comfortable. She took a bite of the egg roll, chewing but not tasting.

Derek came to her side of the desk. He leaned his hips against the edge of his desk, resting his palms near his thighs—the same place Melissa had rested her hands and tapped her fingers. Melissa's pussy had lain against the same spot as Derek's ass. The same spot Nichole had imagined her own pussy being as the blond man-turned-Derek thrust into her. It wasn't hard to imagine Derek facing the opposite way, leaning over her—

Nichole blinked, and the image disappeared. Derek reappeared in front of her. "You're not eating?" she asked.

"I'm not hungry." Only the way his eyes traced her lips made his words a lie.

Nichole took a gulp of water.

Derek's gaze slid to her throat.

"I like watching you eat."

Notebook Nichole hadn't had a chance to become firmly in place yet. If she had, Nichole would've sucked lightly on the egg roll, running the tip of her tongue down the side and over the top, before pursing her lips softly and kissing and nibbling her way down its length. All the while, she'd keep her eyes on Derek, watching his eyes go smoky and his lips go soft, while his tongue peeked between his lips, following the curve of his lower lip, making her—

"Nichole?"

She blinked again and focused on Derek. His eyes were dark. His lips were soft. She put the egg roll back, hoping Derek wouldn't see the tremor in her hand. "Sorry. My mind wandered. What did you say?"

"Your thoughts must've been interesting."

"I was just thinking about our phone conversation," she lied, blurting the first thing that came to mind.

Derek's lips curved in a half-smile as he turned away, reaching behind him. He turned back around with a remote control in his hand. Aiming it at a spot beside her, he pressed a button. Nichole turned just as the flat-screen television mounted to the wall crackled on. The screen remained blue, then a moment of black-and-white static appeared seconds before the image of the staircase she'd just walked up flickered onto the screen.

The image on the screen fast-forwarded until Melissa and the blond man were visible walking up the stairs. They were crystal clear and in vivid Technicolor.

Nichole gasped.

"Is this what you were thinking about?" he asked.

Melissa and the blond man were now in Derek's office, standing by Derek's desk. Melissa's face was fully visible, whereas the blond man's was in profile. The angle was much more revealing, showing expressions that had remained hidden from Nichole's vantage point in the bathroom. Nichole turned her head, checking for a camera. Flush against the wall, resembling little more than a nail peeking out of the plaster, was a camera lens. Very small, very expensive.

It had never occurred to her that there would be a video camera in his office. Though, in hindsight, it was dumb of her not to have thought of it.

Nichole turned back to the screen. The blond man and Melissa were still by the desk, with Melissa looking angry. Her lips moved soundlessly.

Nichole felt traces of her own anger begin to swirl in her stomach, with a dab of jealousy and a pinch of hurt thrown into the mix. Feelings that were irrational in sex games being enacted with a man she didn't really know. Nevertheless, they were growing. Why would Derek show her a video starring his ex-lover?

Melissa turned toward the bookcase.

Nichole turned to Derek.

He was looking at her, not the screen. His gaze was hooded.

"Why are you showing me this?"

"Because I want to know why it aroused you."

Nichole's mouth dropped open. "Why . . . do you think it aroused me?"

"Because I saw the expression on your face when you came out of the bathroom. It was the same one you wore when I was lying on The Sex Lounge, staring into your eyes, rubbing my cock."

The familiar spin was happening in the room.

"Just as I saw it in the elevator. The rapid rise and fall of your chest . . ." his gaze dropped to her breasts.

Nichole struggled to keep their rise and fall even.

His eyes returned to hers. "... when I asked what happened next ..."

... do you run your palms down the front of my jeans ... do you reach for the front of my jeans, unbuttoning, slipping a hand inside, touching, stroking ...

Derek's eyes smoldered, letting her know that his mind must have joined hers in the trip down memory lane.

"... let me know that you were turned on. And when you kissed me, your hands on my head, drawing me closer and deeper into your mouth. When my hips pressed you against the wall and you pressed right back, letting my cock be right where it wanted to be, though without the layers of clothing ..."

Nichole didn't need reminders of how that felt, since the same overwhelming desire had been raging through her non-stop ever since that day.

The motion from the corner of her eye drew Nichole's attention back to the screen. The man's hand fondled Melissa's breast. The camera showed Melissa's lips part and her eyes flare.

Nichole's face grew warm as her mind zoomed to what was coming next.

Melissa turned so that her back was to the camera. Her dress dropped to the floor.

Nichole's stomach dropped to her feet.

Melissa's ass was visible. The man's cock was visible as he held it loosely in his hand. He remained still, waiting. Melissa wiggled her ass.

Memories of imagining Derek's cock swam through her head.

"Did watching this video arouse you?" she asked, her voice shaky.

"No."

The breath she didn't realize she was holding wheezed out

of her. She should be satisfied with his answer. Anything more was none of her business. "Why not?"

He stared at her, saying nothing, his expression giving no clue as to what he was thinking.

"I've never fucked Melissa. Or wanted to."

But the media had linked them together as a couple. She wanted to ask more. But his voice—the words sounding as if they'd been dragged out of him—kept her quiet. His eyes had taken on that bland look that she'd begun to recognize as the one he got when he didn't want to talk about something.

She should remain quiet.

She couldn't remain quiet.

"So, what did the video make you feel?"

She thought he'd decided to ignore the question. And then he said, "If you came home and found two strangers fucking in your bed, how would you feel?"

Livid. Invaded. Violated.

His eyes said he'd guessed how it'd make her feel. "Why did it arouse you?"

She glanced back at the video, surprised to find that Derek had hit the PAUSE button without her noticing. Melissa and the blond man were frozen in place in front of the desk where Nichole had last seen them. Only, this time she saw their faces. Melissa's eyes were closed, her lips parted. The man bit his lower lip while staring down at Melissa.

The image in front of her unfroze. The man jerked his hips forward. Melissa's ass jerked and jiggled. "It aroused me because . . ."

Melissa's body continued to bounce against the desk. The man's hips continued to thrust.

Nichole's blood roared in her ears. She resisted the urge to squirm in her seat as her mind, once again, placed her on the desk, imagined Derek's cock deep inside her, her muscles clasping, gripping, clinging.

She raised her eyes to stare directly into his. "It aroused me because I imagined that I was Melissa and the blond man was you. I imagined I was watching you and me."

"Are you aroused now?" His voice was husky.

"Yes." Her voice cracked.

He leaned forward and cupped her cheek in his hand, tracing her lips with his thumb. "You realize that I invited you here for more than lunch, don't you?" he asked softly.

"Yes," she whispered, the tingle caused by his fingers stealing all other thoughts and words.

"Good." He drew back.

Nichole suppressed a gasp of disappointment.

Derek stood and went behind his desk, opening a drawer and reaching for something she couldn't see. When he straightened, he held her baby-blue notebook in his hand. He opened it, flipping the pages until he got to what he was looking for.

He held the notebook out to her.

Her gaze flickered to the words that had triggered the whole series of events landing her here.

"Is there anything missing?" he asked.

10

Lights. Camera. Action.

Nichole's hands shook, rattling the paper, as she opened her notebook and propped it on the bookshelf in front of her. Finally, it was happening. She was going to have sex she had only imagined with a man she had only fantasized about. The teasing and tormenting was about to end. The beginning and ending of Notebook Nichole was about to happen. Adrenaline flooded her body as every nerve ending in her body sparked to life.

She took a deep breath, trying to tamp the arousal swamping her body, so she could string out the fantasy, make it last.

Did she really want it to last?

Oh, Derek ... please.

Her legs trembled.

She locked her knees to remain upright.

When the shakiness passed, she stepped up onto the ottoman Derek had pulled in front of the bookshelf. Her gaze traveled over books and miniature chaises she'd previously admired. Only this time, not a drop of admiration touched her gaze. In fact, the books and models were barely noticeable, as every ounce of her attention strained to detect the presence of the man coming up behind her. As she waited—for him, for his touch—she forced her eyes to read the words that she already knew by heart:

> *Fingertips slipped under her skirt, skimming her thighs.*
> *Nichole gasped and stumbled backward, the book slipping through her fingers as she fell off the stepstool.*
> *Strong hands gripped her hips righting her.*
> *Taking a deep breath, she opened her mouth to scream, and—*

Then Derek was behind her. The heat from his body spread over her back, ruining her concentration and magnetizing her skin, making her need to lean back. To feel *him,* not the mere awareness of him.

Her shoulders against his chest. Her ass against his cock.

Nichole gasped.

Hands slid up her legs, to her thighs, and over her hips, taking her skirt with them. Fingertips slid to the front, grazing her swollen lips.

Nichole stumbled backward.

Derek made a sound of disapproval. "You're not supposed to 'gasp and stumble backward' yet."

"Y-you're not supposed to . . . t-touch me yet."

"Baby, I *haven't* touched you yet." His voice was husky, no longer mocking. He slipped his fingers under her silk panties, moving down and dipping inside, making finger paint out of her wetness as he stroked her swollen folds. Her hips bucked, dancing to the music created by his fingers.

"*Now* I'm touching you."

She jutted her hips forward, wanting more.

He slowed his finger, giving less.

"Feel the difference?"

Her nerve endings, igniting fireworks along her skin, felt it. Her nipples, straining against the too-tight bra, felt it. Her pussy, flooded by moisture she couldn't control, felt it.

"Yes," she whispered, unable to find the strength to speak louder.

His finger went deeper.

Her pussy became wetter.

"Oh . . . More."

He withdrew his finger.

"No," she said, miraculously finding her voice.

He returned his hands to her waist.

"So . . . you take a breath . . ." His voice was strained as he returned to her fantasy.

The sparks under her skin fizzled, leaving her shaky, while the ache in her nipples, and the moisture between her legs left her craving. For him. For release.

Not for the reenactment of a fantasy.

". . . You're ready to scream, and then you . . . ?"

She sighed, almost angry. Her fuzzy brain grappled with his words, clamoring to remember what happened next in the fantasy. And then she . . . And then she . . .

Stopped.

That scent.

Oh yes . . . Nichole drew in a shaky breath, savoring his scent before the air filled her lungs.

A blend of sandalwood, cloves, leather, and man. Only one man.

The man standing behind her, tormenting her with his al-most-touch, luring her with his Derek-smell.

"I inhale . . . you."

"And what does your scream become?"

"A whimper."

His fingertips slid under the waistband of her underwear. "Show me."

Nichole whimpered. A keening sound that she couldn't fake if she'd tried.

"And then what do I do?" he asked, his voice raspy. "*Shhh-hhh...*" *Derek whispered against her neck.*

"You tell me to be quiet."

"Shhhhhh..." His breath caressed her neck.

She shivered.

He drew her panties down and over her hips.

"What—" she said, quoting her book without being prompted, wanting to spur him to go faster, eager to get to the part where he kissed and pinched, gripped and—

"You know what," he said, pulling her back, making her feel his cock, just like she'd written.

Oh yes. She moaned.

He told her to be quiet. "But you can't be quiet, can you?"

She was trying to remain quiet. But after enduring months of teasing, months of taunting...

"*Oh, Derek... please.*" *Nichole groaned and reached behind her. Frantic, needing, wanting... NOW.*

Here. In the library. In—

"Why not?" he asked.

"Because you've made me wait too long..." And he *had* made her wait too long. Mere days felt like months. Her hands reached behind her, seeking, needing. "Oh, Derek... please," she said, uttering the words that had echoed in her mind for weeks.

She ran the palms of her hands down the front of his jeans.

This time, *he* gasped. The sound filled her mind, spilled into her bloodstream, and filled her with power. The power to reverse the roles. The power to reduce him to all-consuming need, sweeping him down the path of mindless desire with her.

Staring sightlessly at the books in front of her, she reached behind her and felt for the buttons of his jeans, trying to pull each one loose just like she'd imagined. Only the slow, one-by-one pace had turned into a frantic pull. She fumbled. They resisted. Until, finally, all the buttons seemed to pop loose simultaneously.

"Do you know what happens next, Derek?"

His groan was his answer.

"You beg me . . ."

Nichole mimicked his actions—tucking her hands into the sides of his briefs, and pulling them down. Fingertips touched hers, taking over the action.

His cock poked her ass.

The air caught in her throat.

"To touch you . . ." She skipped her fingertips over his groin.

He inhaled sharply.

"To stroke you . . ." She stroked his thigh with wispy strokes.

"Touch me." His voice was hoarse.

She tsked. It sounded like a gasp. "That was an order, not a plea."

He slammed his hips against her.

She yanked her hips away.

He hissed.

"Beg."

His ragged breathing filled the air.

She held her breath.

"Please," he ground out.

Her fingertips tickled his cock. "Please, what?"

His hands covered hers, pleading.

"Touch. My. Cock. . . . Please."

The tension in his tone fueled her power. Excitement surged through her, urging her to do more than touch—to jerk her hips back, forcing him inside her, before grabbing his hips and moving them. In. Out. Setting the pace that she wanted. The pace that he needed.

She held back, closing her fingers around his cock instead. Its hardness, coated with a silky smoothness, brought another rush of wetness between her legs.

He fucked her hand. With each stroke, the tip of his cock touched her ass, leaving a trail of wetness on her cheek.

Oh. God. It was a plea of need, not a name used in vain.

His lips touched her neck. His jagged breath mingled with his swirling tongue, leaving her skin hot, then cold. Fingers glided under her shirt, and under her bra. Hands cupped her breasts.

Nichole arched her back, pushing her breasts into his hands, wanting more, needing more.

Fingertips circled her nipples, pinching, pulling.

"Yes, Derek, yes . . ."

She nudged his cock downward with her hands, bringing him close, giving him a taste.

"Do you feel how wet I am?" she panted.

He released her nipple and pulled her head back. "Do you feel how hard I am?" His voice was guttural.

She glimpsed the lust glazing his eyes seconds before his lips caught hers. Possessing, crushing.

He sucked.

She bit.

"Do you know what happens next, Nichole?" he asked into her mouth. The mocking note was back, though weakened by the hoarseness threading the words.

His finger dipped inside her.

The air whooshed out of her.

He chuckled. It sounded like a wheeze. "I guess you do."

As his mouth recaptured her lips, his hand recaptured his cock, taking it from her grasp. His tongue thrust inside her mouth at the same time he thrust his hips, the single movement burying him deep within her.

They gasped, taking air from each other.

They froze, savoring the shock of the entry.

Time disappeared. Nichole floated in a sense of nothingness. Every cell and nerve was trained on the fusion of their bodies.

His cock quivered.

She clenched her muscles, pulling him in deeper.

And the spell was broken.

He gripped her hips. She gripped the bookshelves. He worked his hips, driving into her.

He took. She gave.

She gave. He took.

Each thrust drove all thought from her mind and pummeled her body with sensation. Passion burned inside her, igniting animalistic need. It was raw and hot, infusing her with freedom— the freedom to feel without thought and desire without judgment.

The bookshelves creaked.

Skin slapped skin. Harsh breaths filled the air.

Nichole shrieked as intense heat licked her nerve endings . . . building . . . climbing . . .

"No," she whined.

"Yes," he ordered.

She wanted to make it last.

She wanted to give in.

The choice was ripped from her, as Derek pumped harder. Spears of heat shot through her body, pooling in her pussy. She tightened, fighting to hold in the heat. Derek thrust faster.

Tremors hit her, jerking through her body, releasing the heat.

Derek tensed, his grip almost painful. His groan caressed her ear. His shudders tapped her back.

His grip became a caress.

Nichole opened her eyes, unaware that she'd shut them.

Slowly, the room came back into focus. The books were no longer a colorful blur. The chaise models no longer shapeless blobs.

Fantasy had become reality. Reality had become fantasy. Now, reality was simply . . . reality. Her carriage had turned into a pumpkin.

The room was once again his office. Slowly, sounds that he'd been unaware of penetrated his eardrums—the sighing of Nichole's breath as it became softer and more rhythmic; the loss of wheeze in his own breath. Nichole's body felt soft and limp, her grip on the bookshelves no longer a clench of passion, but rather the practical grip of a woman holding herself up.

The urge to pull her to him and keep her close slammed into him. He was shot through with the need to know if the tension he felt stealing through her body was just an attempt to remain standing. Or was the stiffening of her muscles pressed against his groin because she was feeling what he was feeling—the desire for more.

When the hell had he ever had after-sex urges and feelings? He'd always preferred not to know what was on a woman's mind after sex, unless it was the position she wanted to try next. And the urge to hold a woman close after sex for the sole purpose of offering support had never before made an appearance.

In the past, he performed on automatic pilot, going through the motions of questioning and touching because it was polite, because it was what women wanted and expected, not because it was what *he* wanted.

Right now, he wanted to hold Nichole.

He dropped a kiss on her neck and stepped back.

He watched her tense.

Right now, he wanted to ask her why she was withdrawing.

"That was better than the fantasy," she said, her voice shaky.

"Yes, it was," he said. He pulled up his briefs and jeans, doing the buttons.

"You were better than the fantasy," she said, smoothing her clothes.

Derek dragged his hand through his hair, searching for the words that usually flowed like brandy from his lips. "I . . ."

Nichole finally turned and stared at a spot just below his left cheekbone. Her lips curved into a smile—a smile that looked a bit too bright, a bit too happy. "Thank you."

"I—" he began again.

"I have to get back to Talentz," she said, grabbing her purse.

Stop her.

She picked up her notebook.

Say something.

She walked to the door.

Say something.

"I'll call you," he said.

She exited the room, not deigning to acknowledge his hackneyed line. As he stood there, watching the door close behind her, he cursed himself for uttering such meaningless words.

He'd meant to say something else.

11

I'll call you.

Nichole stared at the phone in her office, willing it to ring to distract thoughts that were once again obsessively looping around those three little words.

Two days after the library reenactment, and she still couldn't believe that those had been Derek's parting words to her. Oh, she'd known there'd never be any kind of a future with him—she wasn't that stupid!—but she hadn't expected him to want her gone immediately after sex. Spectacular sex, even. At the bare minimum, shouldn't that make a man want more sex?

Obviously, it had been spectacular for her and mediocre for him.

Which left her feeling like a cliché—wham, bam, thank you ma'am—and a fool. Because she'd wanted to believe the oldest line in the book. And was still hoping against hope that it wasn't a line and that he really would call.

Nichole ran her fingertips over the now-tattered cover of the damning notebook that had gotten her into this mess. She flipped to the library scene, letting her eyes skim over the words Derek had whispered against her neck, begging her to touch him, making her acknowledge how hard he was, how much he wanted her. True, it was part of the script, but how could he say those words and have them mean nothing? Even great actors got so into their roles that the emotion felt real.

At least for the moment.

Obviously, those words meant different things to men and women. To women, "I'll call you" was a promise. From men, it was a dismissal. And scripts meant different things, too. For a woman, it was a way to act out a secret fantasy. For a man, it was just a way to get quick sex.

Which made her a bigger fool. Because not only did she still want him to call, she couldn't bring herself to destroy her notebook.

Nichole snapped the notebook closed and stuffed it into her desk in disgust. She would get rid of it at home. Host a Shredding Party for One. As she fed each page through the teeth of the shredder, she'd make a toast, and take a sip of her whiskey sour, in honor of her mother. Kind of a cleansing ritual.

Yeah, that'd make her feel better. It'd make her able to put things in perspective, to look at the positive. She'd been Cinderella for a moment, complete with a beautiful dress, and a Prince Charming that gave toe-curling, muscle-trembling, breath-stealing orgasms.

Make that orgasm, singular, as in one. A single orgasm. Once was supposed to be enough. Once was supposed to rid her of Notebook Nichole and herald the return of No-nonsense Nichole.

She sighed and glanced at her watch. Four p.m. Since she wasn't having much luck concentrating, maybe she'd just go home early and get the party started. Then, tomorrow, she'd be cleansed and refreshed—all traces of Derek removed—and able to focus on work.

Uh-huh.

Nichole picked up the phone and forwarded the lines to the answering service. Tidying up her desk, she picked up a couple of file folders and walked to the filing cabinet to put them away. The door whooshed softly open. She turned with a hopeful smile of greeting on her lips. But then, when she saw who stood at the door, her stomach dropped to her toes. She struggled to keep the smile glued in place. "Good evening, Ms. Moore."

Melissa flounced into the office. At least now she was fully clothed. Against her will, Nichole's gaze traveled over Melissa's white spandex-lycra pants, and she remembered Melissa bent over the desk, her pussy gleaming as the blond man whispered dirty words and shoved himself inside her.

There was nothing in Melissa's petulant face to indicate she had let a man use her like that, let alone enjoyed it.

Nichole touched her own face, afraid of what it revealed— that not only had she enjoyed Derek's words and his cock, she craved more. She dropped her hand. Before Melissa could open her perfectly lipsticked mouth, Nichole said briskly, "I'll let Richard know you're here."

She didn't care if Melissa didn't have an appointment. She couldn't deal with Melissa right now. After all, Melissa was Richard's special client.

Nichole turned to leave.

"Not yet, *Ms. Simms,*" Melissa said, using the same tone she'd used when she'd called Nichole a church mouse.

Nichole bit the inside of her cheek, holding onto her professionalism by the tip of her pinky. She remained where she was without inviting Melissa to sit, sending out the nonverbal cue that they wouldn't be chatting for long. "How may I help you?"

"I noticed you hanging around Derek at the grand opening of The Decadent Chaise."

Nichole ignored the jab, reining in the anger percolating in her stomach. "Mr. Mitchell is a major client of Talentz, Ms. Moore." To her own ears, that came out sounding flat and hollow.

It must've sounded that way to Melissa's ears as well, for the smile she directed at Nichole lacked its usual syrupy sweetness, taking on a viper-like quality instead. "Let's not play games, *Ms. Simms.*"

Nichole gritted her teeth at the pronunciation of her name.

"Your interest in Derek is not business. And maybe Derek is interested in . . ." She paused, letting her gaze drift over Nichole. Her lips curved in distaste, as if Nichole was wearing plaids and stripes in clashing neon colors. ". . . slumming it."

Nichole stiffened.

"But that's all it is." Melissa laughed. "My God, you're a mere receptionist! Surely—"

Anger erupted from her stomach, lodging in the back of Nichole's throat. She swallowed hard, trying to dissolve it, attempting to remember that Richard found Melissa Moore to be an asset to Talentz. "My personal life is my own business. Now, is there a business issue that I can assist you with?"

All trace of laughter evaporated from Melissa's expression. "Derek is my business. You mean nothing to him. If you're lucky, he'll give you one night. Don't delude yourself into believing that he'll come back for more."

I already know what I mean to him, Melissa. Nichole pushed away the pang of loss that surfaced with the thought, taking comfort in the fact that at least *she* was being honest with herself as to where she stood with Derek. Melissa seemed to be in denial about the fact that Derek had yet to give her one night.

"Derek is mine. So, be a good little girl and don't be a nuisance. You have a lot to lose."

Red spots danced before Nichole's eyes, bringing to life the meaning of "seeing red." "You're threatening me?"

"No, I'm—"

The anger broke free from her larynx. "Ms. Moore, for some reason, Richard wants you here at Talentz. For that reason, I'm making the effort to be polite to you. But don't ever threaten me again."

Melissa just stood there, her mouth half-open but blessedly silent.

Nichole took deep breaths, trying to get a grip on her temper. She turned to the phone. "I'll let Richard know you're here."

At Richard's affirmation, she told Melissa she could go back, her tone cold. Melissa walked past Nichole. "Ms. Simms?"

Nichole looked up, wiping all expression from her face.

"That was not a threat."

Nichole waited until she heard Richard's greeting and the sound of the door closing before she sank into her chair. The pent-up urge to slap Melissa's smug face made her shaky, as unused adrenaline coursed through her veins.

She closed her eyes. Why had she let Melissa goad her into responding? She'd known that Melissa's spite stemmed from misplaced jealousy. Nichole had resisted the slurs regarding Derek's reasons for being with her, albeit barely, because she knew why Derek was with her. But, the comment about there being a lot to lose had hit home. Nichole had spent two days turning a bout of great sex into a craving for more . . . great sex. She'd been mooning over the phone, hoping it would deliver a call from Derek. Both of which proved that she was in trouble.

She was having trouble returning to the status quo.

That's why she'd lost her professionalism. Because Melissa's words were true. Even though Melissa had no way of knowing—

Nichole's eyes snapped open. Wrapped up in her own emotional reaction to the accusation, she'd totally overlooked

Melissa's veiled implication. That, somehow, Nichole's "involvement" with Derek jeopardized something.

If she hadn't let anger speak for her, she could've tried to find out what Melissa meant by that. Maybe gotten more information about Melissa's involvement in Derek's lawsuits. After all, it wasn't like she wouldn't see him again at Talentz. Professionally, of course.

Damn. She'd missed an opportunity to help.

The soft swish of the door drew her gaze, seconds before Mr. I'll Call You came into the office.

Double damn. She wasn't ready for this, either: Old Home Week at Talentz. True, she had been wishing for a phone call, but that was for personal reasons. It was too soon for business as usual.

"Mr. Mitchell." She forced her frozen lips to thaw and transform what she suspected was a grimace into a natural smile. "May I help you?"

Derek raised a brow. "We're back to Mr. Mitchell?"

Her grimace-cum-smile refroze. "Derek."

"Hi, Nichole." He took a couple of steps closer. "Is Richard in?"

"Yes. He's in a meeting." Nichole picked up the file folders she'd been about to file when Melissa had walked in and went to the filing cabinet, desperate for space between them.

"Good." Derek walked around the corner of her desk.

Nichole resisted the urge to step backward.

"I didn't come here to see Richard." He continued forward, stopping in front of her. The spicy scent she always associated with him hovered in the air between them, almost tangible, making her feel that if she inhaled deeply, she'd be able to take in a part of him, keep it inside, and merge it with her. She held her breath, blocking the scent that sapped her willpower and ignited the craving to lean against him.

"I'd like to talk to you."

She took a breath, forced to inhale him. Desire spread through her chest, crawling outward. "If this is about Talentz business—"

"You know it's not."

"Then, if it's about the other night, there's nothing to talk about." She smiled to show her sincerity, praying it didn't look as false as it felt. "I appreciate you acting out my fantasy. It was . . . fun," she finished lamely.

Once again, he raised an eyebrow. "Fun?"

Nichole nodded.

"'Fun' is going to an amusement park or biking through the wine country. What we did was not 'fun.' "

He smoothed a strand of hair off her forehead.

Nichole's skin sizzled at his touch.

"Hearing you scream my name as your spasms massaged my cock was 'fantastic.'"

Hearing your groan tangle in my hair, as you shuddered against my back, was awesome.

His fingers slid down her face, stopping at her lips. "Begging you to touch me was wildly erotic." He traced her upper lip.

Nichole's desire raced toward a full-fledged marathon.

He smiled faintly. "I've never begged."

I've never felt so irresistible before. And she felt irresistible now, and . . . relieved. Relieved because, whatever the reason had been for him not calling, it hadn't been because sex with her had been mediocre. "Fantastic" and "wildly erotic" came close to matching her definition of spectacular.

"I want to see you again. Have dinner with me tonight."

"You could've called." Oops. Her face felt warm at the way that came out. "I mean, you didn't have to come here to ask me out."

"You would've said 'no' if I'd called."

He traced her lower lip before drifting to her chin.

Had he called, she should've said no. She'd told herself that it would only take one time to exorcise the desire that ruled her body every time Derek came near. And now she had to admit that she'd been wrong. She wanted more than one time.

But was that because she wanted him? Or because she was, in then end, just like her mother—always imagining that all her one-timers might be real lovers?

She looked at Derek, standing before her, his gray suit meticulous but his face oddly vulnerable, and realized she couldn't be sure. Maybe she was like her mother, fantasizing that a temporary passion was real. Maybe she was just imagining his longing.

But he was the one here asking for more, just as he had been the one begging for her touch the other night.

After all, he hadn't called.

But I still wouldn't have said no, had he called.

His hand cupped her jaw, drawing her closer. "And I didn't want to take the chance that you'd say 'no.' "

I don't want to be like my mother.

But she wasn't like her mother. Derek wasn't a loser.

Semantics. Just like her mother's losers, he'd never commit to more than a night—or two. He wouldn't be there when she needed him. She'd open the floodgates on her passion, letting it all rush out, and Derek would take it and walk away.

But she didn't want to think about that. Not now. Just one more time . . . that's what she wanted.

Nichole pressed herself closer, stretching to meet him. His lips touched hers, skipping the gentle, nibbling stage and going straight to hungry and probing. She kissed him back, letting him know she approved of his choice. Her lips moved under his, urging the kiss harder. She slipped her tongue inside, forcing the kiss deeper.

His cock pressed against her pelvis.

She moaned softly.

"Can you tell I've missed you?" he said against her mouth.

"No." Her teasing sounded like pleading.

He pressed closer. "Can you tell now?"

". . . no . . ."

Derek slid his hands to her hips, drawing her forward. "How about now?"

Nichole moved her hips against him, grinding his hardness against her swollen lips. "I feel . . . something." Her voice was husky.

Derek chuckled before returning his lips to hers. The kiss shot through her body, sending bursts of heat down her neck, circulating through her chest, and sloshing through her stomach, before zooming lower.

Derek moved forward, making her take a step backward. And another. All the while, his mouth continued sending the flow of warmth through her limbs.

Nichole felt the doorknob dig into her spine.

Derek broke away and leaned to the right to pull open the closet door. He stepped into the closet, stacking reams of copy paper.

Nichole blinked, trying to make sense of Derek's actions, her mind still numb from the kisses that had ended abruptly.

"What are you doing?"

Derek took her hand and pulled her into the closet.

"Helping you understand the 'something' you felt."

Nichole's mouth fell open.

Derek lowered his head, taking advantage of her parted lips, his mouth once again possessing hers. At the squeak of the door folding closed, Nichole drew back.

Derek moved forward, refusing to let her break contact—persuading, coercing, and bribing her into forgetting the desire to pull away. His hands slid to her hips and he lifted her, setting her on the stack of copy paper.

"Derek, I can't."

"On the dance floor, didn't you tell me this was a fantasy?" His lips nibbled and licked their way down her neck.

Nichole shivered. She focused on the golden carpet near the corner of her desk visible through the slats in the door, trying to stay grounded. "Yes. But . . . Richard might come out of his office looking for me."

"'Seeing, but unseeing,' " Derek quoted. He unbuttoned her blouse before slipping his hand inside, pushing aside the bra. His mouth once again left hers, following the path his fingers had bared, kissing the curve of her breast.

His tongue circled her nipple.

Nichole's tongue traced her lip.

Derek took her nipple in his mouth, swirling moisture while inhaling, making her nipple hot and cold.

Nichole gasped. Her eyelids fluttered closed, then open. The desk and carpet were a gold-and-silver blur.

Derek's fingertips slipped under her skirt and inside her panties and inside her, dipping into wetness she wasn't aware of, stroking a nub that was already hard. His tongue swirled faster, sucking and licking, licking and sucking.

Nichole gasped. Her hands went to his waist, gripping. "Derek . . . please . . ."

Stop.

"Okay." His mouth sucked harder, moving from breast to breast, nipple to nipple.

Don't stop.

His finger moved faster.

Stop.

Nichole's hips gyrated against his hand. Faster.

"Unzip my pants," Derek rasped against her flesh.

Sensation swirled through every part of her body, blocking out all thought and desire, except to follow Derek's hoarse instruction, craving where it would take her.

She fumbled with his zipper, slipping her hand inside and freeing his cock. It strained against her hand, kissing her palm with a droplet of moisture.

Nichole stroked.

Derek moaned.

She gripped his hand with her free hand, stilling him.

Lifting his head, he met her gaze. His eyes singed her mind, the need blazing within stealing all thought.

A door opened.

Nichole tensed. "Richard's coming."

Derek's hand replaced hers on his cock while his other finger continued stroking and circling, persuading.

His cock nudged aside the thin silk of her panties.

Melissa's sneeze drifted to her ears.

Nichole pushed against Derek.

Derek pushed into Nichole, the head of his cock nestled inside. He stared into her eyes. Eyes dark, lips parted, breathing ragged, he waited.

Richard and Melissa entered the office.

Nichole's eyes widened.

Derek's eyes narrowed, his gaze dropping to her lips. He bent down. "Kiss me," he whispered against the corner of her mouth.

Melissa's scarlet-painted toenail was visible through the slat in the door.

"Nichole. Kiss me."

Derek's cock jerked inside her, seconding his plea.

Richard spoke.

Melissa answered.

Nichole tilted her head to Derek. As his lips explored hers, his hands gripped her hips and he slid his hips forward, plunging inside her. Nichole's gasp mingled with Derek's grunt, muted by the connection made by their mouths.

Derek's hands on her hips steadied them as he pumped. He withdrew almost completely out of her before sliding back in with deep, long strokes. His mouth kept the fire stoked, while his cock made the fire hotter.

Nichole's fingernails dug into Derek's shoulders.

Derek's fingertips dug into her hips.

The familiar heat swirled up her legs, caressed her inner thighs, and landed in her pussy. The sensation coalesced and twisted, causing her hips to gyrate.

A desk drawer slammed shut.

Nichole stifled the scream building in her throat.

Derek stopped, his body tense, straining to hold back.

Nichole pumped her hips, reaching the destination she was seeking. Her muscles spasmed and her legs trembled.

Her scream died in Derek's mouth.

Derek's grunt lodged in Nichole's mouth. His body tensed, then shuddered.

Melissa laughed.

Nichole relaxed her grip on Derek and leaned against him, resting her face against his chest. She listened as his heartbeat slowed to a rhythmic beat. His chin caressed the top of her head, while his hands caressed her back. Up and down. Soothing.

How ironic that she felt a strong postcoital connection to him in an almost-public place, whereas she'd felt empty—afterward—when they'd been in private.

Slowly, the world stopped spinning.

"Now, will you have dinner with me?" Derek whispered, seconds before Melissa asked, "Richard, will you help me get even with Derek?"

12

Nichole paused in front of the half-open door of Derek's penthouse suite. Penthouse suite. That sounded like a photo shoot setting for a men's magazine. It sounded like a fantasy setting from her notebook. She peeked in through the opening. From what she could see—the black marble floor and wide mirror—the entryway looked straight out of a fantasy, too.

Nichole steeled herself, loosened her grip on the paper bag she held, and knocked.

"Come in," Derek said from somewhere to her left. As she stepped forward into the spacious foyer, he came around the corner from the living room and into view. A simple black shirt with thin gold stripes had never accentuated a more muscular chest. Faded blue jeans had never hung from leaner hips. And . . . oh God. He was barefoot. How could a man have beautiful feet? No knobby toes. No middle toe sticking out. Simply long, perfectly shaped toes.

Nichole had never understood the fascination some people had with feet. Until now. Maybe there was something to foot fetishes, something that she should look into.

Of course, she should also look into eye fetishes, smile fetishes, and chest fetishes. Hell, she should just save time and look into Derek fetishes.

"Hi," Derek said, stopping in front of her.

"Hi, yourself," she said, lifting her gaze from his feet. She tried to read his expression. Was he surprised to see her? Happy to see her?

He lowered his head and his lips swept over hers, caressing and nibbling, before his tongue slipped inside. Spearmint penetrated her taste buds, while heat penetrated her bloodstream. Nichole leaned into him, chest to chest. Her breath hitched in her throat as his cock nudged her belly.

Derek pulled back.

Nichole opened her eyes, feeling dazed. Wow. She'd guess that meant he was happy to see her.

"I wasn't sure you were coming."

"Really? Why not?"

"There wasn't much time in that closet to discuss dinner plans."

The closet. Nichole shivered at his sexy tone, remembering the shudders that had barely stopped before Melissa's plea for help had caused them both to freeze. Derek's breath had mingled with Nichole's as Richard had denied Melissa, citing the unprofessional nature of her request and tacking on that Derek was his friend. That had been a relief, to hear Richard tell her no.

But, as they'd waited for Melissa and Richard to leave, Nichole hadn't been focused on their discussion. She'd been focused on the discussion playing out silently between her and Derek—a discussion that had nothing to do with betrayal.

"We *discussed* the important parts in that closet," she said.

That discussion had been without words, Derek's body pressed against hers. His cock, resting against her thigh, a wet reminder of where he'd just been. Where, despite the fact that her body was sated, she wanted him to be again. He'd held her, absently stroking her back, rubbing his cheek against her head, as they'd waited.

Once they were alone again, he'd said, "See you at dinner at eight." And he'd handed her a card with his address—this address—before zipping up his pants and leaving her office.

And now she was here.

Just one more time. Really. This is it.

Derek stroked her cheek with his fingertip, bringing her back to the present, seconds before he lowered his head again. His lips once again moved over hers. He kissed her with such tenderness. She remembered all his kisses—in the closet, in the office, even the first one in the elevator. But this one was the most tender, though it still held the promise of passion. She slid her free hand down his chest to his belly and felt the tautness stirring below.

"If you keep doing that, we won't make it to dinner." His voice was hoarse.

"I thought that was part of dinner." Her voice was hopeful.

Derek laughed. "At this rate, it might be." He took the bag from her then laced her fingers through his, and pulled her along behind him. With each step, her sandals sank into the caramel-colored carpet, making her wish that her shoes were off, too, so she could feel the fibers caress the soles of her feet. Black and chrome met her eyes everywhere her gaze landed— couch, coffee table, credenza, and even the walls, dotted with silver-framed black-and-white photos of familiar places, like a fog-encased Golden Gate bridge, and unfamiliar places that resembled ancient cities in Europe. Palm and ficus trees in gleaming black pots were strategically placed throughout the room. While the overall look was clean, contemporary, and expensive, Nichole wondered if Derek ever missed . . . color. Her own apartment was not nearly so luxurious, but it burst with color: rose-colored cushions in the living room, sunflower-yellow walls in the bedroom.

As Derek led her through the apartment, Nichole's mind went back to the closet, the things they'd heard. "Derek, I haven't said anything to Richard. Has he said anything to you?"

"About what?" His voice was polite, but he didn't turn to look at her.

"About Melissa trying to recruit him to get even with you."

"He told her 'no.' What else is there to talk about?"

"Well, wouldn't he have warned you about Melissa's vendetta?"

"Why should he?"

Nichole took a deep breath. Maybe in Derek's life or line of work, betrayal was a common experience. But she, at least, expected more of Richard. "Because he's your friend. And he should warn you about Melissa."

Derek snorted. "Richard knows I have no illusions about Melissa."

"Yeah, but maybe he has some insight. There's got to be some reason why Melissa is gunning for you. Maybe she's told Richard. And maybe Richard knows who that blond guy is—"

"I referred it all to my attorney and the investigator. They'll let me know if they find anything."

His tone was dismissive, letting Nichole know she should give it up. But something made her say, "But what about—"

Derek stopped suddenly and turned, silencing her with a searing kiss. When he was done, miraculously, she couldn't remember what she meant to ask.

With a satisfied smile, he resumed walking.

Nichole remained silent until they entered the kitchen. Then she stopped and her mouth dropped open. Stainless steel appliances filled the room and glossy black marble topped the counters, continuing the motif introduced in the living room. But that wasn't what had her rooted to the spot. Rather, it was the opened and unopened canned goods, the chopped and unchopped vegetables scattered across the countertops. Dirty pots and pans, interspersed with splatters of tomato sauce and other unknown liquids, covered the remaining surfaces.

The kitchen looked like a scene straight out of Martha Stewart Meets Pigpen.

Derek turned, drawing her gaze to him. A question flickered in his eyes until something in her expression must've answered the question. His smile was sheepish. "I make a bit of a mess when I cook."

"A *bit* of a mess?"

"You should see it when I make lasagna."

Nichole started, realizing she'd like to see that. "Do you need some help?"

"No. I need you to sit here." He pulled a leather-cushioned bar stool away from the breakfast bar. Black, of course.

Nichole sat.

He peered inside the bag she'd brought and removed the bottle. "Sparkling Pear Cider?"

"I've never seen you drink, so . . ." He stared intently at her, his expression suddenly blank. "I mean, I've seen you offer others a drink but . . ." She squirmed under his gaze. "It's imported from Italy. I hope you like it."

She smiled uncertainly.

Derek remained silent.

Her smile disappeared.

"My father was a drunk." His tone was emotionless.

Oh. What did one say to that?

He seemed to be waiting, expecting something. Did he expect her to judge him? Or ask probing questions? Or change the subject? A jolt of longing pierced her. She wished she knew him well enough to know how to respond. Or, that she *had the chance* to get to know him well enough to know how to respond.

But she didn't, so she took a guess. That he really meant, *My father was a drunk so I don't drink because I don't want to be like him.* She shrugged. "My mother was called the town slut." *And so I keep my fantasies locked away so I won't be like her.*

His lips curved into a small smile. "Well. That calls for a toast."

"It does?"

"Yep." Turning, he took two wine glasses from the cabinet. "Would you like wine?"

"No. Cider, please."

He filled a champagne flute halfway and handed it to her. Lalique crystal, she noticed as she took it from him. His fingers grazed hers, sending a zing of prickles over her hand and up her arm. She gripped the glass as his hand moved away, afraid the weakness caused by his touch would cause her to drop the flute, thereby reducing the finely etched angel to shards.

He raised his glass.

She raised her glass.

"Here's to being ourselves," he said.

He hadn't uttered a meaningless "I'm sorry," or worse, asked questions she wasn't ready to answer to a statement she'd never said out loud. "Thank you," she said softly.

Derek tilted his head in acknowledgment.

Glass clinked and understanding arced through the air over the rim of their glasses. She'd said the right thing. He'd said the right thing. Warmth swirled through her body, carrying the emotional connection formed by his look and their words, heating her blood as it flowed, kindling sexual tingles along the way.

Nichole sipped.

Derek sipped.

He set his glass down and reached out, hooking a fingertip under her chin and drawing her closer.

Nichole followed willingly. Lips met, tongues mated, and the flow of tingles became a flood, overwhelming her system.

Nichole drew back. "If you keep doing that, we'll never make it through dinner," she said, quoting his earlier words. Her voice was breathy.

Derek pressed forward. "Dinner can wait," he said. His breath caressed her lips. His hands cupped the side of her face, holding her in place, while his lips resumed their attack on her senses, pressuring and persuading.

Her mind reminded her that she wanted to wait, to hold on to the closeness that had budded over a glass of nonalcoholic cider.

Her pussy throbbed with a heartbeat of its own, causing her to return the force of his kiss, to let her tongue explore his mouth, roving, seeking, wanting.

Stop.

She slanted her head in the opposite direction, deepening the kiss, moaning in the back of her throat.

Derek's hands dropped to her shoulders, slipping under the collar of her blouse.

Stop.

This time, she managed to pull back.

Derek opened his eyes. The fever burning in the emerald depths drew her back to him. She caught herself, searching for a distraction. "I'm . . ." *think of something* ". . . hungry."

"Me, too," he said, his gaze on her lips, his fingers drawing circles on the back of her neck, sending shivers skittering up and down her spine.

"For . . ." her gaze drifted to the countertop ". . . bell peppers and onions."

His eyes smoked. "I'm not sure I'm pleased that you prefer bell peppers and onions to my kiss."

She didn't. But while his kiss heated her body, his words heated her heart. This moment of conversation was too rare to pass up.

Nichole picked up his hand, tracing the spidery lines on his palm. "Bell peppers and onions sliced by your hands." She raised his palm to her lips, flicking her tongue across the middle, and down over his thumb.

Derek's pupils dilated, obscuring the green in his eyes.

Nichole puckered her lips, kissing the pad of his forefinger. "I want to hear..." Swirling her tongue over his skin, she mixed his tangy saltiness with her saliva.

He stared intently at her mouth.

"... the words from your lips." As she traced her lips with his fingertip, her mouth heated under his touch, and cooled with its absence, leaving behind mere wetness.

She slid his finger into her mouth, and sucked. "I want to watch you, imagining what these hands will do to me..."

He inhaled sharply.

Nichole removed his finger, and lowered his hand, placing it on top of a bell pepper. "... later."

Derek's gaze moved from her lips to her eyes. Her heartbeat spiked at the sexual glaze shining back at her. "Well. Guess I'd better hurry up with dinner, then."

He made no move to "hurry up with dinner." Instead, he remained rooted to gleaming hardwood floor. "You sure?"

Nichole nodded.

Derek sighed and then turned. Placing his hands on his hips, he surveyed the mess in the kitchen.

Nichole surveyed him, nearly drooling at the way the shirt hugged his back. She reached for her cider to stop herself from reaching out to stroke the jeans outlining his round ass.

She should've asked for wine. Or, better yet, a whiskey sour. She sighed.

He cocked his head toward her. "What was that for? You're getting what *you* want."

Nichole laughed at his sulky tone.

He smiled. The slow, sexy one that sent lust darting through all parts of her body. Especially the needy, throbbing parts.

"Your new job is to take my mind off of what *I* want," he said.

"Okay." She pressed her legs tightly together, trying to take her mind off of what they both wanted.

Derek turned away, moving to the cutting board.

Nichole turned back to filling her mind with images of his body. This time, she was treated to a side view. From the flat stomach to the not-so-flat groin, where her eyes lingered, thrilling at the bulge she'd caused. A bulge that twitched under her gaze.

"Staring at my cock does not take my mind off what I want."

Nichole grinned. "Oh. I didn't think you'd notice."

"I notice everything about you."

Her pulse jerked. "Oh, really?"

"Yes."

"Okay then, name one thing." She kept her tone light, making the statement a challenge as if they were playing a game of truth or dare.

"Hmmm. You mean besides the way you hold your breath when I enter you?"

The breath swooshed out of her.

Derek smiled, keeping his attention focused on slicing and dicing. The long fingers of one hand were loosely wrapped around the pepper, similar to the way he'd wrapped it around her breast before squeezing.

"Or the way you chant my name in the most arousing way when you're seconds away from coming?"

His hands were steady as he chopped.

Nichole felt shaky inside.

"Or the way your eyes darken and your lips part and your neck arches when I drive into you the way you want—"

He stopped chopping.

"—the same way you looked in the lingerie ad?"

He set the knife down, resting his hands on the countertop.

Nichole stared at his close-cut fingernails, noticing that there was not a ragged cuticle in sight.

Silence wound through the air, forming a noose around her neck, which cut off her air supply and forced her to look up at the same time. Derek was no longer smiling. Arousal still swirled in his eyes but it mingled with something darker, deeper.

"It's a beautiful look, Nichole."

She'd felt beautiful in that photo, just as she felt beautiful with Derek.

"But it bothers you." Despite the raised eyebrow, it was a statement, not a question.

Nichole didn't hear idle curiosity in his tone, nor see judgment in his gaze. In fact, both indicated that he wanted an answer. An honest answer.

She opened her mouth to skirt around the truth. "It doesn't bother me."

His expression didn't change. He conveyed neither belief nor disbelief. He simply waited.

"I was proud of that photo," she said, once again uttering words she'd never said aloud. "It revealed a part of me I'd never seen before—a part of me that I liked. But . . ." she shrugged, removing all emotion from her voice. ". . . the photo became public knowledge in my hometown and I lost my job, so I moved to San Francisco."

She fought to hold back the pain struggling to surface at the loss of a life she'd loved. How someone at the optometrist's office where she'd worked had found out. Next thing she knew, Dr. Swenson had called her into his office and let her go. Then there were the whispers from the old-timers in town about her being just like her mother.

She'd left because she couldn't deal with the humiliation.

"A new beginning," Derek said.

"Yes. Writing X-rated stories in which I'm the star." Her attempt at levity sounded false.

"I would never have made your notebook public, Nichole."

She looked at him in surprise. "I never thought you would."

"Why not?"

She smiled at his surprise mirrored back at her, relaxing now that they were back on safe territory. "Derek, what could you possibly have to gain by making my notebook public?"

"I've been accused of stealing showroom and chaise designs."

Nichole snorted. "Uh-huh. Like I believed that. You'd already established yourself as a designer par excellence before that Jag City lawsuit. And, after coming up with dozens of your own chaise designs, out of the blue, you decided to steal designs from a lone designer?" The laugh she'd been about to utter died in the back of her throat at the look on Derek's face. He looked like he'd just found a hair in a glass of water he'd just sipped from.

"Uh." Her face grew warm. "As I said before, I try to keep abreast of Talentz's clients."

"You believe all that because you read it somewhere?"

"No. I believe that because that's the kind of man I think you are."

His expression immediately shuttered. Turning, he scraped the diced vegetables from the cutting board into a skillet. Those that landed in the skillet sizzled, while others landed soundlessly on the floor.

The spicy aroma of onions, peppers, and garlic wafted under her nose, sending a rumble through her stomach.

"Don't believe things just because you want them to be so."

The icy note in his voice chilled her, sending a ripple of hurt under her skin. Had he interpreted her admiration as a cry for more from him? It wasn't.

But, I do want more from him.

But she'd never let him know that. She hadn't been trying to ask him for more. She'd simply been stating facts. If he'd stolen everything he was accused of, shouldn't she see signs of that in his character? Sure, he was a private person. But he'd looked out for Richard, helping him save face as he'd become wasted. And he'd been totally honest with her, never giving her the impression he was offering more than the enactment of a fantasy or two from her notebook. Spectacular sex or no, there was no way she could fall for him if—

Oh shit.

Fall for him: she'd said it. She'd been trying to deny that she wanted more than sex with him. Trying to convince herself that her "just one more time" comments had been solely about more sex. But her slip meant she'd been lying to herself. If she really wanted just one more sexual encounter, she'd be able to concentrate at work, instead of waiting for the phone to ring, craving the sound of Derek's deep voice.

It wasn't just sex.

Mere sex had never caused such a . . . disruption in her life previously. On the other hand, there'd been nothing "mere" about the sex she'd experienced with Derek.

"No one is ever who you want them to be, Nichole."

His words interrupted her musings, again. She turned her attention back to him, noticing that he was stirring the vegetables with more force than was necessary. Relief flooded her, dimming the shockwaves of her recent revelation. She had misunderstood him. He wasn't disgusted with her because he thought she was asking for more from him.

Her secret was safe.

"Then, you're saying that you did steal the designs?"

"No, I didn't steal the designs. But there's no reason for you to believe I didn't. What evidence do you have?"

"None. Except my gut, which I trust."

Bitterness tinged his laugh. "Trust your gut? That's simply giving yourself permission to believe something you want to believe. In this case, to believe that I'm who you want me to be."

Nichole was confused. What was really going on here? He said he was not guilty of what he'd been accused of, and yet, he accused her of believing in his innocence because she needed to believe he was innocent. And he was convinced that no one was who you wanted them to be.

She stared at his clenched jaw as he continued to sauté vegetables in the skillet.

This was a lot of emotion about what *she* believed—which made her think that maybe this wasn't really about her. Instead, maybe there was someone who wasn't who he, Derek, wanted him to be.

She raised the cider to her lips and stopped. Lightbulbs flashed behind her eyelids.

"What did you want your father to be that he wasn't, Derek?"

Derek flinched, as if, instead of whispering the words, she'd walked over and slapped him.

Nichole flinched, wishing she could take back the question.

Derek's stance reminded her of photos she'd seen of military cadets standing at attention before their drill sergeant.

Her eyes roved his body hungrily. She wanted to walk over to him and slip her hands around his waist, offering him comfort. But, she couldn't. That was an emotional response, while this—what they had—was about sex.

The hand stirring the vegetables picked up speed, as if he were whipping cream.

Nichole slid off the stool and walked to him. Since this was about sex, that's what she could offer him. Sex. While for her, it would be about more than sex. But he'd never have to know that.

She slipped her arms around his waist.

He stiffened even more.

She stood on tiptoe, kissing his neck, while giving her hands free rein, letting them touch him where they wanted. His chest, his abdomen, his hips, reveling in the tight muscles under the palms of her hands. Even though the muscles were partly tight with suppressed anger. At her? Most likely. At his father? Probably. At himself? Maybe.

Nichole's hands moved upward, smoothing over his thighs and angling inward, stroking another hard muscle. A long, thick one that reached for her hand through the denim. She smiled, pleased that at least one muscle's hardness wasn't due to anger.

Derek inhaled sharply.

"I'm not hungry for bell peppers and onions anymore."

Derek remained unmoving.

Nichole slid her hands under the waistband of his jeans. His hands halted her progress.

She shoved aside her fears that he was rejecting her forwardness. This wasn't about her. It was for him. "Kiss me, Derek."

She thought he was going to ignore her request, instead keeping them frozen in a tableau in front of his stove. Then, he pivoted, catching her off balance. Nichole saw thunderclouds dancing in his eyes seconds before he lowered his head and took away her awareness of everything but the lips moving over hers. They demanded her surrender. They stole her strength. His tongue thrust inside of her mouth, not asking for permission, not asking for a taste, stealing both, instead.

His hands grasped her hips, and yanked her against him, forcing a moan from her throat.

Nichole wound her hands around his neck, stretching her

body against his, pressing her chest against his, wanting to get closer, wanting to kiss deeper.

Derek pulled back, his breathing ragged.

"What—"

Derek half-turned and shut off the burner, before leading her in the opposite direction from the one they'd taken to enter the kitchen. More chrome and black, until they stopped at an in-home entertainment room. Royal-blue velour drapes framed the floor-to-ceiling screen and four rows of seats—sixteen seats plusher than any she'd ever seen in a movie theater—sat toward the back of the room.

9½ Weeks was frozen on the screen, just like in her notebook.

She met his gaze.

"I can't promise I'll be able to stick to what's in your notebook." She heard the restrained passion in his voice but she still could not read his expression.

The unknown emotion she'd seen smoldering in his eyes minutes ago in the kitchen caused her to say, "This time, I want to do whatever you want me to do."

13

Derek stared into Nichole's chocolate-brown eyes. She was looking up at him, waiting for his answer.

He swallowed, fighting the panic building in his throat. Panic because he'd been seconds away from telling Nichole about his father. His childhood was off-limits to everyone, even Richard. And yet he'd *wanted* to tell her.

A woman he'd known less than a week.

She blinked and his panic went up a notch. That . . . look was there. The one she'd had in the kitchen when she'd told him he was innocent of the thefts he'd been accused of committing. The one she'd had when she'd called him beautiful. The one she'd had at Talentz when she'd described his chaises.

The look that said she *cared* for him. And worse, she cared for him because of the man she believed him to be, instead of the things he could give her.

Which then made him want her to care about that man. And that made him want to care—

Derek blinked, praying that the act would erase the thought he'd been about to think.

It lingered.

This time, I want to do whatever you want me to do.

Her expression, along with her tone, had been guileless. No ulterior motive that he could see. A request seemingly made out of desire.

She stepped forward.

Derek fought the urge to step back.

Nichole urged him backward until he butted against the wall. Lacing her fingers through his, she stood on tiptoe, kissing the hollow of his neck before lapping her way up the side. "Would you like to take me right here?"

She wiggled against him, her breasts rubbing against his chest, sending a stab of lust to his cock.

Derek gritted his teeth, catching the moan that'd almost escaped from his lips. Yes, he wanted to take her right here. *Fuck her* right here, against the wall.

No foreplay. No kissing. Fully dressed.

She licked her way up his neck, her pussy getting in on the action, burrowing against his cock.

He moved his head to the side, giving her better access. This time, he couldn't stop the moan that escaped his throat.

"Is that what you want, Derek?"

No. It was what he *wanted* to want.

She untangled her hands from his, moving them to the front of his jeans. The first button popped free.

Her smile was feline. "Is that your fantasy?"

No. Just once I want . . .

Another button came loose. Nichole tugged at his shirt, baring his abdomen. He watched her kneel in front of him, his cock primed for what he knew came next. A drop of wetness appeared on his jeans. Nichole's mouth touched his stomach.

A quiver rippled across his skin. He groaned.

The last few buttons broke free.

"Or is this it?"

He tried to convince himself that this was what he wanted. To feel the lips and tongue sending darts of fire through him, wrapped around his cock, kissing and sucking.

His cock jutted forward in anticipation as she pulled his jeans off his hips.

Derek let his head fall back against the wall and closed his eyes. He placed his hands on the sides of Nichole's head, stroking her hair, guiding her closer, positioning her to give him what he wanted.

"I knew this was what you wanted."

What he was supposed to want.

Just once I want . . . to know what it feels like to make love to a woman.

His hands held her head still. "Not here."

She flicked her tongue through the gap in his jeans, caressing the skin within reach. "Where?"

Her breath sent prickles shooting over his abdomen.

"The bedroom."

I want to make love to you in my bedroom.

"That'll be an exotic location for us," he said.

She laughed, just as he'd hoped.

As he pulled her to her feet, the phone rang. Ignoring it, he led her into his bedroom, stopping by the bed.

"Aren't you going to get that?"

"Huh?"

"The phone."

"Oh. Yeah." He leaned down and plucked the phone cord from the wall. The ringing stopped in mid-note, leaving only the faint electronic trill coming from the living room.

Her pleased smile rekindled the panic in his chest. He bent his head, wiping her smile away with his lips. She returned his kiss, her lips every bit as urgent as his, every bit as . . . desperate. That surprised him. She pulled away, smiling. That Look was back—pleased and sexual and soft all rolled into one.

Derek looked away, preferring the action of her hands to the intensity of her gaze.

Nichole unbuttoned her shirt and slid it from her shoulders. She unzipped her jeans, hooked her hands under the waistband of both her jeans and underwear, and slid them over round hips. Moisture evaporated from his mouth as he stared at the nether lips that he had yet to taste.

The soft snap of her bra drew his gaze upward, just as she shrugged out of the straps. Nichole's removal of her clothing had been matter of fact. Her purpose was to simply take off her clothing, not to arouse.

His cock was harder than if she'd given an award-winning striptease performance.

Nichole stood before him wearing nothing but a smile and That Look.

He couldn't move. He couldn't breathe.

She unbuttoned his shirt and slid it over his shoulders.

It fell to the carpet.

Seemingly unaware of the anxiety building in his chest, Nichole smoothed his hair, watching her hands as they slid over his temples, across his cheekbones to the tip of his nose, and down to his jawline. Her touch ignited nerve endings with connections to his cock that he'd never known existed.

His eyes followed hers, seeing not the reflection of his face, but rather the purity of her unguarded enjoyment. Her pleasure—as if she wanted nothing else but to touch him forever—stunned him. When had anyone touched him simply because it felt good? When had anyone looked at him as if really seeing him—the man behind the flesh—and liking that man?

He vaguely remembered his mother looking at him like that once. Or maybe he'd just imagined it.

His lungs felt too small, incapable of supplying the air he needed.

He drew her hands away from his face, moving them down, brushing them over his cock.

Nichole's smile changed, becoming more sensual and knowing.

Derek inhaled, once again able to breathe normally, once again back on familiar ground.

He slid his jeans over his hips, joining her in her nakedness.

"What's next?" she asked, her voice hoarse.

I want to make love to you.

He backed her up to the bed. She sat on the edge and tilted her head up to smile wickedly at him.

Before he could pull back, he felt the heat of her mouth on his cock.

He grunted in surprise.

I want to fuck you.

He moved his hips away. "I won't be able to last if you do that."

She moved away, falling back onto the bed, her hands palm-up on either side of her face. Her pose was a challenge to him, telling him she'd do whatever he wanted. There were no more written scenarios. He had to tell her what he wanted.

He remained frozen where he was.

She raised a hand to her hair, fiddling with a strand. "Tell me what you want."

With those whispered words, he thought he heard something deeper than a sexual request. A veiled plea of need that went beyond sex. Words he'd always dreaded hearing, but had never yet heard uttered honestly. As he gazed into her eyes, he saw something worse than That Look, the one that meant she saw and wanted Derek, the man. This look said that she wanted him to want her, the woman behind the body. Her eyes had changed to a gooey chocolate, just like a scene from a Hollywood chick flick.

Only this wasn't a Hollywood film. Nor did he dread the sound of her unspoken plea. And the chocolate-syrup look directed his way made him feel shaky inside.

That was the most fucked-up feeling of them all.

Shaky wasn't what he wanted to feel. He wanted to feel strong and controlled. He wanted to feel apart. But she was lying there, giving him That Look . . .

Derek positioned himself over Nichole, thrilling at the little gasp she made as he slid his finger inside her, finding her wet and ready.

So what was it going to be?

I want to make love to you.

I want to fuck you.

She wrapped her legs around his hips.

He made his decision and pressed his hips forward. As he slid into her, he closed his eyes. Though this time it wasn't solely because she felt good. Instead, he was afraid she'd see something he didn't want her to see.

Her heat froze the breath in his chest.

She inhaled noisily, holding the air inside.

The world narrowed to the size of his cock cocooned in her pussy. He stilled, reveling in her soft skin—rubbing against his chest and circling his hips—and the tightness of her pussy surrounding him.

"Don't move," he begged.

"Okay," she said, her voice strained. Her lips nibbled his shoulders, sending daggers of lust down his back. Her hands strummed his back, carrying the lust to his cock.

He didn't want to move.

He had to move. He pulled out of her.

She gasped. "Oh, Derek."

The cry spurred him on. He entered her again. In and out. Up and down.

She clenched and released, holding him in and pushing him out.

"I feel . . . all of you," she moaned, digging her fingernails into his ass.

Derek raised himself above her and stared into her eyes.

The Look blazed up at him.

His chest tightened. His balls tightened. Derek plunged his cock inside her.

Chocolate syrup swamped her brown eyes. She gripped his hips. Her pussy gripped his cock.

Something warm pierced his chest, spiraling downward, increasing the pressure in his balls.

Fuck.

"I . . . like that," she breathed.

So did he. The feel of her. The look of her. The way she gazed at him as if she could look forever and not tire of the sight.

No one is ever who you want them to be.

He lowered his hips.

Her eyes darkened.

He raised his hips.

Her lips parted and her neck arched. "Oh . . . I want you," she whispered.

I want you to be who you seem to be.

Fuck.

He tore his gaze away from her and let the in-and-out motion of his cock take the thought away. Disappearing and reappearing. The urge to come overwhelmed him. He stopped and slipped his other hand between them, sliding a finger between her lips. The wetness made his cock jerk inside her.

Her hips bucked. "Oh . . . Derek . . . Derek."

He gritted his teeth, blocking the sound of need that only he could satisfy, the plea for something more than he could give her . . .

"DerekDerekDerek."

. . . the plea for something he was incapable of giving anyone.

He wanted to give it to Nichole.

His breathing was ragged. His need raged. He pleaded silently for her to come so he could make the thought go away.

His finger moved faster.

Her body went rigid under him. "Oooo—"

Derek didn't wait for her to finish her cry of release before removing his finger and slamming into her. Fast. Deep. Hard. Desperate. And then, suddenly, it was there. The world once again narrowed to the connection between his legs. His cock. Her pussy.

No thoughts.

His orgasm flooded his body, seeming to reach every cell and limb. His cock throbbed for what felt like minutes.

She reached up and her trembling hand touched his face. He stared into her dark eyes, then turned his head and kissed her palm.

"Derek," she whispered.

"Fuck," he breathed. He slid out of her, fearing he'd just given her more than his jism.

Like, himself.

14

"Wow," Nichole said once the trembling in her body had stopped. *Wow* wasn't the most original thing to say after pussy-throbbing sex, but to say anything more required energy that she didn't have. Plus, it had another advantage. It was monosyllabic, thus no sappy emotion could leak out into that simple word.

Her secret was still safe.

She smiled, letting her fingers drift lazily over Derek's back, enjoying the contrast of his hard muscles and smooth skin.

Derek lifted himself off her.

Her smile disappeared and she tensed, her gaze darting to Derek.

He didn't look at her as he moved away to the other side of the bed, near the soft glow of the lamp.

Oh, God. He was doing that distance thing again. That hurt. No, it didn't. She wasn't going to let it hurt. This was just sex, remember?

But was she supposed to scramble out of bed and get dressed? Was it acceptable to use his shower before leaving or should she just wait until she got home? She hadn't thought about this. Maybe if she'd had casual sex more often—more often? How about if she'd had casual sex *ever* before—she'd know the protocol. Remembering Derek's withdrawal after sex in the "library," she decided to err on the side of caution. She rolled to her side, away from Derek, and—

Derek's hand touched her hip. "You okay?"

She stilled, not wanting to turn around and look at him, not sure what she'd see. "Yeah. I—"

"Good." His hand pulled.

Nichole followed the direction of his pull and rolled over, once again on her back. He was on his back, staring at the ceiling.

Okay. He wanted her to stay. At least, that's what she thought "good," coupled with the pull of his hand on her hip, meant. Now what?

He remained silent.

She remained silent.

Her discomfort grew. The urge to run away trickled down her legs. She didn't know what to say. Her brain refused to come up with an appropriate after-sex conversation starter. Instead, all she could think about was how what had just happened was . . . the best yet in a string of spectacular sexual encounters. The best because it felt different, like the connection that had begun in the kitchen had followed them into the bedroom. But she couldn't dwell on that; this was just sex.

Outside of a plea for her to remain still, Derek had been quiet during the whole thing. He hadn't uttered a single word meant to tease, nor given her touches meant to taunt. Instead, his hands had caressed and gripped, as if luxuriating in the feel of her body. His body had relaxed and tensed, as if torn between wanting to make it last and wanting it to end.

And his *fuck,* uttered in the barest whisper at the end,

seemed to contain more pain than pleasure. Surely, that had to be something . . . emotional, right?

All of which told her what words could not. That, this time, it was sex sprinkled with emotion. Liking? Caring? Or, maybe they had finally made . . . love?

She snorted inwardly.

Stupid thoughts like that made her thankful that her tongue felt swollen in her mouth, blocking the formation of words. The blockage prevented stupid thoughts from turning into stupid words and spewing from her silly lips.

Well, no need to waste time analyzing the connection she'd been fantasizing about. It had evaporated when Derek had moved away from her. The two inches now separating them felt like two leagues.

Nichole raised her gaze as far as Derek's left nipple, unable to stop herself from uttering the gauche question hovering on the tip of her tongue. "Do you want me to leave?" Gauche or no, she was pleased the question came out matter-of-factly, as if she was indifferent to the answer.

"Come here."

His quiet words caused her eyes to leave the safety of his nipple. He stared back at her intently.

Encouraged, she rolled onto her side and lay against Derek's side. He raised his arm. She lowered her head onto his shoulder and draped her leg across his hips and . . . relaxed.

He remained silent.

She remained silent, though this time it felt comfortable.

"Thank you," he said finally.

She raised her head and looked at him. "For what?"

His lips smiled. His eyes were serious. "For letting me steal your notebook."

Nichole ignored the translation her mind rushed to supply: *for being here with me.* But she couldn't stop the rush of happiness that her interpretation brought with it. "I can't think of anyone else I'd rather have steal it," she quipped.

She lowered herself back onto his chest.

He remained silent.

She remained silent, feeling even more comfortable.

Finally, she said, "Derek, can I ask you something?"

"Uh-oh. It's usually a bad sign when a woman asks permission to ask a question."

"No. It's an easy question."

"Okay . . ."

Nichole circled his areola with her fingertip. "How'd you meet Melissa?"

Derek's chest vibrated, sending reverberations though her chest, seconds before the laugh erupted from his lips. It seemed to go on for a good sixty seconds.

"What's so funny?" Nichole asked when he'd finally stopped.

"Of all the questions I thought you were going to ask, that one never crossed my mind."

"You mean no one's ever asked you a question like that before?"

"Not under these . . . circumstances."

"Hmmm." She hadn't thought about that. But there'd never been a good time to ask him. It wasn't like they'd been doing a lot of talking. And, when they did talk, it wasn't personal. Well, unless you considered flirting personal.

"Isn't it in poor taste to discuss another woman in bed?"

"Only if you're comparing one person to the other—and the person you're in bed with compares unfavorably."

"Well, there's no threat of that." Derek drew circles against her shoulder, smoothing happiness through her pores and into her bloodstream. "It was two months ago. I was leaving Jag City when Melissa came up to me; she was doing a car ad for them."

Now that Derek had mentioned it, Nichole remembered

seeing photos of Melissa dressed as an executive behind the wheel of an XK convertible.

He shrugged. "We went out. She got drunk and I took her home. That's all."

And that was it? She'd turned into a near stalker after one date? There had to be more to the story than that. Nichole wondered if the drinking was the thing that had turned Derek off. Not wishing to push her luck, she didn't ask. "Do you think that's why she's out to get you? Leading others to sue you?"

"I don't know."

She changed the subject. "And how'd you meet Richard?"

"In high school." Derek chuckled. "I'd never had friends growing up. Richard decided he was going to be my friend, whether I liked it or not."

Nichole's heart turned over. Never had friends? He said that so matter-of-factly, with a heartfelt chuckle, no less. How does one grow up and never have friends? Not wanting to ruin the mood, Nichole didn't ask that question, either. "How'd he do that?"

"He followed me everywhere, talking to me even though I ignored him. It was either become his friend—or kill him."

"That's great that you're still friends after all this time."

Derek made a noise that could've been either agreement or disagreement.

"Did he know your dad?"

Silence. A silence that stretched on for a good fifteen seconds. "No."

"Did your dad—"

Derek stiffened. "Don't ask me about him, Nichole." Icicles hung from his words.

So much for preserving the mood. Since she'd ruined it, she couldn't stop herself from asking, "Why?"

"Because I don't talk about him."

"Maybe—"

"Leave it alone."

Nichole flinched, even though she'd expected his rejection. To distract them both, she trailed her fingers over his chest and over his abdomen. The skin rippled under her fingertips.

He remained silent.

She remained silent.

He was the first one to speak. "Tell me about your life. Your mother."

She wasn't expecting that. This time, she stiffened. "It doesn't work like that, Derek. You don't share, I don't share. Tit for tat."

He remained silent.

She remained silent.

His fingertip resumed its circling against her upper arm.

Her fingertip circled his belly button.

He wasn't going to go for it—as in, open up and share. Since she really didn't have a desire to discuss her mother or her childhood, his rebuff should have left her relieved. Instead, she felt . . . disappointed . . . let down. Not because she wanted to talk about herself but, rather, because she wanted to know about him. The real Derek. Maybe it would give her a bit of understanding of what was behind the blank expression and toneless voice that sometimes surfaced. It had to be related to—

"Tell me about your mother," he repeated softly.

Another burst of happiness zipped through her. He was going to go for it. A deal had been made. But, at the price of talking about her mother. . . . Nichole took a deep breath. "My father ran off before I was born, so it was just me and my mom. Mom . . ." *worked during the day and partied at night, keeping the freezer stocked with TV dinners for me* ". . . provided the basics for me, but . . ." "*Honey, I'll be home late tonight,*" *she'd say. Only, many times, I wouldn't see her until after school the next day.*

Nichole cleared her throat—as if that would make the memory go away. "My mom was . . . busy with her life. Always 'in love' with some guy, until he walked out on her the next week or month."

Nichole remembered the tears and depression her mother would sink into until her next love walked into her life. The loneliness that caused Nichole to create fantasies in which her mother was happy, her father hadn't left them, and everyone loved each other.

"She died from lung cancer four years ago . . ." *still alone and unhappy.* Sadness crisscrossed Nichole's heart, strangling her desire to talk about her mother. "Your turn."

Derek's finger stopped caressing her arm. His body no longer felt relaxed. Every muscle was flexed, turning him into a human two-by-four.

Nichole trailed feathery kisses along Derek's chest.

He remained silent.

She remained silent.

"My . . . Jimmy was a drunk."

Nichole stroked his chest, abs and hips. Back up his body and back down.

"On bad nights, he used his fists."

Her stomach clenched. She forced her body to remain relaxed and her hands to keep moving, hiding her dismay from Derek. She drew a line, separating his abdomen from his groin, with her finger.

"On good nights, he ranted."

Nichole thought of her mother. "About how unhappy he was?"

"No." There was no humor in Derek's laugh. "About how furious he was that my mother died instead of me."

Nichole inhaled sharply. *My God, how could a parent say that to a child?* Her mother had been self-absorbed, but she'd loved Nichole in her own way. Even if it was not the way Nichole needed. But to grow up where physical and verbal abuse was a daily occurrence . . . Nichole couldn't imagine what that would be like.

Derek's body was still stiff.

Nichole forced her body to relax. She let her hand drift away from his abdomen, moving lower, tangling in the crinkly pubic hair. She stroked his balls. Turning her head, she flicked her tongue against his nipple.

Derek's cock twitched. His body remained tense, though she suspected that the reason for his tension no longer had to do with his words. Or so she hoped.

She took his cock in the palm of her hand and squeezed.

He gasped.

She slid her hand up.

Derek's hips moved upward.

She slid her hand down.

Derek's heart thumped loudly against her ear.

Nichole removed her hand and rolled on top of Derek. His cock jerked against her belly as she slid her body up his. She lavished attention on his other nipple, before moving to his neck and lapping along his jawline.

"Know what?" she breathed into his ear.

A shiver rippled through him. "No."

She slipped her hand between their bodies and placed him . . . right . . . there. At her entrance.

"I'm happy that you're here," she said, nibbling his earlobe.

Without giving him the chance to question what she meant— that she was happy that he was between her legs, alive, or both— she moved her body down and slid him inside her.

The air rushed out of him and his hands gripped her hips.

"And I'm happy you're *here* . . ." She raised her hips.

Derek's hands tightened, stilling her downward movement.

She smiled, rotating her hips, teasing the head of his cock still inside. "And I'm happy—"

Derek pulled her down. Her pussy lips kissed his groin and tore a moan from her throat. Moving his hands to her back and rolling his hips at the same time, he flipped them so that she was now the one on the bottom.

Dazed, she looked up into his still-smiling-but-serious face. "Are you happy I'm *here,* too?" he asked.

His cock quivered inside of her.

Her pussy clenched.

"Oh yes." Nichole ran her hands along his chest, before curving around to his ass and squeezing the tense cheeks. She let a hand drift lower, along his hip, and inward, where she stroked his inner thigh before caressing his balls with her fingers. "Especially here." The huskiness in her voice made it barely recognizable.

But Derek deciphered the words. He raised his hips, leaving her pussy, and stared at her.

His eyes smoldered, the intensity nearly blinding her. She didn't look away.

He lowered his hips, giving her his cock, one inch at a time. His eyes dared her to look away.

She wanted to close her eyes, to block Derek from seeing the real meaning behind the words: that she was happy *he*—the man, even more than his cock—was inside her.

She kept her eyes open, daring him to see the reason for her happiness.

Derek moved.

S-l-o-w-l-y down.

S-l-o-w-l-y up.

Nichole's pussy begged for him. Her hips yearned to buck upward, to take what he withheld.

His eyes dared her to take it.

She bit her lip and counted to ten. Keeping her body still and her eyes on him, she let her hands fall away and land on the soft sheets. A gesture of her surrender. A challenge for his surrender. "But I'm happiest that *you* are here."

His eyes flared, his lips parted, and his hips dropped.

Derek's grunt pleaded.

Nichole's gasp praised.

He lifted his hips and plunged into her, jerked upward, and thrust downward. He pumped his hips, his pace fast and hard, picking up speed with each thrust. As if he was seeking escape.

Heat snaked and snarled through her body, making her skin burn for relief. Her breath rattled in her chest. Her lungs struggled to draw in air to replace what the fire blazing within had consumed.

She banked the flames, refusing to look away.

Desperation hovered at the edge of his gaze. "Come, Nichole."

Determination swirled under her skin. "No, Derek."

If she came, he could convince himself that the look in her eyes was mere sexual need. She was not going to make it easy for him. He'd have to convince himself of that on his own. But to do that, he'd have to deny the truth of her gaze.

Desperation gave way to panic. He bit his lower lip and closed his eyes, seconds before his body went rigid and convulsed.

"Fuck," he said in the same pain-laced-with-pleasure tone he'd used the last time.

15

Derek's jerky gusts of breath tickled her neck. His body, seemingly relaxed, felt heavy atop hers. Despite her slight difficulty breathing, Nichole didn't want him to move. Not yet. And not because lust still raged through her body from the orgasm she'd kept locked inside. No, it was because his body felt good atop hers. Because she liked feeling him slowly return to normal—his breathing becoming more regular, his heartbeat steadying, his muscles tightening.

She strummed her hands along his back, reveling in the sensation of skin against skin. His chest against hers. Her palms and fingers against his shoulders and back and ass.

Plus, she wasn't certain what things would be like when he rolled over. Would there be a repeat of the awkwardness they'd faced last time?

Nichole hoped not. Because she didn't feel awkward. She felt . . . relieved. She'd told him, mostly nonverbally, that she care—

Uh . . . that she *liked* him.

And she thought she'd been pretty creative in how she'd made her point. Despite the fact that her body still hummed with unfulfilled desire. Despite—

Derek moved off of her.

Uh-oh. Here we go.

Well, he moved half of his body off of her, throwing his leg over her hips.

Nichole smiled.

"Your turn," Derek whispered. He slid his hand over her stomach to the underside of her breast, tracing with his index finger, before moving to her areola. He circled, then rubbed her nipple.

Her smile disappeared and her nipple peaked.

He turned his head, and captured her free nipple with his mouth, while his other hand kneaded and squeezed, plucked and pinched.

Nichole moaned. Her sight blurred.

She raised her gaze to Derek's, blinking in an attempt to focus.

Derek stared back at her. His gaze was clear and serious. Intense.

He sucked her nipple.

She gasped.

He moved back on top of her, replacing his lips with his hands as he slid his body down. He kissed the fleshy parts of her breasts and licked the valley separating them. Nibbling his way down over her stomach, he paused at her groin.

His hands continued to caress while his eyes remained serious. His lips left her skin. "I want to see you."

Nichole blinked, her fuzzy brain trying to translate. Okay. Since he was two inches away from her pussy, she didn't think he was requesting her permission to look.

Spears of heat arced from her nipples to her pussy.

She inhaled sharply and placed her hands on top of the

hands playing with her breasts. "I can't . . . think with you doing that. . . . See me? You want to see me?"

His hands continued to caress her breasts.

"You . . . can't see me?" she asked stupidly.

Derek's lips quirked. "See you later."

You can't see me later? . . . You can see me later? . . .

This time, Nichole's gasp had nothing to do with his finger's effect on her pussy. "You want to see me later?"

Keeping his eyes on hers, Derek lowered his head. Slowly, seductively, his tongue appeared between his lips and . . . touched . . . her . . . clit.

Her hips jerked.

He licked.

"Oh!" Her hips bucked.

He nibbled, and then paused. Heat rolled off of his tongue in waves, fueling the desire in her pussy.

"Oh," she said, this time in frustration.

He waited.

Why was he waiting? Why—

I want to see you.

Oh. He was waiting for her answer. Feeling like one of Pavlov's dogs, Nichole thrust her hips forward. "Oh yes. I'd like that."

Derek's tongue returned, feeding her craving. He lapped and laved, sending her body spiraling toward the cliff.

She grabbed his head. "No. Wait. I want you inside me."

Desperate to keep the desire building, she pulled Derek up and pushed against his hips, urging him onto his back.

He obliged.

She lay on top of Derek, rubbing against him, her pussy kissing his cock. Once again, he grew hard.

His hand pushed her hair aside and his lips met her neck, kissing, sucking, biting. His other hand slid along her hip, urging her hips up off him.

Nichole obliged. She reached between their bodies, putting his cock where she wanted him, then eased down. *Oh God, that felt so good.* She stopped moving and squeezed Derek's cock with her pussy, holding on to the feel of him inside her, filling her—

The phone in the living room rang.

Nichole jerked, startled.

Derek gripped her hips, pulling. "Don't stop."

"I-it might be i-important," she blurted, the No-nonsense Nichole making an appearance before Notebook Nichole could stop her.

"They'll call back." He guided her hips down.

Nichole gasped.

Derek grunted.

"God, Nichole. That's good."

"Oh yeah," was all she managed to get out as the thin beige lines in the sheet faded before her eyes, as all awareness turned inward to the juncture of her flesh joined with Derek's.

She stroked upward.

The phone in the living room rang.

Derek cursed.

He moved his hips, meeting her.

The phone rang again.

"You should get it." Nichole said, shifting to get off him.

Derek held her in place with one hand. He shifted under her, twisting his body, and reached for the phone cord before plugging it into the wall.

With his hand poised above the phone, he looked at her and smiled. "Don't stop."

"Hello," he said into the phone, his gaze on her.

Nichole tuned out his words, concentrating on his eyes. She rested against his groin, her thighs hugging his hips, and cupped her breasts in her hands. She could distract him from his call, just this way. . . . She squeezed and fondled, while rotating her hips, swirling his cock around inside her.

His eyes darkened and he bit his lip as he thrust upward, adding his spin to her swirl. "Uh-huh," he said to whoever was on the phone, his voice just a tad bit unsteady.

Nichole smiled, moving her hands down her abdomen.

His eyes followed their movement, the hunger burning in them searing her skin where he looked.

Spreading her labia with one hand, she rubbed her clit with the other hand. The heat stoked by her fingers joined the heat from his eyes, igniting flames within her.

Derek stiffened.

Nichole gyrated her hips faster, lifting off his cock and back down. Lust began the now-familiar climb in her body.

The fire in his eyes fizzled, his gaze still on her but unfocused.

The fire in her body fizzled. She stilled abruptly.

"I see. Are you sure?" said Derek.

The person on the other end must've been sure, for Derek nodded.

"Call me when you have something else."

Still holding her in place, he leaned over and put the phone back before turning to her, his gaze cold as if fire had never blazed within.

"What is it?"

He didn't say anything for a moment. Just stared at her. Nichole suppressed the urge to shiver.

"My investigator thinks he knows who's behind the lawsuits," he said finally.

Her sexual haze instantly disappeared with his words. "Well, that's great!" He looked anything but happy. "Isn't it?"

"It appears that numerous phone calls were made from Talentz to Barbara Randolph."

"But—"

"And . . ." Derek's smile was cold. ". . . the calls were made from your extension."

Images of Melissa's sudden appearance at Talentz, frequent unexpected office visits, and request for Richard's help flashed through Nichole's mind. "Melissa?"

"Nice try." The arctic glare in his eyes matched his icy smile.

Nichole couldn't prevent the shiver this time—a shiver that had nothing to do with desire. The time for a romp in bed had passed. "Well, who?" She shifted, making to move off of him.

Derek's grip tightened, holding her in place. "You."

Nichole's mouth dropped open. "Me?"

Derek said nothing.

"But, why me? We heard Melissa—"

"My lawsuits started before Melissa ever met Richard."

"But—"

"Plus, she's stated that her only involvement with Richard was a convoluted scheme to catch my interest."

"How do you know she's telling the truth? That doesn't mean—"

"There was no sign of break-in at the Decadent Chaise that night my files were stolen. You're my only witness that there was actually a break-in."

"So? I'd have given the police a statement at the Decadent Chaise. You never asked."

"And you were with me in my office the night the reporter was pushed down the stairs. No witness that I didn't do it."

"Again, if I'd known that you needed me to give a state-ment, I would've done it. Have you been blamed for pushing her?"

Derek's lips twisted.

"So. Just like that, this 'evidence' has convinced you that I'm trying to frame you for thefts you didn't commit?"

His cold glare was the answer.

Nichole's mind scrambled to make sense of what was going on. Derek's accusations didn't make sense. On the basis of phone calls, he'd convicted her? Just because she worked at Talentz at the time his problems started made her suspect? And the fact that she'd been with him when the things started happening proved her guilt? Once again, it seemed like an emotional response that didn't fit the situation.

"Derek, I was not involved in this . . . smear campaign against you." Her voice softened. "And after what we did tonight—"

"There's nothing special about tonight, Nichole."

Nichole winced. "I see."

She made to move away again.

Again, Derek tightened his grip, stopping her.

"What's your hurry? You were happy riding my cock a few seconds ago."

Nichole stiffened. *How dare you!* "Fuck you."

His hands squeezed her hips in a parody of a caress. "I've already been fucked, Nichole. But don't stop now."

Anger blossomed inside her, sending a blast into her bloodstream so strong that she was shaking. Her brain froze in a blazing red cloud, preventing speech and thought, taking away awareness of everything except the bright flash of red. As the cloud receded, she saw anger and something vaguely resembling hurt on Derek's face. She tried to remember that his horrible childhood had left him distrusting and unable to seek or receive love. And that that was part of his reason for lashing out at her.

But she couldn't hold on to the memory of those thoughts. She was not his father or Melissa or any of the other women he'd been with. Nor had she done anything to give him the impression that she was like them. Regardless of the spin she tried to put on it, he had hurt her—was still hurting her—deeply.

Fine. He thought he'd been fucked, far be it for her to argue with him. She forced her hurt to dissolve into anger.

Her lips curved in a smile identical to his. "You're right, Derek. Why stop?"

She leaned down and kissed him, moving her lips lightly over his unresponsive ones. "And you're right about me being out to get you. I made up fantasies I didn't feel and then planted the notebook, making sure you'd find it."

She nibbled his lip.

"And I knew you'd fall for it because, even though you ignored me every time you came into the office, I knew you had the hots for me."

She parted his lips with her tongue, slipping inside, exploring his mouth and seeking a tongue that refused to meet hers.

But his breathing was jagged.

"And I knew you'd fall for me the exact day of the Decadent Chaise break-in and you'd take me there the exact hour of the break-in. Even though you and Richard were planning to play racquetball."

She shimmied her hips.

His body remained rigid but his cock twitched inside her.

"And I made you tell me to wait upstairs for you the night of the party."

She moved her lips from his, trailing her tongue over his chin, and down his neck.

His Adam's apple bobbed.

She continued over his collarbone, arching her back to reach a nipple. It pebbled under her tongue.

"And I jumped you the second you came into the office, making you kiss me until the reporter fell down the stairs."

Nichole reared up, placing her hands on Derek's abdomen for balance as she gyrated her hips. His cock felt hard as granite inside her.

She stared into Derek's face, noticing the clenched jaw, his look of intense concentration, as if he was totally focused on not responding.

She moved her hips faster.

Derek bit his lower lip.

"And here's the coup de grâce . . ."

Nichole jerked up, off of his cock, and thrust back down.

Derek gripped her hips, trying to hold her still.

She ignored his hands, pumping up and down. Hard. Fast. Furious. In between strokes, she got out the words:

". . . I . . . fell . . . for . . . you . . . for . . . the . . . sheer . . . 'joy' . . . of . . . knowing . . . that . . . my . . . feelings . . . would . . . never . . . be . . . returned."

No sooner had she finished than a lump formed in the back of her throat—the lump that always preceded a sob, seconds before tears usually overflowed her eyes. Jerking back, she reared off of Derek and off the bed. She bent down and yanked her clothing from the floor, clutching them to her as she rushed to the door. Placing her hand on the doorknob, she paused and turned back to him.

He hadn't moved. His eyes were riveted on her, their expression, as usual, unreadable—which reminded her of the words he'd uttered in the kitchen.

No one is ever who you want them to be, Nichole.

She swallowed, dislodging the lump, but her vision suddenly blurred. "You're wrong, Derek. People are always who *you* want them to be."

Silence assaulted her ears and pierced her heart as she exited the bedroom.

16

Nichole smoothed the towel over her wet hair one more time, and then slung it up on the rack. She yanked her hair dryer from the basket sitting on top of the toilet set, then set it back down. She didn't feel like drying her hair. So she'd just go to bed with it wet—and either wake up with dreadlocks or die of pneumonia. That would serve her right for being so incredibly stupid.

She turned off the light and stalked to her bed. Throwing back the covers, she slid inside and burrowed under her worn flannel—not *his* 400-thread-count Egyptian combed cotton—sheets. The cherry blossom fragrance of her shampoo—not *his* spicy sandalwood, cloves, and leather scent—wafted under her nose.

She was in *her* house and all traces of Derek were gone.

Really? Then why was she still on the verge of tears?

I've already been fucked, Nichole.

Yes, Derek had been fucked. But, contrary to what he believed, *she* hadn't fucked him. Well, except for that last time.

No, stupid fool that she was, she'd made love to him. A man totally . . . unworthy. A man who believed everyone else—even Melissa, for crying out loud—instead of her. And for the most asinine reasons. Talk about running scared. Derek was the Running Scared Olympic Champion.

Okay. Maybe "running scared" was wishful thinking on her part. Just because she was stupid enough to start caring—there, she'd said it. Not "liking" but "caring"—for Derek, didn't mean that he cared for her. As such, just because he was grasping at straws, wanting her to be guilty, didn't mean he was afraid.

Nichole flopped onto her side, taking the covers with her. She was upset—no, make that livid. She was hurt—no, make that her heart was breaking.

She snorted in disgust. *My heart is not breaking.*

Exactly. She refused to let a man—a man too dense to realize the truth if it reached out and grabbed his cock—break her fingernail, let alone her heart.

She flopped onto her other side, her face landing in the wet spot made by her hair. Damn it, she should've dried it.

Nichole turned her pillow over and tried deep breathing techniques. *Breathe in . . .*

You were happy riding my cock a few seconds ago.

How dare he say that to me?

But he did have a point. She *had* been enjoying his cock. The feel of it buried inside her, the joy of moving it just the way she wanted, hitting the spots she wanted hit, stroking—

Damn. She hadn't even gotten an orgasm before she left. Funny how that always happened. The guy always got his—

Derek didn't get his. You left him hanging.

Well, he'd deserved to be left hanging. He deserved to hang. Nichole frowned. Wait a minute. He had not been left hanging. Unlike her, he had gotten his. Before.

Nichole sighed. Who got theirs was the least of her concerns. What really bothered her was how he'd turned on her, how—

Enough. Breathe in . . .

. . . after everything that had happened, she was not deluding herself. Something *had* happened between them. And yet, he could just forget about it and hurl ridiculous accusations at her!

Breathe out . . .

Fine. So be it. She wasn't going to give it another thought. She'd had fun. It was supposed to be a one-time thing, anyway. She'd go back to No-nonsense Nichole like she had planned to do. Go back to Talentz . . .

Breathe in . . .

Talentz. What was going to happen to Talentz? Derek would probably blame Talentz, and Richard, for hiring "that traitor" Nichole in the first place. He'd probably drop Richard as a friend. Then Derek would be alone. Poor Derek.

Poor Derek, my ass. She was not going to start feeling sorry for him. She'd better start thinking about her own situation. Hmmm. When this made the news, what was going to happen to *her*—and business at Talentz? She snorted. Business would probably boom. In this day and age, a scandal meant instant sales, instead of blackballing. Derek, on the other hand . . .

Stop it.

Breathe out . . .

. . . He must be crushed, despite his unwillingness to admit it.

Breathe in . . .

. . . She was crushed, despite her unwillingness to accept it.

Breathe out . . .

. . . She was not like her mother . . .

She drifted into an uneasy sleep.

. . . Glasses clink. Laughter swirls through the air. Deals are discussed, even though this is not a party for deal-making.

Chaise lounges, reclining in their mini-rooms, are sprinkled among the hovering guests. But Nichole doesn't care about any of this as she walks through the room. Every cell in her body is tuned in to Derek, who's standing in the middle of the crowd. His white tux gleams. He smiles and his teeth sparkle like a toothpaste ad.

The smile makes her heart race.

She pauses, letting her eyes roam his body, admiring the chest that she's rubbed her hands over; the hips that she's grabbed and massaged, pulled and pushed; the cock that she's tasted and ridden.

The cock that she will taste and ride again.

She takes another step forward.

He looks up and sees her. His gaze drops to her breasts. Does he see her nipples, hard as stones, poking through the gauzy material? His gaze drifts lazily down her legs and back up. Does he know that he's started a rush of moisture between her legs?

He's looking at her eyes now. His smile changes, glimmering with knowledge. It's a secret smile, just for her, that says, "Yes, I know. I know that I can make you crave me without a single touch."

Her heart throbs. An answering beat throbs in her pussy.

She smiles and stops. Watching. Waiting. Knowing that he will act on the promises made by that smile. Soon.

"The Sex Lounge," Derek announces to the crowd, his eyes still on hers. "My favorite of them all."

"My favorite, too," she whispers.

His eyes say he's heard her. He continues. "This scene is made for . . ."

She licks her lips as if he's just given her a juicy treat—slowly, letting her tongue caress her upper lip, before winding around and down to taste her lower one.

He bites his lower lip, as if nibbling the same treat.

". . . seduction," he says.

". . . seduction," she says. She hooks her fingers in her dress at the neckline and pulls. She feels the finely woven strands rip, imagines that she hears the tiny pearl buttons ping against the glossy cement floor when they hit. She moves her hands to the tear in the material that has bared her breasts.

She pulls.

The cool air from the air conditioning caresses her breasts. The shocked gasp from the crowd makes her smile.

Derek's eyes caress her nipples, turning them to a hardness that hurts—hurts with the need to be sucked and pinched, suckled and nibbled.

She slides the dress off her shoulders. It pools around her feet, leaving her in nothing but a black thong and her white Victorian lace-up boots.

Derek's eyes are such a dark green, they look black from a distance.

His cock is so hard, pressing against the zipper, she wonders if it will break free. She hopes so.

She walks toward him, adding an extra swing to her hips. The spiky high heels of her shoes and the sway of her hips cause her breasts to jiggle as she walks. The bounce of her breasts excites her.

Derek is excited. Even if she couldn't see his cock straining to reach her, she would know this. The flames dancing in his eyes . . . the jerky rise and fall of his chest . . . the hands clenched at his side . . . the nibbling of his lower lip . . . all of these things tell her that he wants her.

She stops in front of him. With one hand, she motions to the reporters and guests behind her. With the other, she taps the back of The Sex Lounge. "Tell them what this is for."

Derek swallows hard. "The chair is made for . . ." his gaze devours her with its hunger ". . . i-intimate moments."

She smiles, unable to hide the victory curving her lips. She has never before heard Derek stammer.

But her victory is short-lived because, suddenly, Derek is naked and she is on her back. This time, *her* hips are against the smooth fabric, buoyed by the cushion's softness. This time, the crimson velvet is cupping *her* thighs, caressing her skin as she writhes against it. And she is writhing, because Derek's head is between her legs, his hair caressing the sensitive skin of her inner thighs, while his tongue is inside her, exploring and seeking.

"Oh, Derek." The moan slips out before she can stop it.

She thinks she is saying his name over and over again as she bucks her hips against his mouth. But she's not sure. She's not sure of anything but his tongue lapping and laving, making her clit so hard and hot that she almost wants him to stop. Because the light flickering behind her eyelids and the darts of sensation sparking in her stomach and shooting down her legs is almost too intense.

She grabs his head to make him stop.

He plunges his tongue into her pussy.

Her hold on his head turns to a caress as she tangles her fingers in his hair. "Don't stop . . ." It's a prayer and a plea and a curse all rolled into one sound.

Now she knows she is saying his name repeatedly because she can hear herself, in between the whimpers. She is whimpering because the light flickering in her eyes has turned into lightning bolts, and the sensation that was sparking and shooting is now burning and flaming her body. Derek's tongue is spreading the heat in her pussy to every cell and nerve, igniting her skin and muscles.

His name has turned into gibberish spewing from her lips.

Her body has turned into one big nerve ending that is tingling and quivering.

She tenses her body and she grabs Derek's head. She thinks she wants to stop what is going to happen next.

But her body disagrees. Her hands once again guide Derek's head. Her hips gyrate, setting Derek's pace. And her body . . . there's a soundless pop and the heat explodes, flooding every micrometer of her body.

She can't stop the shudders that roll through her.

She can't stop the scream that escapes her lips.

She can't stop the feelings that are not sexual from wrapping themselves around her heart.

After all this, she thinks she is finished, that the orgasm that has ravaged her has left her satisfied. But she is wrong. She is surprised to feel her pussy pressed against the back of The Sex Lounge. As she feels Derek behind her, she knows she is not finished. And as she feels this cock nudge her swollen lips, her hips jerk back to him, letting them both know that she has not had enough.

Maybe she will never have enough.

As Derek thrusts into her, her gasp bounces off the walls of the showroom. A part of her realizes that the music is no longer playing. Another part of her realizes that everyone is staring at them. But the most important part of her—the part that Derek is moving inside of—does not realize any of this. All this part realizes is what Derek is doing to her.

He is gripping her hips, his fingers digging into her flesh. He is pumping his hips, slamming into her. He is kissing her neck. He is nipping her earlobes. She hears faint words caress her eardrums. Words that sound like *I care . . . I want you . . . Stay with me.*

She wonders if she is imagining this.

But she has no time to wonder. She has no ability to think. Because that feeling that only Derek can give her is zinging through her body. Sending her grasping . . . climbing . . . needing . . .

198 / *Rachelle Chase*

She is struggling to stay upright, so she uses The Sex Lounge for support, bending at the waist over the back of the chair.

She knows this excites Derek—can hear it in his gasp, feel it in the way his hands tighten—which, in turn, excites her.

His hips pump faster.

Her pussy grips him tighter.

"Come for me, Nichole," he begs.

She wants to tell him that he does not need to beg, that she is coming. But the breath has frozen in her chest, the world has stopped.

As her body begins its familiar climb, she thinks that the world must have really stopped because she is aware of the people in the room for the first time—neighbors from Yuletide, San Francisco reporters, friends, and strangers. They all appear locked in place, like mannequins rented to decorate the showroom for the party.

All except for Melissa and Richard. Melissa is staring at her, her gaze filled with anger. Richard is looking away, his body language saying he wishes he were not there.

Nichole knows Melissa's stare should fill her with shame and embarrassment.

Instead, her nipples tighten and the desire that has been frozen inside her bursts free.

Derek quivers inside her.

Her pussy spasms, her legs tremble, and her body shakes.

But she does not look away from Melissa's gaze.

Finally, she closes her eyes and smiles. This time, she knows she has been satisfied. For now.

A ringing sound makes her open her eyes. She is confused. The guests have left the showroom. She stands, looking behind her. Derek has left.

"What—" she begins, then turns back around when she hears the sound of a laugh.

Her mother is in front of her, smiling.

The shame she has not yet felt floods her body. She makes a feeble attempt to cover herself with her hands.

"I am *so* proud of you," says her mother.

Nichole closes her eyes, wanting only to disappear.

The ringing sound once again makes her open her eyes. The room is dark. Who has turned out the lights? She looks for her mother but can't see her. She is relieved. Then she looks for Derek but can't see him either. This makes her sad. She can't see anything, not even her white dress on the floor in the pitch black room. What—

. . . The ringing sound . . . where the hell was it coming from? Nichole opened her eyes, finding not pitch blackness, but the sunflower-yellow walls of her room and daylight streaming in through the French doors leading to her small balcony. She blinked. Why did she expect darkness? Why—

She'd been dreaming. Sex with Derek . . . her mom's appearance . . . the ringing . . .

The phone—the ringing was the phone. Nichole flung the covers back and scurried out of bed. Where was the phone? It rang again, alerting her to where she'd left it. She jogged to the kitchen and scooped it up off the counter. Disappointment zinged through her when she realized the number on caller ID was not one she knew.

Nor was it the man she had hoped would call.

She answered anyway.

There was no one there. She must've missed it. Nichole set the phone on the counter. With a yawn, she glanced at the clock on the stove. Seven fifteen a.m. She'd slept in—not that that was surprising, considering she'd tossed and turned all night.

Until the dream.

Her face grew warm at the memory. She'd ripped her dress off and fucked Derek in a roomful of people. Strangers and hometown neighbors alike. And she'd looked them all in the eye, feeling not one iota of shame, and continued fucking Derek. And, by God, she'd enjoyed it. Loved it. Had one orgasm and was about to have another one, if she hadn't been interrupted.

All those people watching had only added to the pleasure.

It proved she was a slut. That's why her mother was smiling at her at the end. She was proud because Nichole was a slut. "Fruit doesn't fall far from the tree" and all that.

That was probably why Derek hadn't called, why he didn't trust her. What did she expect?

Shaking her head in disgust, Nichole yanked the carafe from the coffeemaker and filled it with water. She went through the ritual of pouring the water into the coffeemaker, grinding beans, and waiting impatiently for the first cup to brew. Finally, a cupful had dripped out. She poured it into her GOOD GIRLS DO! mug.

And stopped.

She stared at the mug, at the cartoon angel's smiling/winking face, as if really seeing it for the first time. She'd bought the cup at a consignment store when she'd first moved to San Francisco. Good Girls Do what? Pretend to be "good" for the world to see, while really being "bad"? Nichole hadn't even managed to do that. Ever since the lingerie ad, she'd worked so hard to be good, she didn't have to pretend. She'd been so good her life had been utterly . . . boring. Passionless relationships with safe men—as in, dependable, white-picket-fence-slash-sex-every-Thursday-night-type men. And not even many of those.

Until now. Now she was being bad. Now she was living up to the slogan printed on the mug.

But was she really being bad? She'd experienced more passion in a week with Derek than she'd ever experienced in her entire life. And she'd felt . . . alive.

That had felt *good*.

Maybe caution had led her to make the wrong choices. Just like she could've made the wrong choices out of passion.

Like her mother.

Nichole grimaced. If any of the men in her mother's life had made her feel half as much passion as Derek had made Nichole feel . . . hell, Nichole could understood why her mother kept choosing the wrong men.

And maybe Derek was the "wrong" man . . .

Nichole took a sip of coffee, swallowing the bitter thought with the bitter coffee. She shrugged. Well, so be it. Maybe something good came out of being bad. In this instance, she'd taken a risk. She'd experienced passion.

That did not make her a slut. Nor did Derek's inability to trust have anything to do with her. It was not because of something she had or hadn't done.

She took another sip.

The phone rang, causing her to slosh coffee onto the counter as she slammed her cup down to get it.

It was the same number that had come up earlier.

Not Derek.

She was pathetic—again—hoping for a phone call that probably would not come. Well, she was not calling him. She answered the phone.

"Ms. Simms?" inquired a man's voice that sounded vaguely familiar.

"Yes."

"This is Don Evans from the *Bay Area Tattler*. I'm doing a story on Derek Mitchell and wanted to ask you a few questions."

"Why would you want to ask me questions, Mr. Evans?"

He chuckled. "Well, you and Derek seem pretty . . . friendly, so I figured you might have some information."

Nichole stiffened. "Good-bye, Mr.—"

"Ms. Simms, I was at the grand opening at The Decadent

202 / Rachelle Chase

Chaise. I saw how you and Derek looked at each other. Especially at that one chaise lounge. What was it called? The Sexy Chair?"

Nichole's heart started beating twice as fast. Someone had been watching them at the party? Someone had seen—

"The Sex Kitten?"

"The Sex Lounge," she replied automatically. Someone had witnessed her shock—or worse, her desire once the shock had worn off—over the thong. She remembered how she'd felt. Lust had raged through her veins, making every inch of her body hot, driving every drop of moisture to her pussy to quench the heat. If she'd been feeling that, there was no way she could have prevented it from spilling over into her expression. And the way Derek's eyes had darkened was proof that it had. Who—

"Loved that dress you were wearing, by the way. So sens—"

"The blond guy!"

"Uh . . . I beg your pardon?"

"You're the blond man."

He chuckled again. "I don't know what you mean by, 'the blond man' but, yes, I am blond."

"Why were you watching us . . . I mean, me?"

"I am a reporter, Ms. Simms." His voice was extra patient, as if Nichole had hung up the phone and a three-year-old child had taken her place. "I look for stories. And your boyfriend is quite the story these days."

"Derek is not my boyfriend—" *though I wish he was.*

"Semantics, Ms. Simms."

"Mr. Evans, you have two seconds to get to the point."

"Well . . . I'm looking at a photo of a woman who looks remarkably like you. And she's wearing a pair of underwear that's remarkably similar to the pair on The Sex Lounge. Nina Ricci, I believe?"

Nichole forced air into her lungs then back out. Breathe in. Breathe out. She could handle this.

"Ms. Simms? Are you still there?"

Her phone beeped, letting her know another call was coming through. Dazed, she checked caller ID. Derek. Shock kept her from feeling happy that he'd called. She couldn't click over.

"Where did you get that photo?" she asked, turning her attention back to Don Evans.

"A good reporter never reveals his sources."

"I was unaware that you were a good reporter, Mr. Evans."

He laughed. "I like you, Ms. Simms."

She ignored his comment. "Was your 'source' Melissa Moore?"

His pause gave her the answer she needed.

"Mr. Evans, it's extremely irritating to ask you repeatedly what you want with me."

"I was thinking we could make an exchange. This sinful photo, which I'll hate to have to remove from the wall of my cubicle—in exchange for a few answers about Derek."

Once again, Nichole forced herself to breathe normally. This time, in anger. "A threat, Mr. Evans?"

"I prefer to think of it as . . . barter."

So this was what Melissa had meant by the threat she'd issued at Talentz. She'd stated that Nichole had a lot to lose. And what did Nichole have to lose? Richard already knew about the photo, so she wouldn't lose her job. Okay, so there'd be the humiliation of it being public once again. But somehow, after all the things she'd done with Derek this past week, the photo of her in something not much more revealing than a skimpy bathing suit seemed almost . . . tame.

"Ms. Simms? Are you still there?" His tone was patronizing.

Nichole smiled, despite the anger still swimming through her body.

"Great," he said, as if she'd answered him. His tone was cocky. "Here's what I'd like to know—"

"Here's what I'd like *you* to know, Mr. Evans. Go ahead and print the photo. And please . . . get my name right. It's spelled N-i-c-h-o-l-e. A lot of people spell it without the 'h'."

She could almost hear his surprise.

"But if you continue to slander Derek, turning allegations into fact, it'll be your ass in the papers. Literally."

"A threat, Ms. Simms?" His voice mocked.

"A fact, Mr. Evans. Tell Melly that this *church mouse* got a perfect view of you pumping away in Derek's office. It's captured on tape."

Background noise buzzed in her ear.

"Mr. Evans? Are you still there?"

"How—"

"Now, while you might relish the idea of your ass immortalized in print, Ms. Moore may not. The camera did not capture her best side."

"Ms.—"

"Good-bye, Mr. Evans." Nichole disconnected the call and laughed. She laughed until tears were in her eyes. God, that felt good. And what felt even better was that she honestly *didn't* care if he printed her photo.

She took a sip of coffee and grimaced. It was cold. She poured it out, staring at the smiling angel once again.

The angel's smile.

Her mother's smile.

Nichole almost dropped the cup as the similarities hit her. In her dream, her mother had been proud of who she was, proud that she'd lived her life the way she wanted to, regardless of what the good citizens of Yuletide thought of her. Her smile had said "you're like me" in a good way.

Wow. Nichole stared sightlessly at the various items in her

kitchen. Her mother's smile had said she was . . . proud of Nichole. For finally living her life the way she wanted to.

Nichole's gaze focused on the bear cookie jar sitting unused on her counter. It was one of the few things she had remaining from her childhood. Her mother had occasionally filled it with homemade cookies, sometimes baking Nichole's favorite chocolate chip oatmeal cookies. Nichole set the mug down and pulled the cookie jar forward. She removed the lid, the top part of the bear's head. She stared at the dust bunnies that had somehow gathered inside. Picking it up, she washed and dried it and set it on the counter. Maybe she'd fill it today with homemade chocolate chip oatmeal cookies.

She smiled.

Someone knocked on her door—banged, was more like it—causing her heart to jerk within her chest and her smile to disappear. Who could that be?

Her jangling heart told her who it wanted to find on the other side of the door.

She walked to the door and drew it open. "Derek." Her voice was breathy.

"Nichole." His voice was angry.

She stared.

He glared.

Finally, he asked, "Are you going to let me in?"

17

He was beautiful when he was mad. His eyes flashed and his hands clenched into fists and that mouth—the one that had licked and tasted every centimeter of her body—tightened. Yeah. Really beautiful when he was mad.

Wait a minute.

He was mad? At her?

Nichole frowned. Less than twenty-four hours ago, Derek had slung crushing accusations her way and now he'd shown up with an attitude? She remembered his question about letting him in. "Depends."

"Nichole." He appeared to be struggling to remain calm. "I've tried calling you—"

"I was on the phone. And furthermore—"

"Who were you talking to all night last night?" His words were clipped.

Nichole closed her mouth, unaware that it had dropped open until that moment. "What gives you the right to ask that question? Last I remember, you accused me of fucking you—literally and figuratively—"

"Nichole—"

"Right before telling me that we hadn't shared anything, which was right before—" His words finally penetrated the red mist of anger that had begun fogging her brain. "Wait. What do you mean, last night? I didn't get any calls from you last night."

"How do you know? You were on the phone."

She hadn't been on the phone. She'd been sleep. Dreaming of his cock pleasuring her for the enjoyment of hundreds of bystanders. Had she been so engrossed in her dream that she'd slept through his calls?

Obviously.

Nichole's eyes widened at the sight of Derek's clenched jaw. *My God, could he actually be . . . jealous? No. It had to be her imagination.* But the thought made her anger dissolve a bit. A smile tugged at her lips at the childishness of their conversation. "Why were you trying to call me anyway? You made it pretty clear you never wanted to see me again."

"I changed my mind."

Just like that?

"Let me in."

Despite the attitude—or possibly because of it—her curiosity was piqued. She had to hear what he had to say. Nichole stood aside for him to enter.

God, why did he have to look even sexier than she'd remembered? Not that she'd thought such a thing was possible, that he could look any better. Nichole turned and let her eyes roam his body while his back was to her. Both his jeans and his black T-shirt were wrinkled, as if he'd slept in them. Or had left them wadded up in the clothes basket after removing them from the dryer.

No. He had to have slept in his clothes, for she couldn't imagine Derek doing his own laundry.

The thought that his rumpled appearance could have something to do with her caused a frisson of pleasure to ripple over her stomach.

Nichole smiled at the prospect.

Derek's gaze circled her condo. As she let her gaze follow his, seeing what he saw—her dark rattan furniture topped with rose-colored cushions and foam green and rose pillows, potted plants sprinkled throughout the room, giving it a junglelike appearance—her smile disappeared. What must he think of her little place compared to his penthouse suite? Did he feel pity?

Nichole straightened her shoulders. She didn't care what he thought. This was her place and she liked it.

Still . . .

He finally looked at her, letting his eyes dance over her body. Past the fuzzy robe and satin pajamas, to the naked skin that craved his touch.

His eyes didn't look quite so angry when he returned his gaze to hers.

Her flush no longer had to do with annoyance when she returned his gaze.

"So who were you talking to?"

Or so she thought. Nichole stiffened. A little jealousy was a good thing, but this possessiveness was an entirely different story. "I told you. No one. Not that it's any of your business."

Derek stiffened and sighed. "I'm asking because I want to know if I'm wasting my time."

"Why don't you tell me why you're here and I'll let you know if you're wasting your time."

He raked a hand through his hair and turned away from her, staring at colorful squiggles of her framed Joan Miró lithograph. "Your place looks like you."

He made the words sound like a sexual endearment. Nichole wasn't sure what he meant, but the husky note in his voice caused the blood to stampede to her head. She didn't think she could handle asking him for an explanation. She needed to be strong, to have her mind filled with logical and rational thoughts instead of allowing it to go soft and overflow with wanton images of Derek. Like how deliciously decadent it felt to be under him and on top of him and—

Squaring her shoulders, she moved forward to pass by. "Would you like—"

"Yes." He reached out and grabbed her arm. And just like that, her mind turned to mush. Despite the fact that the thick terry cloth prevented the feel of his flesh, her body rushed to refresh her memory. Of these same fingers dipping inside her to test her, stroke her, and prepare her for what she really wanted. Him.

"Uh . . ."

His hand moved up her arm before moving down and fingering the lapel of her robe. The back of his fingers grazed the swell of her breast, sending ripples of heat to her nipples.

She shivered. "I-I was going to ask if you wanted coffee."

His expression said that coffee had not even crossed his mind. Anger and passion, spiked with vulnerability, seemed to flicker in their depths.

His fingers caressed.

Her body hummed.

"I made a mistake," he said.

"Huh?"

His lips quirked slightly. "Last night."

Oh. Right. *I've already been fucked, Nichole.*

No shit, she wanted to say. Instead, all she could do was stand there as if someone had stuck her feet in a bucket of cement, and stare up at him with what had to be a glazed, lights-are-on-but-nobody's-home look. Because, with each stroke of his finger—which had now moved up to trace the curve of her neck and loop around to the nape of her neck, following her hairline—her brain went to sleep and her body woke up. Blood that was needed to help her think, that was needed to remind her of his past words and focus on his current ones, evaporated from her brain cells. Instead, her blood rushed downward, snaking through her chest and turning her nipples to marbles, before circling her stomach and dipping lower.

Her pussy urged her to press her lips against his palm, and lick his life line, and nibble his heart line. To tell his future with her tongue. A future that went as far as her bedroom. That's as far into the future her tongue was capable of seeing.

Think. Remember that other parts of you want a future beyond the bedroom.

Nichole blinked. Derek must've sensed the feelings roiling inside of her, for his eyes had darkened and his gaze had moved to her lips. His head bent toward her. His mouth was inches away and . . .

And desire was urging Nichole's body closer, shouting for her to tilt her head an inch or so for the kiss that would lead to naked bodies and thrashing limbs.

Nichole took a step back, breaking his hold on her arm. "Y-y . . ." She cleared her throat. "Yes. You did make a mistake. A huge mistake."

She stared up into his eyes, waiting.

He stared down at her, looking . . . uncomfortable. He chewed his lower lip.

There was nothing sexual about the act. She knew from a lot of experience that nervousness had a way of drying out one's lips. Derek's tongue peeking out to moisten his lips was most likely such an act. Then why did she have the urge to lean forward and force his tongue to taste her lips? To press her body against his, feeling everything that was hard pressed against her. His chest, stomach, cock . . .

Nichole resisted the temptation to look down and check out his cock. To see if he wanted her to feel him where she did.

Instead, she asked, "Why did you accuse me of making calls to Barbara Randolph?"

Derek remained silent.

"And why didn't you believe me when I told you I hadn't?"

Derek ran his hands through his hair. "I—"

"And why— Oh!"

His hands left his hair for the sash of her robe. One quick tug and Derek's mouth closed over hers, stealing her mind and taking control of her body. A moan escaped her lips and she did the unforgivable: she swayed forward, letting her pajama-clad body press against his, and savored the hardness she'd been imagining. His chest and abdomen and—

Another moan escaped her.

Oh, God, his cock.

He pulled back. His lips nibbled her jaw and caressed her earlobe. "Because you were right when you said 'people are who you want them to be.'"

Her body, still reeling from the feel of him, had no interest in words. It commanded her hands to wind their way around his back and pull him closer. Her brain, attempting to take control, ordered her to speak. "But . . . why? I mean, why did you want me to be involved in the smear campaign against you?"

His chin moved to the side of her head, caressing her temple in a side-to-side motion, while his hands stroked her back.

Once again, his actions were nonsexual.

Once again, her body made it sexual, urging her to rotate her hips against his. And make him forget about words, devolving to a mindless state made up of only sound and sensation.

The tension filling his body broke through her sexual fog. She pushed aside urges and forced herself to relax, hoping that would help dissolve Derek's stiffness.

"You didn't believe me because . . . ?" she asked again.

He slipped his hands underneath her robe. "I didn't believe you because . . ."

He unbuttoned her pajama top and slid his hands between the folds, cupping her breasts. "... I'm good at *this*." He rubbed his thumbs across her nipples.

Nichole gasped.

He bent his head to her breasts.

Nichole grabbed his head, her hands intending to push him away, but burying themselves in his hair instead. "Derek ..."

His tongue flicked out, lapping her nipple, before taking it in his mouth.

He sucked.

She stumbled.

Derek drew back. "But I'm not good at ..."

He placed the palm of his hand against her left breast. "This," he said softly.

"Wha—"

He picked up her hand and placed it on his chest. "Or this," he said.

Her breast. His breast. Nichole blinked, barely suppressing the desire to shake her head to clear it. Sometimes she wished Derek would just speak English, instead of using cryptic codes or, in this case, sign language. How was a girl supposed to think when one second he was kissing her, then the next he wasn't? One second he's licking her nipple, swirling his tongue around it in that way that sent moisture directly to her pussy, blowing hot air and then sucking the heat from her skin and making her nipple cold in that way that made her knees buckle. Then the next, he's placing his hand over her breast as if instructing her on the Pledge of Allegiance and—

Heart. Her heart. His heart.

"Oh," she whispered, pressing her palm over his breast—his heart.

"I'd like to ..." he chewed his lower lip, then stopped. "... to work on it. With you."

"Oh."

She stared, shock keeping the words locked in her chest. She'd hoped that Derek would call and apologize, maybe suggest that they start over, but she hadn't expected—

"Derek, I'm having a little problem . . . concentrating. What are you saying?"

His hand wrapped around her hand, trapping it against his chest. "I'd like to see you again. And again."

He removed her hand from his chest, lifting it to his mouth. He kissed her palm.

She inhaled sharply.

"And again." He slipped her finger in his mouth and suckled. "And again."

Nichole gasped.

He withdrew her finger. "I know that you did not call Barbara Randolph."

His tongue traced her forefinger, dipping into the vee between it and her middle finger. "I know that you are not responsible for those lawsuits."

"W-who is?"

"I don't know."

Her heart was happy. Her body throbbed. Her mind was scattered. "Maybe . . ." *What?* " . . . Don Evans knows something. Maybe that's what he wanted to ask me about." Nichole took her hand away and frowned. Once again, she'd been hasty. "Damn. I should've at least let him ask me his questions."

"That name sounds familiar. Who's Don Evans?"

"He's a reporter with the *Bay Area Tattler*." Nichole told Derek about her morning phone call.

By the time she finished, he was touching her again. His thumb traced her lip, swiping important thoughts with each pass. His eyes were soft and liquefied, beckoning her to enter an inviting emerald forest that she could lose herself in. Forever.

"You told him to print the photo?"

She nodded.

"Despite the way you feel about it?"

She shrugged. "Suddenly, it didn't bother me anymore. Somehow, having a stranger discover my fantasies . . ."

Nichole turned her head and kissed Derek's thumb.

Derek's eyes flared.

". . . and my belief that my *Eau de Baise-moi* had been shared with the world and—"

"I'm sorry."

Those two words carried a mixture of anguish and discomfort. Anguish because of her imagined pain and discomfort because . . . well, maybe he didn't say sorry that often. At least that was the impression she was getting.

Her heart flip-flopped. "After the initial shock, it was no big deal. I think it helped."

"I should have believed . . ." He stopped.

Nichole's heart felt too big for her chest. In her dream, a stammering Derek had surprised her. In real life, a nervous Derek stunned her.

"I should have trusted you." His lips twisted. "Emotion, other than anger, is a bit new to me."

Yep, her heart was definitely inching toward explosion. She grinned. "I'm getting good at it. I can teach you."

He was easing her toward the couch in the living room.

"No." Nichole stopped and stepped away, moving to within thinking distance of Derek. "If we keep walking that way, I'll never finish a single thought. Where was I?"

Derek walked to her couch and sat down. "Don Evans. Photos of you, revealing the glorious curve of your ass that begs the palm of one's hand—*my* hand . . ." He paused to use the hand in question to pat the place next to him.

When Nichole didn't move, he continued, ". . . to follow

that curve of your ass cheek like this . . ." His hand caressed the cushion.

Nichole's laugh was shaky. "That's not where I left off." Her voice was husky. "I didn't tell you the best part. Don Evans is 'the blond guy' in your office video." She told him about her threat.

Derek laughed when she'd finished. *His* laugh was sexy and seductive, sending bolts of lust through her. "I don't think you have to worry about your photo appearing in the paper."

"Probably not." Her mind went back to the blond man and Melissa. "You were right about Melissa only being interested in getting you."

"I wish someone else was interested in getting me."

"Derek, I'm trying to stay focused."

He patted the couch again. "Can't you come over here and focus?"

"No."

"I promise not to touch you."

Nichole snorted.

Derek grinned. "I could take my clothes off. You could tell me if I look good against green and pink flowers."

Nichole imagined his naked body on her couch the way he'd sprawled on The Sex Lounge. His eyes had been hungry. His body had been taut, hard with need. His cock had been weeping. She had no doubt he'd look good posed on her couch. "Derek, would you please try to concentrate?"

"I have been concentrating, Nichole. Ever since I walked through the door. No, make that ever since I read your stories. Focused on getting you out of your clothes, stoking the fire I glimpsed slumbering in your eyes, uncovering—"

"Derek."

"Okay." He leaned back, spreading his arms and resting them on the back of the couch. His legs were parted in a vee. It was all Nichole could do to prevent herself from walking over to him and crawling into his lap.

She paced instead. "Okay. Since Melissa was trying to interest you, it seems unlikely she'd be behind this. . . . Anyone could've used my phone at Talentz . . ."

The sound of Derek pressing the keys on his cell phone drew her attention.

"My investigator's looking into it. Let me call him."

Nichole listened to his side of the conversation. After Derek hung up, he turned to her.

"There were five calls placed from Talentz to Barbara. All on weeknights after ten p.m. He's going to try to see if there's any significance to the dates. Like, right before court dates or depositions or . . ." Derek shrugged. "So the question is, who would've used your phone late on weeknights?"

Nichole rarely hung around the office after eight p.m., preferring to work from home whenever she needed to work late. "Clients are never in the office that late at night. So, that leaves the cleaning people or—"

She jerked her head up and looked at Derek.

"Richard," she said, her tone disbelieving.

"Richard," he said, his voice vibrating with anger.

18

Nichole glanced uneasily at Derek. Given his reaction when he'd thought she was behind the lawsuits, she didn't know how he'd react to betrayal by his best—only?—friend. Derek's jaw was clenched as he stared out the window, his gaze seemingly focused inward.

She walked to the couch and sat down next to him, placing a hand on his leg. "It's possible it isn't Richard."

Derek's eyes moved to her, his gaze glacial. His lips twisted. "Right."

Yes, she knew the possibility of it being someone else was remote. There was no reason for anyone other than Richard to be in the office late at night. But believing in the impossibility was preferable to believing in Richard's betrayal. "I'm sorry," she said softly, her hand massaging his leg, attempting to smooth away his pain.

"I know you are." He gave her a smile that did little to melt the ice in his eyes. Placing his hand on top of hers, he lifted it from his leg. He kissed her palm. "I need to go."

The flicker of heat in his eyes thawed a bit of the ice.

Her pulse throbbed in her wrist.

He cupped his hand behind her neck and pulled her forward. His kiss seared. His lips were restless. His tongue demanded, delving into her mouth, searching, seeking answers. Nichole suckled his tongue, sampling his anger and hurt, his need and desire.

He pulled back. "I'll call you."

Nichole was beginning to hate those words, despite the fact that he seemed to mean them. Lately, he seemed to leave her adrift at the best parts. She sighed, struggling to force her needs to the background and focus on his. But his lips, glistening from their kiss, and his eyes, smoky with want, beckoned her closer. She pressed her lips to his, tasting him again.

A few seconds later, she pulled back.

Richard. She was supposed to be thinking about nailing Richard.

Derek stood, still holding her hand. He pulled her to her feet.

Nichole rose, forcing her thoughts to Richard. "Wait. I have an idea. Richard oftentimes works on Saturdays. We could call, see if he's there, and . . . confront him."

"No. Richard won't admit anything without proof. I'll have my investigator start looking for evidence. And get my attorney to file suit."

"We could show Richard our evidence."

"Phone records would hardly convince him to confess."

True. But Derek's thumb was caressing the palm of her hand, sending delightful prickles skipping along her skin. Prickles that were, unfortunately, impeding her ability to think.

She removed her hand. Reluctantly. And began to pace again—to stomp out the heat that Derek had ignited in her body—and attempted to concentrate. "We could make Richard think we had something, some proof . . ."

Like what, though? They had proof that Barbara Randolph

had been called from Nichole's office on nights that Richard had to have been there. They knew that Barbara Randolph was suing Derek for theft of the interior designs for Jag City.

"We could say that someone at Jag City told us . . . no, that won't work." How would anyone at Jag City know anything about the lawsuits? Barbara wasn't a Jag City employee. Jag City was simply caught in the middle. The only connection they had to Barbara was her brother, Jeremy.

"We could say that Jeremy Smith told us his sister confessed."

"Confessed to what? We don't know the extent of Richard's involvement with her." Derek came up behind her. His hands brushed her skin, moving her hair out of the way, seconds before his lips nibbled her neck. "It's sweet of you to try to help me."

She didn't want to be sweet. She wanted to be naughty and nasty.

His hands circled her waist, moving her against him.

"I want to help." She covered his hands with hers, moving them down her hips and across her thighs. "Let me help."

"You are helping." His hands took control, sliding under the waistband of her pajama bottoms. His mouth slid along her neck, sucking and biting.

Nichole gasped.

Derek breathed heavily.

"I want to help . . . in a . . . different way," she whispered.

"I want you to help in this way," he said against her neck. His hips pumped against hers.

Nichole moaned. She wanted to help in both ways. But not now. Now, she could only do one.

Remember Richard.

She stepped away. "We could try to trip him up. . . . Tell him we found out someone is trying to ruin you. . . . Ask him for his help."

Derek pulled her back. "Mmmm-hmmm."

His cock pressed against her.

"We could say someone confessed." Her tone was desperate.

"We could say I confessed." His tone was teasing.

She ignored his joke. She tried to ignore his hands as they slipped to her pussy and parted her lips.

"Oh!" she gasped.

"Yes," he rasped.

"I have to think." She moved his hands away.

This time, he let her.

"Or . . . or . . . we could say we suspect Melissa. And think Richard has information, since he's been seeing a lot of her."

"We'll ask him questions and his ego will cause him to correct us," said Derek. His hands returned to her body, caressing her stomach and fingering her breasts.

"Yes," Nichole breathed. "Exactly. Our minds think alike." And right now, her mind was on the same page as his. The page where his hands cupped her breasts, the nipples sandwiched between his fingers as they massaged and kneaded. Darts of heat would spear her pussy—

"And we'll catch him," said Derek. "I saw that episode of *Cops*, too."

She tried to be indignant but those fingers . . . "Derek, b-be serious." Using every droplet of willpower, Nichole stilled Derek's hands and stiffened her body. Taking deep breaths, she waited for her body to cool, for her vision to become focused. When she felt the tiniest bit normal, she said, "We could say that Melissa confessed to . . ." *wanting his fingers to move a few feet lower, move a couple of inches over to the left and . . .*

That was the confession on the tip of Nichole's tongue, on the verge of being stated by her body.

She ignored the need buzzing inside and concentrated on her thoughts.

They could say that Melissa had confessed to calling Barbara Randolph or . . .

The buzzing grew stronger. She fought to ignore it.

. . . had confessed to getting even with Derek . . .

Derek licked her ear.

She shivered.

. . . had confessed to asking Richard to help her get even with Derek . . .

Derek bit her shoulder.

She gasped.

Nichole spun around, grabbing Derek's forearms. "That's it! We'll say Melissa told us that she'd asked Richard to help her get even with you. And we know that Richard said no."

"And that would help to . . . ?" His voice was hoarse.

Now that the words were out, she didn't know. But two seconds ago, when Derek had been making her hot and shivery, it had made perfect sense. Because, as usual, she couldn't think.

She frowned and took a deep breath, trying to get the blood to return to her head. That would help to . . . to . . . to . . . do absolutely nothing. The only way that would work would be if it were true: that Melissa had asked Richard to help her and he had said he would, and his help included the smear campaign against Derek. But that wasn't true, at least the Richard saying yes to Melissa part.

She gripped Derek's arm, excitement making the blood rush to her head. "I know! Remember when we were in the closet—"

"Oh yeah. One of my favorite memories."

Nichole sighed. That sounded so good. He sounded so good. No. Back to the moment. "Melissa asked Richard to help. So we can have Melissa tell Richard she knows why he wouldn't help her. Because he was getting even with you himself!"

Derek didn't say anything. Finally he said, "Hmmm."

Nichole waited.

"That one has potential. One problem: we're not Melissa."

"I could call Richard and pretend to be her."

Derek smiled. "You could never be Melissa."

Nichole frowned. "What—"

"That's a compliment."

"Oh. Well."

Derek's smile disappeared, his look now thoughtful. "We e-mail Richard, pretending to be Melissa." He snapped his finger. "No, we *instant message* Richard."

"Yes! Richard's always on IM." Nichole high-fived Derek, then grabbed his hand and pulled him down the hallway into her home office. She plopped into her chair and booted up her PC. Derek leaned down behind her, his hands braced on the desk, his breath caressing the tiny curls at the base of her neck.

Nichole shivered. She launched AOL Instant Messenger. Her list of buddies popped up. Richard was, indeed, online. Yes! "Okay, we need a screen name for Melissa . . ." *Bitchofthe-week . . . Bimbo4u . . .*

Be nice.

Nichole typed. M-e-l-i-s-s-a-M-o-o-r-e.

An error message displayed saying it was taken.

She tried again. M-e-l-i-s-s-a-3-8-D-D.

It was available. She grinned.

Derek's chuckle behind her stroked the baby hair on her skin.

"Okay. Now the message . . ."

He reached around her and placed his hands on the keyboard. "Allow me."

His arms seemed to brush against her more than was necessary to type a simple message. His chin stroked the top of her head, moving gently side to side as his fingers passed over the keys. The spicy smell of him teased her nose.

"This okay with you?" he asked.

Oh yeah, it was more than okay. If she just leaned backward, her head could nestle against his throat. Afterward, if she arched her neck, her lips could reach his jaw, her tongue could lap along his jawline, encouraging his head to dip, and his mouth—

"Nichole?"

She focused on his words, happy he wasn't looking at her suddenly flushed face. She really must learn how to stay focused when she was around him.

"Yes, that's fine. Though maybe you should tell him that you're upset."

He took her suggestion and then hit ENTER. The words sat silently on the screen while they waited for Richard's response:

MELISSA38DD: Richard, I'm upset. Now I know why you wouldn't help me get even with Derek.

Two seconds later, Richard's response appeared:

RichardAtTalentz: Melissa, I don't know what you're talking about.

"I'll just keep typing. Let me know if there's anything you don't agree with."

Nichole nodded, afraid the usual breathiness would give away the direction of her thoughts. It wasn't good for Derek to know that his slightest touch infused her with lust. She needed some semblance of pride.

She watched the messages appear on the screen.

MELISSA38DD: Don't play stupid. You wouldn't help me because you're already getting even with Derek. I know about Barbara Randolph.

She wanted to lean back against Derek.

RichardAtTalentz: I can tell you're upset. Let's talk. I'll be at Talentz in thirty minutes.

She wanted to kiss the underside of his jaw.

MELISSA38DD: No, it's too late to talk. I'm on my way to Nichole's. I'm sure she'll be interested.

She wanted to grab his chest and pull him down to her.

"There. That should do it." Derek logged off before Richard could reply. "Now, we wait for him to call."

Nichole blinked, turning the blobs on her screen back into words. "What if he decides to call Melissa?"

"He probably will. If we're lucky, he won't reach her. But if he does . . ." She felt Derek shrug. ". . . he won't know it was us. And we'll go to Plan B."

A couple minutes later, the phone rang. Nichole picked up the cordless handset on her desk. The number on caller ID was familiar. She smiled up at Derek and answered the phone. "Hi, Richard."

"Hi, Nichole." He sounded anxious. "Uh . . . I was wondering, did Melissa call you?"

"Yes. Right before you. She sounded really upset."

"Yes, uh. I got the same call."

Nichole snorted. "Well, I can understand why she'd call you. But I can't imagine what she wants with me. She's on her way over."

"What? Right now?"

"Yes . . . Richard, is everything okay? You sound funny."

She winked at Derek.

He blew her a kiss.

"Yes, yes. Everything's fine. But listen, Nichole. Melissa's upset. She's probably going to tell you a bunch of lies. I'm on my way over."

Nichole smiled while feigning confusion. "Richard—"

"Just don't believe a word she says until I get there to explain."

She agreed and hung up. "He's on his way," she said to Derek. Her smile turned sly. "I don't suppose we have time for . . ."

Derek's eyes lit up at her suggestive tone.

". . . a kiss?"

19

Suggesting a kiss had not been a good idea. Shortly after Nichole had ended the call with Richard, Derek had made a phone call and one kiss had turned into ten, leaving her aroused, breathless, and unfulfilled.

After zipping up her pants, she fluffed her curls, seconds before the doorbell rang. Repeatedly. As if the visitor was being chased. Which, in a sense, he thought he was. It had to be Richard.

Nichole entered the living room and glanced at Derek. "I'll be in the kitchen," he said quietly.

She nodded and walked to the door. Taking a deep breath, she dusted off her acting skills and pasted a sad look on her face.

Which was hard to do, considering that minutes ago, Derek had stroked her body to feverish degrees, taunting her flesh, then left her burning. They'd run out of time. But the sooner she could get this over with, the sooner she could get back to him. Provided he got through this . . . confrontation all right.

She swung the door open.

"Hey," said Richard.

"Hi," she said somberly, ushering him inside.

"You all right?" he asked, looking around. "Is Melissa here?"

"No. But she called. Right after . . . Derek." At the mention of his name, she forced a tremor into her voice. Nichole flashed back to sex at Derek's suite.

I've already been fucked, Nichole. But don't stop now.

She let the hurt and anger planted by his words swirl through her mind. She summoned the lump that had formed in her throat as she'd stared at Derek's implacable face, seconds before she'd run out the door.

Tears filled her eyes.

"My God, Nichole, what's wrong?"

"I'm sorry, Richard. You came here to talk about you. It's just that Derek called and . . ."

Richard's lips tightened.

Nichole halted the tears, before they could flow from her eyes. Richard would buy eyes watering, but crocodile tears and sobs would be unbelievable, not to mention overkill. That was so not her. "Would you like to sit down? Or can I get you something to drink?"

"No, I'm fine. Tell me what's wrong."

Nichole sat on the edge of her couch. She smiled sadly. "You were right. About Derek. I was so stupid."

"What'd he do?" His jaw was clenched.

"The short version: he said it had been fun, indirectly letting me know it was over. Not that it ever really started."

Richard cursed.

"Really. It was my fault."

Richard's laugh was humorless. "It wasn't your fault."

"He never made any promises. I just thought I'd be different, because I am different from the women he usually dates."

He held her hand, rubbing his thumb over her knuckles. "If you had chosen me—"

The pang of sadness was real. "Richard, please don't. Anyway, I don't want to talk about it. I just feel so . . . angry. So, if I'm curt with Derek at the office, well, I just wanted you to know why. But it won't affect my professionalism."

"I know that Nichole. I'm just so . . . sorry. He never deserved you."

She squeezed his hand. "Now, let's talk about you. Melissa made some serious allegations."

"Don't believe her."

She raised a brow. "Aren't you going to wait until I tell you what she said first?"

He gave her a tight smile. "Okay."

"She said she asked you to help her get even with Derek and you said 'no.'"

"That much is true."

"She said that the reason why you said no is because you're already getting even with Derek. Both lawsuits . . ."

"That's a lie."

". . . the reporter who claims she was pushed at the Decadent Chaise . . ."

"That's a lie."

She removed her hand from his and rubbed his arm. Comfortingly. Comradely. "Richard, she said you've been bribing Barbara Randolph."

"I have not been bribing Barb."

It was "Barb," was it? She softened her voice. "Richard, I know you're working with Barbara. I've . . . checked the phone records and seen the late-night calls you've made to her."

Richard remained silent.

And now, the *coup de grâce*. "I'd . . . I'd like to help," she said softly.

"What?"

"Oh, not in a big way." She gave him a rueful smile. "I understand, now, why Melissa asked you to help her get even."

She reached over and gave Richard a hug. "I'd like to help," she repeated softly, feeling like a weasel. If she kept this up, she'd be crying for real. For despite the fact that Richard's actions were wrong, she still felt sorry for him—for what was about to happen.

This time when she drew back, the sadness shimmering in her eyes was real. "Maybe I could help pay off Barbara."

Richard looked at her intently, disbelief and ... hope ... flickering across his face. "Nichole, you don't know what you're saying ... You're angry—"

"Yes. I am."

"You're hurt."

"Yes. I am. I want to help."

"Nichole, I'm not involved with—"

"I want to get even."

Richard remained silent. Considering it? Believing her?

"Please," she said softly.

"Nichole, this is not like you."

Nichole twisted her lips and dug within for bitterness. "It is the new me, Richard. I'm tired of running away. I want to fight back."

Richard stared at her hand on his arm.

Nichole held her breath, remaining silent. Finally, she said, "Melissa will be here any moment. We don't have much time. Let's confront her together."

Finally, he sighed. "I guess I could use a little help. Barbara is expensive. I'm paying her court fees."

"Are you paying the chaise designer's too?"

Richard laughed, this time with humor. "No. That one was free."

"What do you mean?"

"Jared Morgan was hard up, which is why he consented to a work-for-hire arrangement with Derek. I simply planted the seeds, encouraging him to take back his agreement—Derek's only proof—and sue."

Nichole frowned. "But Derek didn't give him back his agreement."

Richard smiled. "The break-in at The Decadent Chaise."

Nichole's mouth fell open. "Jared did that?"

Richard shrugged. "I don't know if he did it or hired someone."

"And the reporter's fall? Did he do that, too?"

Richard shifted. "That was an accident."

"You did that?"

"I was drunk. She asked me questions earlier about how it felt to be friends with the 'fabulously successful Derek Mitchell.' Right in front of Melissa the night of the party."

Nichole remembered Richard standing next to Melissa, looking grim that night. She hadn't thought anything of it. She'd been so happy he was entertaining Melissa, so relieved that he wasn't drinking, that she hadn't questioned things further. A quiver of remorse trickled through her. She should've asked what was wrong. Maybe she could've prevented it.

"So you pushed her?"

"No! It was an accident. I was drunk, on my way to Derek's office to sleep it off. She came up the stairs. I said, 'Hey' and reached for her. Only, I stumbled, and pushed her. It was an accident." Richard shuddered. "Thank God she didn't get hurt worse."

Nichole didn't know what to say.

A sound in the doorway drew their gaze to the kitchen. Derek walked into the living room, his expression cold.

"What—" stammered Richard.

"No. I think the question is 'why?'"

Richard looked from Nichole to Derek in stunned silence. As the seconds ticked by, Richard's face changed to a mottled red.

"Why did you do this, Richard?" asked Derek.

But Richard was staring at Nichole. "Why, Nichole?"

"Because what you were doing was wrong."

"And what you did to me just now was right?"

"It was the lesser of two evils."

Richard's lips twisted into a snarl. "Derek is the lesser of two evils? You really are stupid."

Derek stepped forward, his fists clenched. "Apologize."

Richard glared, remaining silent. Finally, he muttered an apology.

"Now I asked you why," repeated Derek.

"You know none of this will hold up in court."

Nichole couldn't believe the Richard before her. Resentful. Petulant. Vengeful. "Why do you hate Derek so much? He was your friend."

"Friend? The man who screwed me out of business when we got out of college?"

"You bankrupted it with your drinking. I saved it."

"Right. And tossed me bones at Talentz to assuage your guilt. And got all the women, including Nichole."

Derek shook his head in disbelief.

"So. Good luck proving all this." Richard turned to leave.

"I don't want to prove it," Derek said. His voice was soft. His tone was deadly. "I want you to make Nichole a partner in Talentz."

Nichole gasped.

"I want you to confess you pushed the reporter down the stairs and that Jared Morgan is responsible for the burglary. And I want you to stop paying Barbara Randolph."

Richard snickered. "Yeah, well, we all want a lot of things, Derek. See you in court."

Nichole sank against the couch after Richard left. Once again, she was speechless. She looked up at Derek, taking in his clenched jaw and clenched fists, and patted the seat cushion next to her. "Come here," she said.

He walked over and sat.

She brushed the hair off his face with her fingers. "You okay?"

"Yeah. I don't get it, but I'm okay."

She stroked his forehead. "Do you think he'll really let you take him to court?"

"I don't know. But I don't want to talk about it."

Nichole told herself his rejection didn't matter. After all it wasn't the first time. Plus, intimacy didn't happen overnight. Especially with someone from Derek's background. These things took time.

She pasted a happy smile on her face.

His fingertip caressed her upper lip. "I don't want to talk about it *now*," he said quietly. "I want—"

His words were interrupted by the doorbell.

Nichole rushed to the door, thinking maybe it was Richard. She yanked open the door. "Are you Nichole Simms?" asked a man in a blue uniform.

"Yes."

He motioned to the men behind him, who carried a huge box up the stairs and to her door. "I didn't order anything," she said, confused.

"I have a delivery here for Nichole Simms from The Decadent Chaise."

Nichole turned around to look at Derek.

He grinned and shrugged.

The moving men placed the box in the living room and ten minutes later it was just her and Derek.

She ran her fingers along the dark wood and traced the soft red fabric of The Sex Lounge, letting the memories overwhelm her. The photo taped to a page in her notebook; Derek's hips propped against the red velvet, his cock glistening; her thong strewn haphazardly atop it. She gazed at Derek. "Thank you," she said.

He stood up and stripped off his T-shirt, unzipped and pulled off his jeans and underwear, then reclined on the chair. "If you really want to thank me . . ."

Her heart burbled with happiness at the look he gave her: Passionate. Protective. Loving. Within seconds, her clothing was off and she stood naked before him. She walked forward and crawled on top of him.

"Should we get your notebook?"

Nichole smiled. "No. I don't need that anymore. Its usefulness is over."

With that, she leaned forward, pressing her lips against Derek's. "What do you say we start making new stories?"

His cock jerked against her belly, giving her his answer.

Here's a hot sneak peek at Rachelle Chase's

Sin Club,

coming soon from Aphrodisia . . .

Prologue

Transcript of interview with Dr. Tommy "Love" Jones on San Francisco's #1 morning television show, *Wake Up Bay Area*:

Wake Up Bay Area theme song plays in the background. A red leather couch flanked by two brown suede chairs is situated in front of a floor-to-ceiling backdrop of the Golden Gate Bridge. Dr. Tommy "Love" Jones, wearing a black scoop-neck T-shirt and khaki pants, sits on the couch, arms spread along the back, legs crossed, looking out at the audience with a smile.

A glass-topped coffee table, empty except for a red ceramic coffee cup, sits immediately in front of Dr. Love.

Wake Up Bay Area cohost Lisa Mann, dressed in a powder-blue suit, sits in the chair to the right, diagonal to the couch, with her legs crossed, coffee cup in hand, smiling faintly, her profile to the camera.

Music ends.

Announcer: Wake up, Bay Area!

Lisa: (*to audience*) Good morning, Bay Area. Today, we'll be talking with Dr. Tommy "Love" Jones, host of the popular radio talk show *Sin Club*.

(*turns to Dr. Love*) Welcome, Dr. Love.

Dr. Love: (*smiles*) Thank you, Lisa.

Lisa: *Sin Club*—such an interesting name. I know our viewers are dying to know the answer to this question: How did *Sin Club* get its start?

Dr. Love: (*laughs*) By accident. When I took over the midnight show at KPSX several months ago, I kept the format open. Listeners could call in and talk about whatever was on their mind. Before long, I noticed a pattern. More than half of the folks seemed to be calling in with relationship problems. So I focused the show on relationship empowerment and called it *Sin Club*.

Lisa: (*frowns*) But . . . *Sin Club* . . . what does that have to do with relationships or empowerment?

Dr. Love: (*leans forward, his expression serious*) Most people who called in were unhappy in their relationships, but rather than doing anything about it, they settled—and complained. So I encouraged them to "sin."

What's the accepted definition of "to sin"? To commit an offense. To these people who were settling and complaining, taking action to solve the relationship problem was *offensive* to them.

So my definition of "to sin" is to take action. To go after what you want. If you're not happy in your relationship, do something about it. If your partner is not treating you right, don't accept it. If your old methods of getting what you want are not working, try new ones. If you want that man or that woman, go after him or her. (*laughs*) Well, only if you're both single.

Lisa: (*nods and sips coffee*) You make it sound so simple.

Dr. Love: It is. Deep down inside, I believe people know what they want, know what they should do. They know when they should leave a relationship and they know when they should stay. Part of "sinning" is listening to that little voice, breaking out of your comfort zone, and taking action.

Lisa: If it's so simple, why is your show so popular? (*leans forward, sets cup down on the table, and grabs her notepad, reading notes*). I mean, in less than three months your show has gone nationwide. Your midnight broadcast is replayed twice daily. (*looks up*) Why can't people heed your advice on their own?

Dr. Love: (*shrugs*) Why do people with a drinking problem join Alcoholics Anonymous? Why do people with a weight problem join Weight Watchers? For support. Whenever you're trying to break a habit, it helps to have encouragement. *Sin Club* is a safe, anonymous environment for people to get the encouragement needed to make hard decisions—and to report back on their success and failures.

With 50 percent of all marriages ending in divorce and about half of those still married being in unhappy marriages—not to mention the single folks in bad relationships—unhappy relationships are a big part of American society. That's why *Sin Club* is so popular.

Lisa: Unfortunately, we're out of time. Is there any advice you'd like to leave our viewers with?

Dr. Love: (*grins*). Yes. Go sin.

Lisa: (*chuckles*). All right. Great advice. Thank you for taking the time to chat with us today, Dr. Love.

Dr. Love: Thank you, Lisa. It was a pleasure to be here.

Lisa: *Wake Up Bay Area* will be back after these messages from our sponsors.

Wake Up Bay Area *theme song plays in the background. Dr. Love is leaning forward, forearms resting on his knees, listening to Lisa. Lisa is talking, gesturing with her hand. Dr. Love nods and laughs, then begins talking.*

Music ends.

Cut to commercial.

1

_____

"*T*oday is the day to sin . . ." Tommy "Dr. Love" Jones's voice seemed to whisper the words directly into Jessie Anderson's ear.

Jessie turned from the window and frowned at the stereo speaker from which Dr. Love spoke. "I'm *trying* to sin," she muttered.

"Take charge—" continued Dr. Love.

"I am."

"Be bold—"

"I am."

"Do something you've never done before—"

"I am!"

"—something that you've always wanted to do, but never thought you could do. Because you were too scared to go after it. Or scared you might actually get it—"

"I'm not scared I'll get it."

"—or scared you might *not* get it."

"Yeah, well, I am a bit scared of that one."

"So be bold. Take charge. Do it. Go sin. It's all about you . . . Tonya M., you're on the air."

Jessie turned her attention back to the window. She parted the gauzy curtain, careful to keep her nakedness hidden. As she peeked outside, she idly listened to the radio show. As Tonya M. described her deep-seated desire to give up psychiatry and become a mortician—and how her career unhappiness was affecting her relationship—Jessie shook her head. Why did the grass always look greener? Here Tonya wanted to flee the living and work with the dead, while all Jessie wanted to do was inject some life, some excitement, some . . . *sex* into a member of the walking dead: Martin.

And today—tonight—was her last chance to save their relationship.

Jessie reached over and switched the radio off. She turned on the CD player. Sade's "Ordinary Love" soothed her frazzled nerves as she gazed out the window, ignoring the beauty of the ocean below. Instead, her gaze sought the backyard of the vacant single-story house next door. She stared intently into the blackness, able to make out the dark shadow that was the gazebo, nothing more.

No flicker of red light.

Jessie dropped the curtain and began to pace, her quick strides causing the flames of twenty candles to flutter erratically as she passed.

Where was Martin? He should have arrived more than thirty minutes ago. She was sure her written instructions had been clear: "Be at the gazebo of the vacant house next door. Flash the light on your key chain at 9:00 P.M. sharp." Though Martin was a genius with numbers, erotic rendezvous were not his forte. But surely even Martin couldn't screw that up?

Maybe his penlight had gone out.

Heart racing with anticipation, body thrumming with excitement, Jessie rushed back to the window. Was that the signal? She craned her neck. Yes, a definite red flicker. She took a deep breath.

Take charge.

Be bold.

Do it.

Go sin.

Summoning the sexy vixen sleeping within, Jessie smiled in the direction of the signal and flung open the curtains.

Nick Ralston gazed out over the ocean, admiring the moonlight as it bounced off the waves. He loved the sound of the ocean, so peaceful, so different from his life. But that was about to change. Making a fresh start wasn't going to be easy but he'd taken the first step by buying this house. His house. Well, technically it wasn't his yet, but it would be by next Friday. For added insurance, maybe the "For Sale" sign out front would "mysteriously" disappear when he left. He smiled at the image of the large sign hanging out of the passenger side of his Porsche Boxster.

Leaning against the gazebo, Nick lit a Marlboro Light. He exhaled the smoke before it could enter his lungs and withdrew the cigarette from his lips, staring at the glowing tip. With a wry smile, he flicked his wrist and sent the cigarette spiraling to the damp grass. He ground the toe of his shoe against it, extinguishing it forever. He sighed. No women, and now, no cigarettes. Which one would prove harder to swear off?

With one last glance at the ocean, he turned to walk down the path separating his house from his neighbor's, heading to his car. He'd only taken two steps when a movement in the second story window of the neighboring house caught his eye. He glanced up and stopped in mid-stride.

A woman in a red see-through number stood in the window, silhouetted against a backdrop of flickering candles. Nick watched her lean forward and open the window. Muted strains of drums, guitar, and piano drifted over to him, accompanied by a sultry feminine voice. It took him a moment to realize that the throaty lyrics were not recorded with the music, but rather, were coming from the woman herself.

As she straightened, the hot curves of her body were once again visible. The bouncing light shone through the thin material, perfectly outlining the small waist and flaring hips that merged into lush thighs. Thighs that parted and hips that began to gyrate suggestively as he watched.

"What the hell . . . ?"

As if in answer to his question, the woman took a step backward into the room. Candlelight illuminated her face enough for Nick to see her lips curl into a seductive smile. He watched her long, slender arms rise above her head, her wrists and shoulders rotating in sync with her hips. Her fingertips slowly traveled down her body, brushing lightly over her breasts, over her stomach, down her thighs, then back up, this time caressing her inner thighs and taking the hem of her gown with them. His breath stuttered in his throat as her hands stopped at her pussy, her fingertips making vertical circles while her hips moved back and forth to meet them. A brief glimpse of dark hair was visible with each upward movement.

Nick's hand went to his crotch.

The urge to unzip his jeans and stroke himself in time to the woman's swaying hips surged through him. Instead, he moved his cock to a more comfortable position. He knew he should leave. But, he couldn't. Her hips mesmerized him, keeping him rooted to the spot. Unlike the erotic acts he'd been forced to endure at bachelor parties, this woman's routine seemed . . . personal. Her movements unpracticed, spontaneous and aimed directly at him, at his satisfaction. He didn't know why or how she even knew he was here.

But, hell, did he really care?

Her fingers stopped their lazy circling, the clingy material dropping back into place around her thighs.

"No . . ." Nick's whisper of dismay escaped him of its own volition.

Ignoring his need, the woman buried her hands in her up-swept hair. A quick shake and ebony curls cascaded over her shoulders. She threw her head back, drawing Nick's eyes to her throat, infusing him with the desire to trail his lips along her neck, down to her shoulders, to nibble at her collarbone before licking—

His visual fantasy ended abruptly as her head snapped forward and she crooned to the waning music. Her lips—coated a glossy red that shimmered with each word she sang—plucked a chord tied directly to his cock. A smile spread slowly over her face, as if she knew exactly what was happening to Nick. Then she spun around and sashayed to a chair he hadn't even noticed was in the room. Her back to him, she shimmied in front of the chair, her hands grabbing her ass, squeezing and massaging, her fiery nails glistening with each grasp.

Nick licked his lips and reached in his back pocket for the emergency cigarette before remembering it lay mutilated in the grass.

He let his hand fall back to his side.

The music changed to something slower and the piano was replaced by keyboards. As the moody notes of a saxophone cascaded over his eardrums, the woman's hands caressed their way up her back and slid the straps of her gown over her shoulders.

Nick held his breath, waiting, hoping, praying . . .

As if in slow motion, he watched the slinky material slide over her skin, hugging her hips for the briefest moment, before gliding to the floor.

His erection surged against his jeans as he stared at the most perfect ass he'd ever seen. No anorexic model here. This one would give Marilyn Monroe a run for her money. Before he could look his fill at her backside, she turned around and Nick's mouth dropped open.

She was holding a stuffed bear. Only this was no innocent bear from Saturday morning cartoons.

She trailed the bear's face over her body, giving the impression it was bestowing kisses, licking and laving its way across her breasts. She held its head against one breast and rubbed it slightly back and forth.

Nick groaned. An unbidden desire surfaced . . . to feel her hands threaded through his hair, pressing his face against her plump tits, to let his tongue flick across her dusky nipples, to feel them harden in his mouth . . .

He watched her change the bear's position, dragging it across her abdomen, lower, lower . . .

His breath became ragged. "Oh yeah . . . that's it," he breathed, as she brought the bear's face to the dark hair that hid what Nick desperately wanted to see, to explore.

Suddenly, she turned around, her back once again to him. The bear's lower body dangled obscenely between the vee of her thighs as she threw her head back and rotated her hips.

Nick closed his eyes, blocking out the sight of her full ass swaying back and forth. He inhaled deeply and concentrated on getting his pulse and hormones back under control. He had to get out of here.

Now.

He'd ignore her. He'd walk back to his car, not once looking up at that window. Yeah, that's what he'd do.

He opened his eyes and took his first step with determination. By the second step, he felt his eyes drawn back to the window. Okay, he'd take one last look while he was walking. Before he'd completed his third step, he stopped and gaped at the window.

The bear had disappeared and the woman stood gloriously naked. Her finger curled and uncurled, beckoning. She turned, smiling at him over her shoulder, then moved from sight.

Nick remained where he was, stunned. This woman—this stranger—had just invited him inside.

His first thought was to take her up on her offer, to run, not walk, right up to that second-story bedroom. But the voice of reason intervened, reminding him of his promise:

No women.

Sandy, hooking him with her flirtatious ways, keeping him with her passion and adoration, and sinking him with her lies, had been the perfect catalyst for his vow. While he'd been walking around proud to be her man, she'd been making other men proud—teasing them, leading them on, and sleeping with them.

No. He had no time for women, no time to try and figure out who was telling the truth and who was lying. He was here to focus on work.

No women.

Silently repeating the promise like a mantra, Nick continued along the path and stalked to the front of the house, determined to ignore the images of his naked neighbor and what she might be doing in bed—without him. When he reached the driveway, he opened the car door and . . . paused. He turned around and glanced back at the now-empty window.

His cock still throbbed. His pulse still raced. Curiosity and anger battled in his mind.

Why the fuck had this sexy stranger beckoned *him*?

Author's Note

After I finish a book, I like to sit back and reflect on what I read. So, just in case you're like me, here are a few things to think about . . .

1. If a man you fantasized about discovered he was the star of your sexual fantasies and wanted to act them out with you, would you do it—accept his offer to turn fantasy into reality—like Nichole did? Why or why not?
2. On the night of The Decadent Chaise grand opening, Nichole feels humiliated when she sees what she thinks is her hastily discarded thong on display for all to see. Do you think her humiliation is justified? Why or why not?
3. After his confrontation with Richard, Derek contrasted his father's words, *You'll never be more than a pile of shit*, with Nichole's declaration, *You're beautiful*. Did he really believe that both of them were wrong?
4. As Nichole watches Melissa and the blond man have raw, unemotional sex in Derek's office, it excites her. Do you think she could have become excited without imagining it was Derek?
5. After Nichole and Derek have sex for the first time, do you think Nichole was right in leaving immediately after sex? Had she stayed, do you think Derek would've said what he was struggling to say when she left?
6. At Derek's penthouse, they share real intimacy during dinner preparation by discussing their parents. Given what you learned about Derek's relationship with his father, was his anxiety about "making love" believable?
7. Derek shows up on Nichole's doorstep after she left him because he accused her of being behind his lawsuits. Should she have forgiven him?